"LET GO OF YOUR BLADE, DELAN. . . ."

Teksan's voice was like an unbearable pressure.
My frozen grip relaxed, and I moved my hand
away from my weapon. *Now he will take it
from me,* I thought, but he did not touch it.
He had woven a Rope of magic and it floated
from his hand like mist, substantial with gathered
darkness. When he tied my waist with it, and
my arms, and my throat, the touch of it was
colder than any ice, burning to the bone. As
it burned, deeper and deeper, into the very
heart of me, I knew it was the death of my
freedom, an utter and irremediable ending. I
was hopelessly enslaved by Teksan's magic, and
I had no choice but to aid him in working
his evil sorcery against the Aeyrie race. . . .

DELAN
THE MISLAID

LAURIE J. MARKS

DAW BOOKS, INC.
DONALD A. WOLLHEIM, PUBLISHER

1633 Broadway, New York, NY 10019

DAW Book Collectors No. 774.

First Printing, March 1989

1 2 3 4 5 6 7 8 9

PRINTED IN THE U.S.A.

For my parents,
Gretchen and Don Marks

Chapter 1

In the spring of my nineteenth year, the elders of my community finally resolved the problem of what to do with me by making me foreman of the ast gatherers. I spent a miserable season increasing my unpopularity among the children, until I realized finally that I really didn't blame them for disliking the work that I myself hated intensely. I gave up trying to impress the people that I knew would take no notice anyway, and my days settled into dreary tedium again.

One day, as we returned from a foray into the Glass Mountains, we were met on the path by Crila, one of my nestmates. She danced delicately on her lively toes, beads and bells jangling with self-importance where they were draped in loops over her hips. "There's a stranger in."

"A stranger!" Jabbering loud questions, the children surrounded her. Even the one with a cut foot, whom I had been carrying on my back all afternoon, wiggled angrily and demanded to be put down. Except for the Traders, who do not care to linger, no one visits the Digan-lai.

"What does he look like?"

"He is very tall. Very dignified."

"Where has he been?"

"All over the world," Crila said grandly. The children sighed with awe. Not one of them had traveled beyond the glowing peaks of the mountains and the dark holes in the ground which they called home. The Traders told tales, of beasts which flew and beasts which swam, and awful dangers awaiting the unwary. Despite these strange and frightening accounts, I used to daydream of following the Trader path to wherever it led me. But lately I had ceased to daydream entirely.

Standing with the ropes heavy on my back, watching the children milling in excitement, knocking each other's hats and baskets askew, I felt something like hunger in the hollow of my belly, and my throat grew tight as well, and my heart pounded strangely. I interrupted the shrill voices of my workfellows. "What kind of stranger?"

She wrinkled her broad nose. "Did I hear something? Phew! Something stinks."

I laid my hand on my glass shard knife, but she only danced away a few steps, laughing. "What do you want to know, Hairy Del, Hairy Del? Who was your father? Your father was a *medog*! Your mother wanted his big—"

I started after her. Crila ran away on her wild, dancing feet, oblivious to the cutting edges of the bare pathway. She sang as she ran: "Hairy Del, Hairy Del, looks like a swamp rat, has a bad smell!" Her red loincloth stood out like an ast flower against the purpling sky. From a distance she shouted, "He bought someone. Someone we don't want. Guess who!"

That was how I found out what I was truly worth to my people. They had sold me to the stranger for a packet of crich, which would give a lucky few some nice dreams, a bolt of blue cloth, a box full of beads, and two great baskets full of lowland sweetbread. This the children gleefully told me as I was waiting in the dormitory for the elders to send for me. I did wonder dully why everyone accepted that I was a thing to be exchanged, and not a person belonging only to myself. But I knew why. It was a lesson I had learned by rote, one in which I was drilled day in and day out until I could not distinguish it from the air I breathed or the food I ate. I was ugly and useless, only half human. If I had looked like everyone else, or thought like everyone else, no one would ever consider doing this to me. But I was Hairy Del, Delan the Freak, and I deserved no better.

My people the Digan-lai are not much like me. Their leathery skin insulates them against the harsh sun and the killing wind. They have long, nimble, many-jointed spinner's fingers. They can see in the dark, but bright light can permanently blind them. Except for their heads, they are hairless.

· I have soft skin the color of clouds in a spring shower, and a short, pudgy body, thickly covered with fur. The hair of my head is a wild and unmanageable mane which grows down my neck and blends into my body fur. I can look at the mountains and even the sun without losing my sight, but I cannot see in the dark. My fingers have only four joints rather than seven. As if this were not enough, my back is marred by a hideous birth defect: big, bony protrusions, ugly lumps of tender flesh which make it impossible for me to lie down on my back.

I am told I looked fairly ordinary when I hatched. I grew into my ugliness like some people do into their beauty. Yet, as early as I can remember, the people of my community would screw up their faces and avert their eyes when I passed by, and go to great lengths to avoid touching me.

Being a pragmatic people, the Digan-lai would probably have forgiven my ugliness had I not been incredibly clumsy as well. But at the age when my clutchmates were working, I still could not do even the simplest of tasks without breaking or tangling something, or hurting myself or someone else.

The Digan-lai live and hibernate in caves, for without maintenance no structure can long stand against the winds of winter which come roaring down the jagged, barren slopes of the mountains, stripping the surface bare of sucker plants and exposing the glass to the sun. Only I looked upon the mountains in the months of winter, having ceased to hibernate when I was very young, and was not blinded by the brilliance of the sun in the exposed glass. The months of winter were a very lonely time for me, but not much more lonely than any other season of the year.

After the hibernation of my first year I had not developed male genitals and so it was decided I must be female. But after the hibernation of my thirteenth year when all of my nestmates awoke from sleep to find they were adults, I remained unchanged. My breasts were little more than sensitive places under my fur. I felt none of the sexual urges which seemed to govern their lives. But I was seventeen years old before I discovered my ultimate deformity, which I had the wisdom to keep a secret: I was neither male nor female. I had no genitals at all.

My people wished they had recognized my defects and exposed me as a hatchling upon the jagged ridge where the spirits of the dead join again with the howling wind. But after the day I realized that even the cheapest kind of love was denied me, no one could have wished more passionately than I that I had not been allowed to live.

In despair and bitterness I learned how to fight. I fought with my tongue, and I fought with my hands. I found a vicious sliver of mountain glass which I bound to a wooden handle, and which made me feel dangerous, although my attempts to use it were laughable. Slivers of glass are rare and valuable, and my people thought mine should be sold to the Traders so the entire community could benefit from my luck. I told them they could sell my glass knife if they could take it away from me. Apparently they decided it was easier to simply sell me.

I had been waiting in the dull darkness for some time when finally one of the elders, a wind-dried old woman who had never been particularly unkind to me, came to bring me to the stranger. I asked as I followed her through the passageway toward the main hall, "What does he want with me?"

"He wants a companion, he says, someone who can work and travel with him. We warned him that you are clumsy and can't see in the dark."

At this I stumbled in the unlit passageway, as I had been doing my entire life. I said bitterly, "Did you tell him I am ugly beyond description? Did you tell him I am a half-beast?"

The elder stopped short and turned to me. I felt her gaze studying me in the gloomy passage. She spoke eventually, but her tone was not angry. "You have this one opportunity to impress him. If he dislikes you, he will cancel his agreement. If he likes you, neither you nor I can even imagine what will become of you, whether good or bad. But you do not belong with us, and you never have. Think carefully about your choices, Delan."

I thought carefully. When they took me into the main hall, where out of respect for their guest a few light wands were burning faintly, I went up to him as modestly as I knew how, with my eyes on my toes.

"This is Delan," said the elder.

"Sir," I said. When I looked up, it was to find my fellow Digan-lai staring at me in some amazement for I was famous for my foul temper and bad behavior. The stranger, a Walker male as tall sitting down as the Digan-lai were standing, examined me from head to foot. I looked at my toes again.

"What are you?" he finally asked. "I have never seen anything like you."

"I don't know," I said.

"I see you have a weapon. Are you a trained fighter?"

"I can fight."

One of the elders interrupted anxiously, no doubt seeing his crich dreams going up, as they say, like smoke. "The young ones, you know how they are; they give Delan a hard time, and she scares them to make them leave her alone. But she has never—"

"It might be useful to have a blade with me. If she can use it."

"I can fight," I said again. "Sir."

"Can you read?"

"I can learn."

"How do you know?"

I looked up at him, forgetting modesty. "I want to. So I can." It was the truth. My hands might have been clumsy, but my brain definitely was not. I have often wished this were not so, for my abundance of wit only made it more difficult for me to endure my unendurable life.

The stranger seemed amused rather than offended. "Sit down and have something to eat."

I did as I was told, though I was not particularly hungry. It took the sudden relaxation among the elders to make me realize that I was truly going away with the stranger, into the mysterious world where monsters lurked. My appetite abruptly came to me. Monsters or no monsters, I could imagine no worse fate than that of having to stay with the Digan-lai.

We left at daybreak. It was a purple morning, cold with spring chill. Most of the Digan-lai came out to watch my owner, Teksan Lafall, teach me how to balance and secure the load of goods on the back of his draf. I had seen drafs before, and was fairly certain of their gentleness. But when he turned to look at me mournfully, as he stood unsteadily under his tremendous load, I was not so certain of his lack of sentience. I said under my breath, "Don't blame me, I have to do as he says just like you do." But the draf only shifted his six feet and swayed, sighing heavily and drooping his shaggy head.

"Good-bye! Safe trail!" the Digan-lai called politely as we started away.

Crila was among them. "I hope you enjoy your share of the sweetbread," I said to her as I passed. She turned away, but not before I saw, to my astonishment, that her face was wet with tears.

It had been with Crila that I discovered I was not female. Knowing her perversity all too well, I had never thought it was because she liked me that she crawled into my bed that night two years ago. Yet my loneliness was such that I had been friendly enough. We had never talked about that night, she and I. Now it occurred to me too late that I might not be the only freak among the Digan-lai. What would become of her now that she had no one to point her finger at, thus keeping notice away from herself? I should have been delighted to think of her as my replacement, but I was not.

We had been walking a long time when I finally looked up from my feet. The draf was making his sure-footed way down a steep part of the path. The mountain peaks that I had looked at my entire life were behind me, and before me were yet more mountains. The path lay twisted and shining as a stream of water between the matted plants.

My companion trudged in silence. I looked at him through the corner of my eye. Something disturbed me about him, though his appearance was ordinary enough. He wore brown, plain clothing, without ornament. His graying hair hung in limp strands to below his ears. He had a high, frown-creased forehead, and he squinted in the gentle spring sun. He put his feet down without much attention, as if his thoughts were on higher things.

I said, "Sir? What is there in the world besides mountains?"

When he turned his gaze on me, something in his eyes opened a hollowness in my stomach. "You don't know? What do the Digan-lai teach their children?"

"How to spin. How to gather ast."

Teksan Lafall snorted, and fumbled in a woven satchel that he carried over his shoulder. He took out a stiff roll, and spread it out, thin as a leaf, so I could see what was drawn on it. "This," he said, "is a map of the world. These are mountains, this is ocean, and this is the lowlands."

The world did not seem very big. The lowlands lay like three splashes of spilled soup between the mountains and the ocean. Each splash was connected to the other only by twisting lines like badly spun threads, running through the jagged mountains. "Those are trader paths," Teksan said. He tapped a thin finger to one of the twisting lines. "This is where we are. We are going here, to the Lowlands of Derksai."

I stared at the map, wondering what kept the ocean from spilling over the edges of the world. I finally asked, "Why?"

"What do you mean, why? I live there. I am the teacher for the Community of L'din."

"You're a teacher?"

He frowned at me. "I am a scholar!"

"I beg your pardon." Much humbled, and wondering at my own fear, I looked at my toes again. "What do you want me for?"

"Cooking and cleaning."

I did not speak again. I wished rather wearily that the desire to read had never occurred to me. To be always longing after what was denied me was a miserable business. I tried to convince myself that cooking and cleaning rather than gathering ast would be a nice change. But I could not feel excited by the prospect.

When evening came, we stopped in a flat place so the draf could spend the remaining light tearing plants from the mountain surface. Teksan sent me to find a nearby stream to fill the waterbags, and to gather fuel for a fire, not an easy chore this time of year when the only thing which burns is medog pellets. The stream ran silently in its narrow channel. The inner surface was as smooth and red as my glass knife. I looked up from filling the waterbags to see something like a speck of dust crossing the blazing sky, but before I was sure I had seen it, it was gone.

I went back to where Teksan lounged on the plant mat, a book open on his knees. The draf was still chewing, meditating on the sun which blazed yellow and red fire onto the mountaintops. I put down the waterbags and took a sling, and headed to an area we had passed earlier, where the panja was blooming, panja blossoms being a medog's favorite food. But I had no luck there, and cast about farther, beginning to panic as the wild sunset faded. I could not see in the dark—but what would Teksan do to me if I returned empty-handed? So I encountered my first monster through all but stepping on it in my distraction.

It was lying on its side on the ground, with what seemed to be a great mass of gleaming black leather spread about it. Its body was shining faintly in the fading light. I stared at it, too mystified to even be afraid, wondering at the way the light lay upon it in rivulets, not having even realized yet that it was a living creature. Then it turned its head, and I was looking into a sentient face, dark skin showing through darker fur, and deep, unquiet eyes.

I felt inside as if all the knots which held me together were coming untied. But I would have felt foolish running from those eyes. Suspended between fascination and terror, I stood where I was and babbled, "Pardon me, I didn't know anyone was here."

The mass of black leather moved, lifted, spread, and then, with a terrible, impossible grace, the monster was on its feet, with its huge spread wings folding again, and I, breathless at the beauty of it, standing in its wind. If this was one of the rare carnivores of earth, surely it would be a privilege to be eaten by it. But it only examined me from head to toe as if as fascinated by me as I was by it. Then it said, "I am just awaiting my onfrits. Who are you?" It had a husky, soft voice that put a shuddering into my bones.

My reply stuck in my throat, but I wrestled it out backwards. "Someone's mistake. Delan of the Digan-lai."

It said, "Delan the Mislaid would be a better name."

"If I am mislaid, then where do I belong?"

"Only you can answer that question. Why are you so far from the Digan-lai community?"

"I am traveling with Teksan the Scholar. He bought me."

"Ah." The monster smiled to itself, seeming to understand far more than I had told it. "Even among the Walker race it is not considered legal to buy and sell people. Therefore it is your decision whether he owns you or not."

I said irritably, "You monsters are all alike with your word games. Am I supposed to guess what your riddles mean? If I do, will you eat me anyway?"

The monster stared at me. Then it began to laugh. After a while I began to laugh, too; I couldn't help it. A creature like a huge flying insect appeared out of nowhere. I ducked as it seemed to lunge at my head, but it was only aiming at the monster's shoulder, where it clung with clawed feet, examining me, its eyes bright, its huge ears twitching. "Happy?" it said.

"Funny," corrected the monster. "Delan, I am Malal

Tefan Eia. Malal and Tefan are my parent names, and Eia is my own name. I am a person, just like you are. And I am not a carnivore. This is Ch'ta, an onfrit, one of my companions."

"Sorry, I didn't know. I have never met anyone like you before. Please, are you male or female?"

"Both," it said. "What are you?"

"Neither," I said, without thinking. My heart thundered as I realized I had divulged my most terrible secret, but the winged hermaphrodite nodded, as if both this oddity and its own were entirely normal. Still I waited, disbelieving, for it to look away, embarrassed by my ugliness, to make some awkward casual remark and find a reason to go away. I waited, but it did not happen.

"We are both travelers, too," Eia said. "Where are you going?"

Stumbling over my own words, I answered. Having accepted that it was a person, I realized slowly that except for its wings and the incredible musculature of its torso, it was not so different from myself. It seemed no less furry than I, and was dressed in a soft white garment of fine astil across which the light lay so wonderfully, with a long knife hanging at one hip, tied in the sheath and strapped to the thigh.

When I was done talking about Teksan's business, the being reached into a satchel much like the one Teksan carried. What it brought out was so small that it lay in the palm of only one hand, a ball of fur from which huge ears stood out, and bright eyes gleamed. "I have a problem, this onfrit hatchling. She will begin talking in about fifteen days, and grow wings soon after. Would you like to have her? She is not so much trouble to take care of, just keep her warm and feed her whatever you eat. . . ."

But I was already reaching for the onfrit, feeling hew claws grip tightly to my fingers as I took her out of the person's hand, saying something, I do not even remember what. "Good," Eia said. "It was not healthy for the onfritling to travel in my satchel all the time, and receive so little attention. Better not tell your master how you got her, though. His kind doesn't like my kind. If you tell him you found her in a crack, he'll believe you. What do you want me to do for you in return?"

I held the warm, furry, trusting infant to my chest. My hands were trembling. When the winged being moved slightly, I looked up wildly, ready to defend with everything I had should it change its mind and want the onfrit back. But Eia was smiling, and the only thing beyond that smile was an inexplicable sadness. I said, "I don't suppose you know where there is a pile of medog pellets."

"Actually, I do," said Eia, "You see, we *are* both people; we both want a fire. I spotted the fuel before I landed."

It was not far. As we walked, two more onfrits appeared, but shyly kept their distance as they swooped earthward and rose up again on fluttering wings, munching flowers.

"Is everyone of your race both male and female?"

"Yes. My native language, H'ldat, has only one pronoun: Id, meaning a person of any gender. We use the H'ldat pronoun when we speak the Walker tongue also, since the Walkers consider the word 'it' to be an insult. They seem to think there is something special about being only one sex!"

"Id?" I said, bewildered by too many new notions coming at me much too quickly.

"Id, idre, ids. She, her, hers."

"Id, idre, ids," I said to myself, scooping medog pellets into my sling, as Eia did the same into a nearly transparent bag that floated in air, as weightless as a wind pod. More than once our hands touched casually. I kept wondering why Eia did not draw away from me. It was not easy for me to get accustomed to having someone so close that I could feel their body heat.

"I am wind-drift," it—id—said. "My nests are burning behind me, but as for where I am going—" Id shrugged, wings whispering in the still twilight. "I don't know. Nowhere." The onfrits chirped and played nearby, like leaves swirling on a whirlwind.

Our bags were full too soon. Eia straightened, a black shadow against a darkening sky. "Delan," id said, but did not continue.

I said, "I have to go back while it's still light. I can't find my way in the dark."

"I know. Walk carefully, child, it is a tricky path ahead of you."

I waited to watch idre leap off a point of rock and seem to float like a stormcloud. And then ids great wings beat down and the onfrits swirled in ids windy wake. Id was gone, leaving me with a raw rent of pain and wonder inside of me.

By the time I reached my own camp, I would not have been able to believe that any of it had happened, if not for the onfrit clinging to my fur inside my shirt and making a comfortable, warbling sound which I took to mean she preferred my chest to Eia's bag. Perhaps, if Eia had been wrong, this would be a much different story. But Teksan believed my tale of finding the onfrit in a crack, and let me keep her. I named her Dulcie.

Chapter 2

On the outer edge of the town, the sight of a green field made the draf stretch his neck longingly away from the dusty road. It was already summer hot here in the lowlands. The road dust burned like hot ashes underfoot. A stream bumbled past the field, singing sweetly in its rocky bed. Neck-deep in a pool below the footbridge, bright clothing hooked on bushes at the shore, children splashed and shouted. I looked at them in amazement as we passed overhead: My people are not great swimmers, and I in particular had never been trusting of water. But it would have been wonderful to dip my tired feet in the cool water.

The draf's hooves tapped on the wooden bridge. "Look at the hairy person!" one of the children cried.

They scrambled out of the water, shouting and pointing at me. I hastily put my arm around the draf's neck, pretending to be checking his girth straps. My onfrit Dulcie scrabbled about on my shoulder, looking wide-eyed at the children, and chirping breathlessly with wonder.

"Mind your manners," said Teksan sharply to the children. As one they drew back, still staring, some of them gesturing respectful greeting to my master with their fingers at their foreheads. But I glared at Teksan from behind the shelter of the draf. Only at his convenience did he ever protect me from ridicule or remember that I was capable of hunger or thirst or weariness. My fragile pride would have survived utter indifference with far less damage.

Six days ago, the trader path had taken us around a sharp bend. Suddenly Derksai lay below us, like a flat blanket spread between the knees of the mountains. The way was steep and treacherous here, with a gulf of empty air at one elbow, and a wall of sheer glass at the other. We were making this part of the journey in the pale light of dawn, to avoid both the darkness which my vision could not penetrate and the glare which could have blinded Teksan.

He edged along the path, hugging the side of the mountain. But I felt a strange thing as I walked that terrible way: a joy at the emptiness below me, and a powerful desire to fling myself over, as if, like the unforgotten monster, I could trust the air to carry me on its back.

The thick, humid air of the lowlands gradually embraced us. As the path flattened, Teksan surreptitiously wiped sweat from his face. Of all Walkers I had ever met, I alone did not share this fear. It was my love of steep places, in fact, which had led the Diganlai to conclude that I was brain-damaged—that and my clumsiness, a combination which, like Dulcie's curiosity and fearlessness, did not seem designed to promote survival. As we came to flat land, though, it was my turn to become uneasy.

During my first few days in the lowlands, I had to absorb a great many new concepts all at once: plants that grew tall, soil, families, great numbers of people, buildings and farming and complex commerce, and all the colorful, wonderful and disorienting artifacts of civilization. But the one thing I did not seem able to become accustomed to was the sky stretching unobstructed from horizon to horizon. My fears were exactly the reverse of normal: I delighted in high places, but felt trapped and insecure on flat ground. With each step I took under that dreadful expanse, I missed the mountains.

The chattering children trailed behind us, pulling clothes on over wet skin as they walked. In the busy farms surrounding the town, clusters of people in bandannas and wide straw hats raised dust with their hoes. I had learned that by midday the fields would be abandoned, but the workers would return at sunset and work half the night.

Before us, the streets of the town were crowded. It was market day. I cringed inside my skin, and drew closer to Teksan. In another town, on another day, a child had thrown rocks at me, as several adults looked on, glaring as if something I had done had made me ugly and crooked, something so bad that I deserved to be stoned as well.

Oblivious to my fear, Teksan led the way into the crowd. Drafs and wagons and baskets jostled me. Startled and shocked faces jerked around to stare at me. I fixed my gaze miserably on Teksan's heels, wondering how I had ever imagined that things might be better away from the Digan-lai. They at least had been used to me.

We turned down a quiet side street. "Wait here," Teksan said, pointing at a curbstone. Red curtains hung behind open shutters, and a flagon of ale decorated a wooden sign over the door.

Sighing, I sat on the curb. "You can lie down if you want to," I told the draf.

"Drafs are not sentient," Teksan said.

"Yes, sir."

As Teksan went through the open door, the draf began to kneel with admirable grace, one set of legs at a time, until he was on the ground beside me. He tugged affectionately at my sleeve with its teeth. The children who had followed us whispered and giggled in the middle of the empty street.

"Are you a traveling menagerie?" one of them shouted, and they all laughed uproariously.

I said, "No, poor ignorant child. I have come from a distant, dangerous land where monsters live, just to look at you."

The children backed hastily away. Dulcie chirped in my ear, and crawled down the front of my shirt to be petted. "Are you hungry, sweeting?" I murmured, and gave her a bit of bread out of my pocket. She warbled in her throat as she crunched on the dry crust.

Teksan was gone long enough to consume more than one mug of ale. When he came out, another was with him. Though Teksan had told me there were a hundred different Walker races, I was still surprised when not all people looked like the Digan-lai. This man was even taller than Teksan, and so thin his limbs seemed like sticks. He wore an eyeshade against the afternoon sunlight. He squinted at me and said in an offended voice as thin as he was, "This?"

"This is my servant, Delan. Delan, this is my friend, Presle, who is a land-seller."

"Sir," I mumbled, and said no more for fear I might be insolent rather than merely unfriendly.

"Well, get up," Teksan said.

I nudged the draf, who sighed and scrambled to its feet, and we followed the two men down the street. The children trailed behind us, at a cautious distance.

Teksan's house was like all the others in town: a flat building made of manufactured sandstone blocks the color of dust, with a small courtyard where sunlight filtered through a slat roof. The interior was cool and musty, and squares of blinding sunlight lay on the dirty floor.

Except for the cheap roadhouses where we ate and slept on our journey, I had never been inside a building. Teksan and Presle having gone down to the cellar, on my own I explored the house. It was plain and colorless, with the hard, dull light outlining its unsoftened angles. Its rooms included a kitchen, a storeroom, and a bedroom with a lock on the door. At the top of an irregular stairway, I found an empty garret. Dust powdered the floor. The window shutters squawked as I opened them. In the street below, a few adults stood with the children, talking vehemently and waving their hands in the air near the courtyard entry. Brown tiled rooftops stretched to the edge of town, where lush trees overhung the stream. For the first time since we left the mountains, I took a deep breath. It was a cramped, dirty little room, but it was safely above ground. I hoped this was where I would sleep.

I went out into the neglected garden, where the shed leaned wearily to one side and the few flowers were blots of faded color behind dense vegetation. Teksan had told me that my duties were to include gardening, but I had seen soil and cultivation for the first time in my life only five days ago. As I stared helplessly at the mess, Dulcie crawled down my back and my leg, and nibbled a few leaves before finding on a bush a red berry which she consumed completely, warbling with pleasure and licking the juice off her toes afterward.

A voice said, "Are you sentient?"

I turned sharply, heat coming into my face. An older woman leaned on the chest high-wall, her head covered with a blue kerchief. The gloves on her hands were black with dirt.

"Of course I am," I said.

"You're a sorcerer's creation, then?"

I schooled myself to politeness, though my heart sank. I knew that tone of voice: a busybody. "No, ma'am. I am the schoolmaster's new servant." I went over to the wall and looked into her garden, which was a humbling contrast to mine. Profuse flowers bloomed along neatly raked pathways. Vegetable plants thrived in straight, weedless rows.

"Where are you from?" she asked.

"The mountains."

"I suppose it gets cold there." I felt her eyes examining me, as she tried to imagine what kind of environment could shape a Walker into something like me.

"You have a nice garden," I said, although the truth is that I found it dull in its overwhelming orderliness.

"Yours is a mess. Teksan is not much of a gardener."

"Where do I begin?"

"With the weeds."

"Which ones are weeds?"

"You don't know? You poor thing." She scrambled nimbly over the wall.

By the time Teksan came looking for me, I had brought the draf through the gate. He willingly consumed everything I told him to eat, as I followed around after him, pulling up the remains by the roots. Alyk, the neighbor, had been amazed that I did not even know plants had roots, but no more amazed than I had been upon learning that she had never in fifty years set eyes on the Glass Mountains, or even, except on a few occasions, traveled outside of the town limits. "Why should I?" she asked. But I was speechless.

"Well," Teksan commented, unimpressed by my industry. "Come in before you get heatstroke. There's the unpacking to do."

I tied the draf in the shade where everything within its reach was a weed, woke Dulcie from her nap between rocks, and went into my new house. When I came out again in the evening, the draf was gone. One of Presle's offspring had come to take him to a farm at the edge of the village. I had known that the draf was only borrowed, yet I spent a long time wandering vaguely among the plants he had cropped. A draf was not much of a friend, but I missed him, even so.

"Delan. Delan."

The room was glowing, red and gold. The dull stone walls glittered in the light. I got up from my makeshift bed and went to the window. The streets of the village below were empty. Each building stood in sharp-edged clarity, bright against black shadows. The air was cool and fragrant. The light of sunrise tipped my fur with fire.

"Delan," the chirpy voice said again. Dulcie fluttered up to the window on wings like stretched astil.

"Dulcie!" I whispered. She landed awkwardly on my shoulder, clinging frantically to my short fur and flapping wildly until she was balanced. Then she folded her astonishing wings into neat bundles, only to spread them again for my admiration. As soft as powder under my touch, the membrane both gave and resisted, to embrace the wind and yet control it. I stroked her soft fur. "How wonderful you are!"

Something unknown and mysterious ached inside of me, ragged with unattended hunger. I watched the sun until the light began to dull, and a few figures appeared on the street below. But my sadness did not fade. My new place was rich at least in possibilities. Yet, mistake or mislaid, I was still a freak. Only once in my entire life had another person seemed unaffected by my ugliness. But now even the memory of the beautiful, gentle-spoken flying monster gave me pain.

"The Aeyries use them as message carriers," Teksan said when he saw the onfrit fluttering around the kitchen. "They actually believe they are intelligent beings."

I put a spoonful of black honey into a pot of boiling water, and stirred in the grain, handful by handful.

The first time I had tried to cook porridge it had been full of lumps, and Teksan had made me do it again. I frowned at the pot. My unreasonable fear of Teksan had lingered, and I was not willing to risk arguing with him. I decided to teach Dulcie to talk only to me, rather than prove to Teksan that he was capable of making a mistake. I said, "Who are the Aeyries?"

Immediately I was sorry I had asked. He said violently, "How can you not know? They hold the earth in thrall! They snatch the bread from our children's mouths!"

He continued on in this way all the while I stirred the pot, and was still declaiming when I served breakfast. "Why?" I asked when he finally paused to take a mouthful of food.

"Why what?"

"Why do they do it?"

"They are not human, of course. They think they are better than the rest of us. They think they deserve to spend their days in dreaming while they live on our honest labor!"

"But if they give us machines, and books, and new ideas—"

"Give us? Sell us! Knowledge is a right, not something to be sold at a price so high it keeps us in poverty. While they live in luxury, wearing nothing but astil, raising up their spoiled, fat children to look down upon us from the top of their mountains—"

I was to hear a great deal about the Aeyries during the months that followed. The entire population of L'din, and Teksan's friends in particular, hated them for the luxury in which they lived: their wastefulness, their leisure, and above all for the fact that it was thanks to them that the Lowlanders had to pay taxes. The Aeyries lived in unapproachable strongholds in the mountains. They were not like Walkers. But no one knew what they looked like, or anything else of

use about them, except for the fact that they exploited
hardworking people.

Occasionally, I did wonder that the Walkers so resented something that they did to me every day. Teksan
insisted that knowledge was a right, yet when the
school doors opened he refused to allow me to attend.
Teksan said that it was wrong for anyone to avoid
what he called honest labor, but I did all the honest
labor in our household while he spent his spare time in
the tavern or behind the locked door of his room,
doing mysterious, smelly, sometimes noisy experiments.
Not one of those who railed against the Aeyries would
have dreamed of living in a mud hut rather than houses
made of sandstone manufactured in the Aeyrie designed foundry, or of burning wax candles rather than
using the Aeyrie designed air lamps. My neighbor
Alyk would happily complain about the Aeyries for an
entire afternoon as she watched me work in my garden. But her prize flower, a night-blooming lily which
glowed red in moonlight, had been bought from a
peddler of Aeyrie goods.

I was smart enough to avoid pointing out these
inconsistencies. Growing up among the Digan-lai had
taught me what little good it did to argue against
common opinion. I had no interest in calling attention
to myself. All I wanted from the residents of L'din was
that they become blind to my fur, and all I wanted
from Teksan was that he have no reason to regret my
presence. It did not seem like too much to want from
life.

I worked hard. I joined the informal club of gardeners that met at Alyk's house. My garden thrived. The
floor in the kitchen sparkled in the light of the air
lamp. I learned from others or taught myself how to
cook, how to grow ornamental plants in pots in the
courtyard, and how to strike hard bargains at market
so I would have money left over to spend on kipswool

to recover the old furniture Teksan had bought, and woven grass blinds to soften the light. I came in one day from working in the garden, and was myself surprised by the welcoming, warm colors of the unused parlor. How beautiful I had made it! But for what purpose?

That afternoon I scrubbed the kitchen floor in a fury. I rasped the metal bush accidentally across dry sandstone, showering stinging sparks across my hand. I threw the brush at the wall. With a startled cry, Dulcie headed for the ceiling and clung frantically to a curved spoke of the air lamp. "I am not happy!" I shouted. "I work hard. I behave myself. But I am not happy!"

The next morning, I told Alyk I had to miss the meeting of the garden club, and I left the house soon after Teksan was gone. I tried to look casual as I went through the village, for it was too much to hope that no one would notice me. Already the day was hot and dusty. I sweltered in my fur. My heart pounded in my throat.

The school was on the other side of the village from Teksan's house, a dull, square, windowless building which opened on the road on one side and an unused alley on the other, where a broken-down wagon without wheels rested on its axles, and full trash bins awaited the dustman. I went cautiously, but the alley was empty of people. The broken lock on the back door of the school, of which I had dutifully informed Teksan several times, was still broken. The knob turned in my hand, squeaking softly, bringing my heart into my throat. It opened into a storeroom, one which, as far as I could tell, only I, the unofficial janitor, ever used. The mop and broom and bucket stood neatly in their corners where I had left them nearly a week ago. The hunter worm, whose web I cleaned out of the corner every week, was hanging from a thread, weaving busily.

I lay down on my stomach on the floor and put my eye to the crack where the door had warped away from the jamb. Chalk squeaked on slate, and Teksan's voice droned in my ear. I shifted my angle until I could see him, holding up his slate with a letter written on it. I dug my stolen piece of brown chalk out of my pocket and wrote on the floor. "Eh," said Teksan. "Eeeeeh." The children murmured in a disorganized chorus.

"Eh," I whispered in the cool, dusty closet.

Only five mornings later, I was spelling out shop signs. I had no idea how remarkable this was until I overheard Teksan commenting proudly on his best student, who was reading simple words after only a forty-day. By the end of a forty-day, I was no longer even going to school.

I ingratiated myself with a locksmith and idly watched her construct a lock and a key for the school. Then I went home and picked the lock on the door of Teksan's bedroom. I was careful to leave no telltale scratches on the keyhole, something I knew how to do thanks to the locksmith's helpful idle chatter. But I was sweating even before the lock was undone, and when the door creaked faintly on its hinges, a gulf of terror gaped suddenly in my belly. "How silly," I said out loud. "He won't be home for hours." But even Dulcie clung to my shoulder, wide-eyed and silent.

I pushed the door open with my foot. In front of me was Teksan's bedroom, no bigger than the parlor. It was sparsely furnished, but wildly cluttered and very dirty. After my first glance, once I had noticed what was in the center of the room, I was not able to focus on anything else. In the center of the room was an empty space where the walls and the house and the smooth sandstone floor ceased to exist. Inside that emptiness I sensed rather than saw a swirling, like clouds in an advancing storm, and the weird flicker of blue lightning.

Dulcie leapt from my shoulder and fled. Her terrified screeching echoed down the hallway. But I stood as if turned to glass. It was a long time before I was able to very carefully close the door again, and snap shut the lock.

"What is the matter with you!" Teksan shouted at me that night. He had come home from the school to find me with my work undone, burning dinner in distraction as the storm swirled in my stomach.

I heard myself saying softly, "I beg your pardon, sir. I think I must be tired."

"Tired? From what? You haven't done anything today."

I said, "Four months I have been working from sunrise to sunset. Haven't you gotten two baskets of sweetbread worth of work out of me yet?" I listened to myself in horror, and yet I could not stop.

He went to his room without speaking. I frantically stirred the pot, trembling with an angry, reckless, heady joy, wondering if I should run away. Too late, I decided it would be a good idea. His returning steps were quick and angry on the sandstone. I looked up into an expression I was all too familiar with. It was hatred, hatred mixed not with the usual fear, but with an awful gladness. He had a cane in his hand.

In that long, horrific moment as I watched the hissing arc of the cane, I knew that Teksan had dearly wanted this to happen, had been watching and waiting impatiently for an excuse to raise his hand against me. And I was nearly as certain that I deserved it, not because I had not worked hard enough, or even because I had done things which he had forbidden, but because my offensive appearance and inexplicable differences were somehow my fault.

The cane caught me on the side. Clumsy as always, I caught my foot on a leg of the table as I tried to flee, and went sprawling. The cane cracked across my backbone, and my body jerked under the impact. It cracked again. I caught sight of Teksan's face, twisted with his terrible joy. I hardly even felt the pain, so great was my fear. He hit me over and over. I knew he was going to kill me. I huddled helplessly on the floor, as if I had no ability either to fight back or to flee. "Stop," I sobbed incoherently. "I'm sorry, please forgive me, stop, oh stop." Then his cane contacted the ugly, sensitive lumps on my back. Agony exploded white lights in my brain, and I fainted.

The sandstone was cold under my cheek. In terror I jerked up my head, and nearly blacked out again from pain. The kitchen was empty. Pieces of the broken cane were scattered around me. The air lamp's light burned in a fog of smoke, but Teksan had taken the pot off the stove.

I forced myself to move. Burning ropes of pain slapped onto my back. I crawled out of the kitchen, and into the dusky parlor. It was a long way to the foot of the stairway. I deceived myself with ridiculous lies as I dragged myself up the stairs: "Just one more. This is the last step." Then deceit worked no longer and I buried my face in my shirtsleeve, sobbing. I wished Teksan had killed me. I do not remember fainting again.

I dreamed that I lay under a soft glow of light, and gentle hands were touching me. There was a sweet taste in my mouth, and a spreading warmth in my belly. A hushed, profoundly angry voice whispered words I could not understand. The touch probed the deformities on my back. Someone's voice moaned, ragged and hoarse. Then there was a coolness, quenching the fire of pain. I wanted to turn my head, but could not. I wanted to speak, but could not.

Later I had another dream, that I had wings, and rode the back of a swirling storm. Lightning flickered around me, and I laughed as I flew.

When I awoke, the light told me it was late morning. I lay in my bed. My clothes were folded atop my small clothes chest. Dulcie huddled against me, warm and quiet. The pain was not nearly as bad as I expected it to be, as if in my dream of being tended I had healed myself.

I got up and went back to Teksan's room, and carefully fiddled my makeshift pick in the lock. This time I shut my eyes before nudging open the door, and went in backward so that what I saw when I opened my eyes was the disordered bookshelf. I escaped with a book this time, as I had originally intended. It was the only one with a title I could easily read. It was called *The World*.

If Teksan was going to kill me, at least the reason would be not that I had failed to be a perfect servant, but that I had chosen to become free.

Chapter 3

The front door slammed. Teksan's footsteps crossed the house to his room. I had returned the stolen book just in time. Now I panted with fear on my cot, where I had spent most of the day reading and thinking and trying to avoid moving. Dulcie huddled in the hollow behind my legs, wide-eyed and silent.

Teksan's footsteps started up the stairs. Under the covers I gripped my knife in a sweaty hand.

He opened the door. My heart stopped beating. My single brave candle guttered before him. He stared at me from black, lightless hollows. His clothing wrapped him like a midnight shadow.

The walls of the room veered abruptly away at impossible angles, stretching into a vast, monstrous darkness. What had been air seemed solid, shuddering and cracking as Teksan moved. He stretched, grew, filled the doorway, filled my entire vision. He became the size of a storm. A thunder rumbled from his arms as he wove his hands in the air, spinning out of the twisting shadows a Rope of darkness.

When he came to me, I could not move. He lifted away the covers. I cringed away from him, shuddering with horror as his cold hands touched me. I felt powerless to prevent him from his purpose. Yet even in this abruptly changed Universe, I still gripped my glass knife in my hand.

"Let go of your blade," he said. His voice was no sound, but an unbearable pressure.

My frozen grip relaxed, and I moved my hand away from my weapon. *Now he will take it from me,* I thought, but he did not touch it. The Rope he had woven floated from his hand like mist, substantial with gathered darkness. When he tied my waist with it, and my arms, and my throat, the touch of it was colder than any ice, burning to the bone. As it burned, deeper and deeper, into the very heart of me, I knew it was a death, an utter and irremediable ending. Eia had been wrong: I had no choice, no choice at all.

He said, "You will be downstairs at your usual time in the morning."

Confused and dazed, I stared at him. In the course of only a moment, all had become ordinary again: the walls and atmosphere of my room, the candleflame straightening and sputtering in the corner, Dulcie shifting nervously against me, and Teksan standing in the doorway, frowning at me impatiently.

"Yes, sir," I said. The door closed, and he was gone. I reached, and found my knife handle again, only a fingerlength away, as hot and sweaty as the palm of my hand.

I told myself the strange thing had not happened. Once it was over, I remembered it no more clearly than a dream. But I knew that it had not been one. On a level of awareness which was new to me I continued to feel the awful, deadening cold of the Rope. Somehow I even knew its name: Despair. But I was no less a prisoner for being able to name that which bound me.

As I had read the stolen book that day, I had daydreamed of following the road to wherever it led me. The book declared the world to be a single gigantic glass mountain hurtling though the air, with the five moons whirling crazily around it. Thinking of the Walkers of L'din, going placidly about their predictable business, I could understand why they might prefer to believe that the world was a flat disk floating peacefully in an infinite ocean, with the moons and the sun tethered to it by pieces of string. But something in me delighted in fearful knowledge.

I had read that, contrary to what I had understood all my life, our world is inhabited by three primary races of intelligent beings, all of which have enough in common with each other to be considered human. My book was apparently a translation of one written by and for Aeyries, for they were listed but not described although some of the Walkers' Hundred were described in detail. The book also mentioned the Mers, the mysterious herdfolk who live in the sea, a migratory people with no language but a wordless song which expresses only emotion. And apparently even the Aeyries had never heard of freaks like me or people like the remarkable winged stranger.

As I read, I had dreamed of heading northward, deep into the Glass Mountains, searching for other Walkers like me who had adapted as I had to the cold wind and the glaring sun. They would be people who even thought like me, who delighted in knowing they inhabited a glass mountain hurtling through space, who wanted to talk to a Mer about the sea and an Aeyrie about inventiveness, who delighted in asking questions even when there was no answer, who wanted to love and be loved.

Now I knew I was not going anywhere. If there was a place on earth where I belonged, I was not destined to find it.

I cooked for Teksan the next day, but I did not eat with him. In the cool of the morning, despite the lingering pain of the bruises and welts across my back, I worked in the garden. For breakfast I ate vegetables

I had grown myself, raw, with the dirt still on them. As soon as the fearful weight of the sorcerer's presence was gone, I broke into his room and stole the book again. Throughout the morning, word by word and page by page, with the book open nearby wherever I was working, I read.

The summer was ending. All day long and far into the night, the harvest songs of the field workers could be heard. Teksan closed school for the harvest, and spent all day in the tavern instead. Sometimes, he brought his friends home for dinner. I eventually realized that everyone knew he was a sorcerer but, rather than being horrified and fearful, respected him for it. His numerous friends were eager to listen to him talk, and equally eager to agree with him. He talked tirelessly and hatefully about the Aeyries, and every word he spoke seemed intended to make the L'din Walkers feel even more victimized and self-righteous.

I listened sometimes from the kitchen, where I dutifully cooked dull and uninspired meals for them. As I listened, I came to understand how easy it is to blame the one who is different for every ill which befalls the people. I had been fortunate to have hatched among the nonviolent Digan-lai, for I was a natural target. It was inevitable that someday someone would decide that Delan the freak had brought a curse upon them, or had caused a drought, or had given their draf some disease.

I used to love going to market, where a few people smiled with welcome when they saw me coming. Some of the crafters in town were accustomed to being visited by me every day: the locksmith, for instance, and the wheelwright, both of whom had frankly told me they wanted to apprentice me. But now it took all my courage to make myself go out into the street, and I did my business in haste.

The Rope which bound me burned into my soul. I

remembered my recent self as if a stranger, remembered my little joys and triumphs: how I had loved the little power of creating beauty and making things grow, how I had felt the day I realized that because I could read, all the knowledge of the world could be mine. I remembered how it had been, but my small triumphs were empty now. Teksan and I both pretended that he had never been maddened by hatred for me, and that I was not a helpless prisoner in his household. But I was unable to forget that joy on his face as he hit me with his cane. Fear made me unwilling to even guess what he meant to do with me. I worked hard and went to bed tired, but I had trouble sleeping at night.

One day I looked at the swirling Hole in his room, and realized I was no longer afraid of it. I thought it must be a door, opening into the ether through which our glass mountain world was falling. I wondered what could happen if I stepped into the swirling emptiness, and whether Teksan could follow me or call me back from that darkness.

The next day I opened one of his books of sorcery. I leafed through it with horrified interest at first, and then with increasing boredom. Its faded pages contained little more than dull listings of ingredients to mix and the order in which to lay out certain stones and say certain words. Perhaps Teksan had the necessary ingredients on his shelves, and perhaps he did not. All his jars and bottles and boxes were unlabeled, and I had no means of identifying them.

Nonetheless, when I found the spell for changing something into something else, I paused to consider. If I could be anything I wanted, what would I want to be? An ordinary Walker, leading a Walker's safe but dull and predictable life? A scholar like Teksan? A child again, an egg to hatch anew? An onfrit? And did I really want any change caused by only a few fistfuls of powder and a few spoken words? What would be the value of a change so cheaply bought?

I closed the book and put it back on the shelf. A sickening dizziness suddenly washed over me, darkening my vision and twisting my stomach, leaving me clinging to the shelf, with the blood throbbing in my ears and my knees weak under me. I stumbled out of the room and shut and locked the door, but the dizziness and sickness did not leave me.

Dulcie found me in the kitchen, where I had built up the fire under the pot. When the water boiled, I had been unable to get up and brew a cup of tea, and the pot was boiling dry. "Sick?" she asked anxiously. "Delan?"

"Dulcie, I should never have touched that book."

She clung to my shoulder, her soft fur tickling mine. "Love you."

"Oh, Dulcie." I petted her, and she chirruped as she always did, happy in my affection and in the simple joy of her simple life. "You went away again today," I said. "Where do you go when you go away?"

But she nuzzled my cheek with her warm nose and did not answer.

Teksan did not seem to notice that anything was wrong. I went to bed that night even more exhausted than usual, and plunged into some deep secret dream place where I had never been before, with wild, bright, unpredictable inhabitants who demanded strange things, and knew without asking, and were both dangerous and desperately beautiful.

I awoke late, with my blankets thrashed and twisted, and stumbled downstairs in a daze to hover anxiously over my cooking as if somehow the laws of the Universe had changed in the night and something awful would happen if I did not pay close attention to the cereal. At last Teksan was gone and I could sink my weary and aching body into a chair. It was autumn, and chilly even near the stove, but my clothes and fur were damp with sweat. All down my back, fierce, piercing pains drove into my flesh like spears.

"Delan, sad?" Dulcie clung to me.

"Leave me alone," I said. "I feel bad."

"Come. Come. Good place." She pulled on my worn out shirt with her sharp teeth.

"You don't understand. I can't go anywhere."

"Can," she said firmly.

I stared at her, offended. "Do you think I haven't tried?" But she kept tugging on my sleeve until I stood up, absurdly angry in my misery, swaying on my feet. "I'll prove it, then!"

She jumped from my shoulder to float on transparent wings. "Come."

I followed her. We went out into the morning-busy street, crowded with people who avoided looking directly at me or my pet, as was their habit. I pretended to them and to myself that I was just running a routine errand. Dulcie fluttered overhead, with cold sunlight shining through her wing membranes, coloring them amber.

When we came to the edge of the town, nothing had yet happened to prevent me from going so far from my house. I said to the onfrit, "Where are you taking me? Dulcie, I am sick."

She came down to me, digging her claws into my worn shirt and bundling up her wings. "Good place."

"Teksan will kill me."

She cocked her head, examining my sweating face with bright eyes, as if I were a puzzle to be figured out. "Love you, Delan. Trust Dulcie."

"Trust!" It was not the first word Dulcie had learned which I never used, but I shook my head in bewilderment. For a while I leaned for support against someone's garden wall, with the countryside spread before me. How shocked I had been when Alyk told me she hardly ever left the town! But since my arrival six months ago, I had not left it either. The hay was being cut, and turned golden where it lay. The workers, wearing red stockings so their coworkers would not accidentally cut their ankles, stood in crooked lines, singing and talking and swinging their scythes. The trees had turned the fiery colors of sunset: red and orange and yellow.

I had never been forbidden to take a walk. It was a beautiful day. I was curious now about why I was so convinced the Rope would keep me from going anywhere, and about how far I could actually go. I straightened up stiffly from my supporting wall, wondering vaguely what could be wrong with my back, to make it hurt so much. My recovery from the caning had been complete, at least in body.

I pointed at a spreading tree which grew near the road, just beyond the first farm. "I'll go that far," I told Dulcie.

When I reached the tree, I sat under it to rest for a while. I felt very hot, and the throbbing in my temples made my vision blurry. The intense, piercing pains in my back had been joined by other pains in my abdomen.

I felt very alone, and awfully afraid. I had never heard of any illness which felt like this. But if I was going to be sick, I knew I would rather be alone than have Teksan take care of me, even if it meant death.

"You're taking me to a good place?" I asked Dulcie.

"Good. Very good."

"Will I get wet if it rains?"

"Rrrains?" she repeated. "What is rrrains?" Of course, this was the first autumn of her life, and she did not know.

"When water falls from the sky." She seemed alarmed. "Never mind, it doesn't hurt anything." I stood up again. But as I walked, she rode on my shoulder and told me wonderful, incredible things about this place where we were going. There was a tremendous quantity of food, and it was high up in the air, and it was "soft," and there were many friends there, and sweet, running water. I finally laughed at her. "You're making this up, aren't you."

"No," she said, but chortled gleefully.

I threw her off my shoulder and made her fly. Even her tiny weight hurt my back.

Somehow, I kept walking all day. The road twisted among scattered farms and hills. The features of the countryside blurred in my vision and in my memory. I realized I was very ill, but my recent wayfellow, indifference, kept me walking. I began stumbling and falling, and yet when Dulcie, sun golden and chirping with anxiety, tugged on my shirt, I got up and walked again. I lost track of where I was or what direction I was going. I left the road without noticing it, following Dulcie deep into trackless, uncultivated land.

Glass shards broke out of the loam to form irregular ragged cliffs. The vegetation became scattered and scrubby. The ground crunched and gave way under my feet. I came to a stream, which led between rising, shining blue walls of glass. When I fell, the sand cut my hands and a thousand beads of blood formed on my palms. It was a barren, beautiful place. When the sun set, the cliffs seemed to glow from within. Light flowed up their riven sides like flame.

I fell again, and lay fainting with pain on the vicious sand. In the fire of the sun, I felt as if I had been burnt to a cinder. I could not go on.

"Delan?"

"Leave me alone," I mumbled into the cutting sand.

Something light and gentle touched my hair, and then slipped under my mane to touch my neck. I heard a ragged sigh of breath. I painfully lifted my head. The blaze of sunfire was fading. Over me bent a great, hooded shadow, black as night.

"How long since you ate?"

"Eia," I whispered in disbelief.

"Yes. How long since you ate?"

I felt as if the glory and anguish of the sunset had gone inside of me. Cool against my fever, the hand rested on my neck. "Since morning," I said.

Dulcie fluttered overhead. The shadow straightened up against the sky. The withdrawal of that touch seemed beyond bearing. "Dulcie, go to my place and tell Ch'ta to bring me some food." Eia bent over me again. "You will have to walk a little farther. I will help as much as I can. Can you sit up?"

I struggled up, dragging my heavy body to its knees. A warm arm slipped carefully around my waist as if somehow the monster knew that if id had touched my shoulders I would have screamed at the pain of it. And then I was lifted in one motion to my feet. The flyer's body pressed against me, supporting me along its length like a wall. Id was fur-soft, and life-warm. Ids wings lifted to cup around us like a shield, shutting out the chill, holding in the warmth.

I huddled there. I had never known such safety. It stunned me with its suddenness. After a while, I began to cry, I who never wept even when I was alone. Then I was quiet, and still the vivid dream (how could it be anything else?) did not fade. My face rested on the flyer's unclothed shoulder. Ids arms and wings embraced me. Under my cheek, was fur like my own, damp with my tears.

I said, "Teksan will come after me. He has a Rope tied to me."

The flyer asked mildly, "What kind of rope?"

"He made it out of darkness. The candle almost went out. He made me let go of my knife. Then he tied the Rope around me, even around my throat."

Id was silent. I realized vaguely that my words were utterly nonsensical. But then Eia whispered, in a voice of such rage that even I was afraid, "It was not enough that he starve you and hurt you? That he make you ashamed of what you are? It was not enough?"

I felt utterly bewildered. How did Eia know these things? "He loves to hurt me."

"Oh Del!"

"The name of the Rope is Despair," I said helpfully. I did not understand what was happening. Above all else, I did not understand why I trusted the monster, or why my pain mattered to idre.

Again there was silence, and the tightening of ids hands around my waist. "Mislaid Delan, there is something uncanny in you. I doubt Teksan suspects that you know and see so much. Despite your binding, you were able to come this far. What does that tell you?"

I said dutifully, like a child at a lesson, "The Rope's greatest power is its ability to make me believe that nothing I can do is of any use."

"Yes. Surely that power will be weakened here, among so much elemental Glass. Teksan will not find you, either, in this maze."

"If he does, he will kill me."

"No. Not until you have done what he wants you to do. Delan, walk with me. I will keep you from falling."

We began to walk, one step at a time, through the heavy, clinging sand. With each step I felt further unbalanced, but Eia compensated for it and kept me on my feet.

"I am sick," I said. "But I like this dream. I don't want to wake up."

"No," my dream companion said. "You are not sick, and you are not dreaming, and you are definitely not going to die."

"Then what? What is happening to me?"

The flyer held me tight against id's side, taking the weight of each step I took onto ids own feet. "How can I tell you so you believe me?" Ids voice was strange and ragged. "You do not see how like me you are?" The black wing was still wrapped around me, and the other one moved like a shadow in the darkness, lifting and folding rhythmically in counterbalance to our joined weight. The body pressing against my fat and shapeless side was muscle hard and sleek.

"I am not at all like you! You are—beautiful."

"And you think you are not?" The shadow head bowed heavily against the starry sky and the glimmering cliffs. "Well, when we have light, I will show you."

Dulcie returned with Eia's Ch'ta, carrying between them a bag of dried fruit. We ate as we walked. It seemed a very long way. The five moons rose suddenly from the horizon in the grouped configuration called The Dance. The stark cliffs lay black and brooding, but edged with white. For a time my pain was dulled by the drug of wonder.

Eia paused at one of these light-edged cliffs, and plucked something out of the darkness. It was a thick rope, lying on the smooth glass like a braid decoration, fastened somewhere above our heads. Id called, "Here I am; is it safe?"

Two dark shadows dove out of the sky, warbling in welcome. Dulcie and Ch'ta shot up to greet the onfrits, and they tangled and swooped wildly in the moonlight.

"You have to climb it, Delan."

Just watching the onfrits' dance had made me dizzy. I put my shoulder against the glass, but even it did not seem solid any longer. "I have to?"

"Take off your shoes and trust your sensitive feet. The rope will make it easy."

I fumbled with my shoes, and Eia gave them to the onfrits to carry away. "I will go up first, to help you over the ledge."

Alone, I watched the rope twist and flap like a live

thing as Eia climbed it. This dream seemed vivid beyond possibility: a death dream maybe, or one which came of playing with a book of sorcery.

"Come up," Eia said from above.

I took hold of the rope, and fumbled with my toes for a place to put them. Solid purchase appeared as if by magic. So long as I did not think about my footing, I found it. It was only when I stopped to consider that I felt my fear. The moonlit, sandy stream dropped away below me, and then instead of rope I was gripping Eia's wrist. Id pulled me up over the ledge. I lay sprawled and trembling, my breath knocked out of me by hard glass, nearly fainting with the pain in my back.

"You said the rope would make it easy," I gasped.

"Sometimes saying something makes it true. Here." Again the strong hands helped me up. "Duck your head; the entry is low."

The faint glow of an air lamp illuminated the ledge and the cramped interior of the cave. There was no bed, only a rug on the floor, piled with blankets the like of which I had never seen. The only furniture was a long-legged stool and table rudely made of gnarled binewood. There were books everywhere, and a disordered pile of paper on the table. On a ledge, nesting among a mess of sticks and leaves and scraps of cloth, all three of Eia's onfrits were grooming Dulcie, who seemed well satisfied with the arrangement.

Eia sat me on the stool and began undoing my clothing. Id was wearing only a knife belt, and behaved as if fur was more than enough clothes for anyone, and so I decided not to be offended at this liberty. Ids face was triangular like mine was, but with sharp, fine bones. Ids mane floated in a soft, hazy tangle, like mine.

I looked in sudden curiosity at id's crotch. Just as with me, there was only fur, coming to a neat point. Eia said, "I have an interior penis, which on appropriate occasions makes its appearance. Sometimes on not so appropriate occasions, which can be awfully embarrassing. Here, sit still." If it was rude of me to be looking for ids genitals, ids voice did not tell me so.

Id pulled off my shirt. The release of tension made me realize how tight it had gotten. I twisted to look at my throbbing back, and did not recognize it. Swollen bulbs of flesh poked out of my silver fur like pale tumors. I stared, shocked and horrified. "Think of them as flower buds," Eia said.

I looked again at idre, at the beautiful, stretched astil wings with the light shining through, outlining the tracery of veins. My horror faded suddenly. I whispered, "Am I growing wings?"

"Yes. And genitals."

"I am—you? What you are?"

"Yes."

"Are there others?"

Eia almost laughed. "Yes, some four hundred."

"Do they ask questions that have no answers? Do they love living on a mountain falling through space? Do they want to talk to a Mer about the water?"

Eia looked at me out of deep, liquid eyes that made my heart turn over strangely. "What do you think?"

"Yes?"

"Yes."

Chapter 4

My memories of the next several days are like pages torn out of a book. On each of those pages is Eia: writing at the table; asleep beside me, curled on ids stomach, black wings drooping; standing out on the ledge in the blazing sun; supporting me in ids arms, holding a cup of water to my mouth. I also have a strangely shattered memory of ids pointed, triangular face, wet with tears. I had been screaming, I think, in delirium or in pain. I remember that, even in my fevered daze, I was bemused by the stranger's caring. I said nervously, "I'm sorry for being so much trouble."

"It is a privilege to attend a l'shil," Eia said. "Someone was a Companion to my passage in this way, and someday you, too, may be Companion to someone. This is as it is supposed to be."

In those days I learned lessons that would serve me well. I learned that it was possible to be helpless and vulnerable without also being hurt. I learned that not all generosity was disguised exploitation. I learned to trust a little.

At last, from a deep sleep, I opened my eyes to a brilliant sunrise, and an uninhabited cave, with even the onfrits missing. The pain and fever were gone. I curled on my side in Eia's bed, so relaxed and peaceful that I scarcely recognized my own self. When I tried to move, air tingled on delicate, incredibly sensitive skin. I felt muscles move in my torso that had never moved before. Something waved on the edge of my vision, awkward as an infant newly hatched, white as a cloud. It was myself.

I knew that Eia was returning because the onfrits appeared in a playful crowd, wrangling lightheartedly over air space. Dulcie swooped over to be petted, chirping with good cheer. Eia dropped lightly to the ledge, ids black wings creating a brief twilight in the cave. Then morning sun burned around ids folding wings, white sun on blue glass. "Delan?" Eia said.

"Eia, they are so heavy." My voice was hoarse with disuse—how many days had it been?

Id came over to me and crouched gracefully, wings briefly brushing the floor. "You have little strength in your flight muscles yet with which to support your wings. And you have lost about half your body weight. Everything will seem heavy to you until you become accustomed to being a small person."

"Half!"

Eia untangled from me the strange blankets, each of which weighed no more than a dried leaf. "Look."

I had never known how pudgy and shapeless I had been, until I looked at myself that morning and saw a stranger's body, stretched across the rug in lean, clean lines, muscles standing out that I had never known existed, kept from spare harshness only by the softening of my charcoal and silver fur. Whoever this stranger was, I thought to myself in confusion, id was astonishingly beautiful.

Eia took hold of the edge of my wing and unfolded it. Though I was lying down, the tip reached as high as the ceiling. It was cloud white, with a pearling of gray on the leading edge and along the ribs. In the sunlight its red blood veins shone through the tough membrane like lace. I lay speechless under its spread, fascinated by the blood pulsing in the veins.

Eia said, "We are a rare people, but Silvers are the rarest among us. And you have such contrasts, so dark and so light!"

"How could it be me? It doesn't feel like me."

"You are not awake yet." Id stroked a fingertip down the leading edge of my wing, where a few silver hairs were sparsely scattered.

That touch riveted and paralyzed me. I had in fact been asleep and numb my entire life. I had never truly felt anything until I felt that touch, brushing across my sensitive, innocent, newborn wing. I felt it, not only in the wing, but in the rest of me as well, in my heart which froze for a moment in my chest, in my tough as glass lightweight bones, and most powerfully in that secret place between my thighs where Crila's fingers had once searched and found nothing.

Eia's voice was too quiet. "You seem to be awake now."

"I am awake," I whispered, wondering in terror and longing what would happen now.

But Eia stood up abruptly, and suddenly was very far away. "Get up, then. We'll have some breakfast. I'll teach you how to fly."

Explaining the mechanics of flight, Eia sounded unnervingly like Teksan in the schoolroom. But unlike Teksan, who talked at length and repeated himself often, Eia said each thing with brevity, and only once. Id seemed to assume that I would remember it, and that if there was anything I did not understand, I would ask. I did remember, and the only thing I did not understand was how I was supposed to continue to remember when I was in the air and terrified.

That was a question I was given no chance to ask. Eia and I stood on the ledge, with the crazy glass maze stretching as far as could be seen below us. Id pointed. "It looks safest that way. Make your landing on the sand. I will count to five and if by then you have not jumped, I will push you."

"But," I began.

"One," Eia said, "Two."

I jumped.

Heavy, unmanageable, and uncoordinated, my wings had been dragging on the floor and banging on furniture all morning. But they spread of their own volition as I went over the ledge. Captured under the cupped membranes, the wind picked me up. I did not fall; I floated. And I was not terrified. All in one moment I knew why I had always felt so misplaced, why I was always longing for high places and felt at home on precipices. My entire life I had been traveling in the wrong element, confined to the ground when I belonged in the air.

I could not help myself. My shout of ecstasy sang in the glass below.

"Turn," Eia said. Id was hovering above me, ruddering gracefully with id's legs, laughing. "You'll spike yourself on glass if you're not careful. Try to think of where you're going to land."

"Nowhere!" I shouted. "Never!" But, nonetheless, I did what I had practiced afoot in the cave, lifting one wing and dropping the other, and so turning away from my suicidal direction and toward the comparative safety of the streambed. It was a long, easy glide. Eia had cautioned me against trying anything more complicated. I had to build up my endurance slowly, or injure myself and thus become unable to fly again until I was healed. I landed messily at the end of the glide, with my face in the sand and the wind knocked out of me.

"Delan!" Eia landed a handsbreadth away, light as a leaf. "If you've hurt yourself—"

I got up on my elbows and turned my head, astonished. "I'm not hurt. I'm just not very good at this."

I saw a motion in id's face, as if Eia was about to put on the serene, schoolteacher mask again, but abruptly decided against it. For a long moment we looked at each other. "You'll get the knack of it," id finally said.

I looked at the sky. The air brushing past me, insubstantial stuff. "I don't believe I just—" The moment of being absolutely certain what I was and why I lived faded. I felt disoriented. I was hatched a Walker. I belonged in the air. How was I to understand myself?

Eia's smile contained at least as much sadness as gladness. "I guess you'd better do it again, then. Until you believe it."

Id gave me a hand up. I shyly put my hand on ids shoulder as we walked side by side back to the hanging rope. Eia's fur was hot with the autumn sun. Ids knife was tied in the sheath and strapped to ids thigh. Id had a fine, thin scar in one wing membrane. In the inside of ids right wrist, a triangle was branded in the flesh. I felt small beside the mass of muscles in ids torso, even though we were eye to eye in height. When our wings brushed accidentally, it left me trembling.

We climbed the rope to the ledge again, for we could not take off from the ground. (Eia had tried to explain why not, but my vocabulary was not adequate to it, and my mathematical ability ended at counting my change at market.) When I looked at idre before my next jump, I spotted in ids face disquiet and self-possession standing hand in hand like old friends. The schoolteacher I had so resented was gone, and never came back. The one who was with me now was a person layered and folded like a winter blanket in a storage cabinet. But with the door open.

*   *   *

When I was so tired that I could not even lift my wings to fold them, Eia finally took pity on me and let me rest. After a meal of cooked grains and draf cheese, I went back to bed. Id drew up the rope and flew out with Ch'ta to fetch supplies from the Walker friends that were providing for idre. I dozed through the afternoon. When I awoke, Eia was still gone, and I was hungry again. Every muscle in my body was sore, and my knees were weak. I ate what I could find, and picked up one of the books.

Later, I lit the air lamp. I sprawled on my stomach on the bed, and became so engrossed in the book that Eia's breathless voice startled me as if out of sleep. "Who taught you how to read?"

I knew enough about flight by then to realize that the incredible control of Eia's silent landing suggested something beyond mere experience. The light of sunset reflecting off the glass shone red and smoky through ids wing membranes, which were half spread to disperse body heat. The tension in me was released in a sigh. I had been unreasonably afraid that Eia would not come back. "Teksan did," I said.

"I am surprised to hear it."

"I spied on his schoolroom. I steal his books, too. He does not have any stories, though."

"You steal them?" Eia gave a delighted laugh, undoing the buckles to loosen the pack strapped between ids wings. "Did you ever read any of his sorcery books?"

"Only once. You know a lot about Teksan," But I remembered that I myself had all but told Eia that he was a sorcerer, when in my fever daze I told about the Rope named Despair. I did not feel it here, I realized suddenly. Beneath my confusion and disbelief over what I had become, moved a dizzying joy.

Eia said, "Teksan came to my community once, before I was winged, demanding to be taught our kind of magic. But he would not understand that our few magicians grow into their magic, and it cannot be taught. He thought we were refusing him because he was a Walker. I have never forgotten him. He frightened me."

"Perhaps he *had* grown into his magic, and you were refusing to help him develop it."

Eia seemed about to burst into angry speech, but took a breath and instead said mildly, "It is true that we withhold too much from the Walkers. But it would have been a mistake to encourage power in a man like him. You know that."

"How is Walker magic different?"

"One of our magicians tried to study it once. Id determined that sorcery's power comes in part from inflicted pain, and would go no further with it."

"Inflicted pain! The book was just a listing of recipes—"

"Del, you are the one who told me that he enjoys hurting you. Sadism is a requirement for sorcery, though most Walkers manage to stay ignorant of the fact, being enamored of the idea of magic. The book which tells how the magic powders are made will give you nightmares, at the very least."

It was a new experience to have someone at least as bright as I, and far better educated, in the same room with me. I said sullenly, "Why do you know so much?"

Eia laughed suddenly. "Please pardon me. I have enjoyed being protective of you, and am not as willing to give it up as I ought to be. I have some berry wine; would you like a cup?"

I decided that Eia was an altogether surprising person. Having emptied the pack, id took a bottle out of the storage box, and filled a couple of pottery cups. I got up willingly from my lazing, for I had never been allowed to taste wine before. After the first sip, which was more startling than pleasant, I liked the wine a great deal. I began to feel as if my head was separated from the rest of my body. I sat on the stool, watching Eia construct a bean and vegetable stew. "I was glad when you came home," I said. "I like being with you."

My own boldness unnerved me, but Eia said quietly, "Thank you. I was glad to come home to you."

"What race are we?"

Eia looked up from slicing, ids face inscrutible. "Aeyrie."

"What?"

"Aeyrie." Eia bent over the pot.

"But—" I fell silent, utterly dismayed.

"I know what you have heard about the Aeyries. We have our misconceptions about the Walkers, too: they are incapable of abstract thought, we say. They are hopelessly narrow-minded and prejudiced. Their world is the size of their village or farm. They treat their drafs better than they treat their children. They prefer simple fictions over complex truths. But none of these things are necessarily true—some of the most complex, broad-minded, courageous people I have ever known were Walkers."

The fur on Eia's sides was plastered down with sweat from the hard flight. Id stood up to shake out cramped legs, and then squatted down again, frowning at the stewpot. The onfrits awoke from their naps and came over in a rush to fight over the vegetable scraps.

I said, "The Walkers say that the Aeyries exploit them, make them pay high prices for what should be theirs by right. They say that if not for the Aeyries they would not have to work so hard, they would be rich—"

"Del, look at your body. Look at how much substance it has."

I obediently looked again at my stranger's legs and torso, which had only the same color of fur to reassure me that they were myself. The sharp relief of bone and muscle made me look underfed, if not starving.

"You can build your endurance and become a tireless flyer, but your entire strength will be concentrated in your flight muscles. Even if you wanted to, do you think you could till a field?"

"I—no."

"Our people used to gather food in the wild and carry it to our homes in the mountains. But now the Walkers call that thievery and shoot us down with their bows. They think we are rich! But the truth is that we live on the edge of starvation."

I said, after a very long time, "If that is the truth, then very few Walkers actually know it."

"You have grown up a Walker. You tell me the answer to this question. If they knew what power they have over us, would they exercise it well, or badly?"

I did not have to consider long. "Badly."

"So," Eia said.

"Do you hate them, then?"

"Most Aeyries do."

"Do you?"

Eia swept more vegetable trimmings to the floor for the onfrits. "No." Id looked up at me. The reflected light from the air lamp glittered in ids eyes. "It is ingrained in Walker culture, that they have rights to the land, that their primary purpose in life should be to form a family unit and reproduce. How can I hate them for failing to be aware of what they are doing to us?

"And they are not entirely unaware, not all of them. I know because I have lived with Walkers, as you have. Two years ago I left my Ula to join the Community of the Triad, which is the only place in the world where members of the three races are trying to live together in harmony. I was a taiseoch-dre, the offspring of the chieftain of Ula t'Fon. My parent disinherited me for going against ids will. You see, I have this difficult gift, which often seems more a curse, the inability to see matters in yes or no, black or white."

Id bent over the little stove which was scarcely bigger than the stewpot id set upon it. I looked at my cup, and was somewhat surprised to find that it was empty. Eia sipped from ids cup, smiling as id watched the onfrits, who having each secured a substantial pile of food were now generously exchanging pieces of it with each other.

I said, "And then you left the Community of the Triad also? Why is that?"

"Well—" Eia hesitated. "I fell in love with a Walker woman. She was in love also, but not with me. I left because my unforgivable behavior was causing me to lose my self-respect."

Id looked up at me then, and laughed softly. "Are you shocked, or just surprised?"

Never in my entire life had anyone talked to me so frankly. I said, "I can't imagine you badly behaved."

Eia laughed again. "You don't know me very well."

"Are you going to go back to that place?"

"To Triad? If I can swallow my pride."

"Haven't you been lonely here, all these months?"

"Yes, very lonely. Not nearly as lonely as you must have been, these twenty years."

"How did we end up living so near each other? What a strange coincidence!"

"No." Id came up to me, until I was bewildered by id's nearness and looked shyly away. I had never seen anyone move like Eia, so spare and flowing, so unlike my own clumsy awkwardness. Eia put a hand to my back, between my wings. I quivered with tension. No one ever touched me, not even by accident. My first reaction was to want to pull away.

Eia pretended not to notice. Ids hand smoothed down my back, like petting an onfrit. "It was not a coincidence at all. I followed you and settled nearby on purpose. My onfrits contacted Dulcie, and she came to visit sometimes. One night I went to you because

Dulcie fetched me. I can tell you, now that we both know you have come out perfect, how afraid I was that he had damaged your wing buds with his cane."

I remembered the dream hands on my beaten body, the hushed and angry voice, the sweet taste that blanked out pain. I wanted to ask why, why had Eia followed and befriended a stranger, why had id done so much and yet not told me what I was or rescued me. At first I was afraid of what the answer to that question might be. Then I was too distracted to care. Eia's hand stroked my sides and shoulders, firmly and purposefully. "Does that hurt?"

"Not very much." I did not tell idre about the other things ids hands were doing to me, the things that were not pain, not quite. I felt a new sympathy with my Walker nestmates, who having awakened to their sexuality, could not care much about anything else.

Behind me, Eia said softly, "I was hard on you today. I do not know what is going to happen, or how much time we have. I don't think your hard work today did any damage, but your muscles are going to be awfully sore."

Ids careful hands kneaded my flight muscles like a baker her bread. I sat quiet, for a long time, though I did not feel quiet.

Then ids touch grew softer, stroking slowly, and finally ceased entirely. "Do you want some more wine?" Eia's voice was not entirely steady.

I turned on the stool, and reached up to touch ids folded wings on the leading edge, touched softly, soft as air. With a jerk they lifted and hooded out in a way which should have seemed menacing. But I was on my feet, the wine cup clattering on the floor, and Eia's arms were around my waist and on my back, pulling me close into the warm and sweat damp musk of ids body. My half spread wings shuddered against ids. The hard nipples of ids breasts pressed into mine. Ids eyes, near and dark and unquiet told me of a losing struggle, a hunger deep and long standing, a loneliness as unremitting and relentless as mine.

Eia said, "Del—" Then a smile, crooked and rueful. "Oh, hellwinds."

Ids fingers stroked my face closer, and ids mouth touched mine. I heard the sound in my throat, like a moan of pain. Fingers dug suddenly into my hair. Eia whispered something; beautiful, incomprehensible, liquid words, yet the meaning was somehow very clear to me.

Eia was playful as an onfrit. My shyness gave way to an intense, demanding, fierce hunger. Untended, the vegetable stew threatened to scorch. Eia leapt out of bed at last, to add water and stir it vigorously, leaving me sprawled where I was, my life's first orgasm still shivering in my muscles, my nipples wet from Eia's mouth and standing up in the chill. Id returned to me in haste, the corners of ids eyes crinkled with laughter, but came gasping and frantic from our kiss, hands trembling as id turned a wing for me.

On my back, I realized suddenly why Eia had seemed afraid earlier, when lying helpless under me, with me so crazed and altogether unknowing of what I was doing. But by the time we were coupling again, I was beyond worrying about such things. Eia sobbed suddenly in the tangle of our bodies. Black wings hooded over us, fluttering against mine, and then they spasmed, and spread, and Eia's wild, sweet voice rang agaist the glass walls.

Later, id lay breathless, holding me close. I wept or laughed, I did not know which. Eia's hand stroked my mane, working out the tangles one by one with ids fingers. A long, sweet time, long after I became quiet, id touched me. It was awfully easy to believe that id cared for me.

We ate scorched stew, sitting back to back on the one stool with our wings spread to make room for each other. Eia said, "Is it so bad, being an Aeyrie?"

I sputtered and choked on a mouthful of soup.

"Is that a yes?" Eia's voice vibrated with laughter. "I fulfilled my obligation?"

"What obligation?"

"As your Companion, to make certain your first lovemaking is a good one."

"This was supposed to happen?"

I tried belatedly to hide my dismay, but Eia said hastily, "I keep forgetting you were brought up a Walker! Yes, the Aeyries do arrange these things. Why leave something so important up to a wingling's lack of discrimination? Oh dear, that will offend you, too."

"Yes," I said stiffly.

Eia sighed. "Well, the Aeyries expect l'shils to be somewhat at the mercy of their genitals, although it is hard to say how much of that is culture and how much of it is truth. A Companion is supposed to be as much parent as lover, to steady you through the transition year and then to let you go. I have worried over it for months, knowing that you were near maturity and I was the only one who could watch over you, but I am entirely inappropriate for the role! I will not, I told myself, I will not touch the child, under any circumstance!"

I could not see Eia's face, but ids voice was at once so distressed and so amused that I might have laughed, except that I had gone from dismay to giddiness at knowing that Eia, beautiful and self-possessed Eia, had utterly failed to resist me.

"So now we are in this difficult situation. You want to be loved, you want it desperately."

I said after a while, "Yes." I felt shy again. Maybe intimacy would never seem casual or ordinary to me.

"And I am—" Eia hesitated, and finished wryly, "entirely overcome. Which feels wonderful and is awfully dangerous. I want to stay your friend. I do not want to hurt you!"

I said, "Well, I will not hurt you."

Eia sighed, and then laughed. "I think you underestimate yourself."

We washed our dishes in a pail. I went out on the ledge as Eia put things away. It was night; the moons had scattered from their dance and the stars were bright and close. Soon the month of rain would be upon us, and after that the winter. I wondered what I was going to do with myself. I thought of the Rope that bound me to Teksan, and wondered how I could become free of it. I wanted nothing more than I wanted to stay here with Eia, but would id ask me to stay?

Eia came out to me. "Del?"

I said nothing. Eia took my hand. "There is a kind of wind, called a hellwind. There is no fighting it. All you can do is ride it, and hope your luck is good."

We drew closer under the star bright sky. Eia left a warm burning place on my wing with ids mouth. I stopped thinking again. We played a game without any rules, wrestling, and laughing with delight whether we won or lost. And then we traveled beyond laughter and came utterly undone together.

In the midst of our lovemaking, I cried, as if I knew that when I opened my eyes in the morning I would no longer be able to avoid knowing the truth.

Chapter 5

Eia huddled in ids wings beside me, ruffled and sleep quiet and musky with sex. Ids tangled mane framed ids relaxed face in contradictory disarray. I lifted a hand to smooth the tangles, but did not. My wit, stunned by my metamorphosis, stirred at last from its shock.

When Eia and I encountered each other for the first time in the mountains, id had certainly known immediately that I was an immature Aeyrie. Id had not told me. Id had known of Teksan's antipathy for the Aeyries, but had not warned me or tried to separate me from him. The night Teksan beat me, Eia had come to me, and cared for me, and yet once again left me ignorant in that house, ignorant even of the fact that I had a friend within calling. Surely id had known long before then the danger I was in, a danger which even I in my naïveté had recognized at last. Eia was brilliant and knowledgeable and widely experienced. Could id have been unaware of the hopelessness and loneliness with which I was living my life?

Surely this tenderness and respect and delight could not be possible without love! But Eia's six-month silence bespoke massive indifference, if not cruelty. I tried to think of a good explanation, and could not. Every possibility led me to the same conclusion: Eia

was misleading and using me. Ids honest and affec-
tionate ways were a mockery, and I, in my misery and
loneliness had been all too easy to be made a fool of.

I lifted my hand to angrily shake Eia's shoulder, but
once again drew it back. I did not want to fight with
idre or, even worse, to discover that I was willing to
accept more lies for the sake of continuing happiness.
I did not want to hear Eia deny or explain, and tarnish
this dizzying brightness in me with either lies or truth.
Perhaps I had been used, but I also had become human in this bed. Somehow I had to keep what I had
gained, even if it meant I had to get up and go away
while my gratitude and my independence both were
still intact.

When I went over the ledge with my clothes tucked
under one arm and Dulcie fluttering in confusion after
me, Eia was still asleep. I told myself that the whole
world lay before me. I told myself that even the tears
which blinded me were good.

I flew through a crisp, pale morning which tasted of
winter. Sun shimmered over the maze. The glass
glowed, but rivers of shadow filled the sandy canyons.
I could not fly far. I landed within the maze, but I
walked quickly, seeking to reach cover before Eia
began to look for me. It was cold and silent here. The
sand whispered under my feet. The cliffs blurred around
me. My stomach ached with grief. I walked in a daze
of tears. The cliffs diminished around me, but I did
not notice.

Too late I sensed my danger. One step beyond the
glass canyon, the Rope had me. In one moment it had
consumed all the warmth in me, like a winter wind. It
even robbed me of my pain. Even as I gave a choked
cry, I was bewildered by my own anguish. What was
the matter with me? What had I lost?

There was some reason why I should not go back to

L'din. But I could not remember clearly what the reason was. Didn't I need food and shelter? Did I have anywhere else that I could go? Yes, Teksan had hurt me, but I had deserved it, hadn't I?

Under the first tree I turned back, searching the cold, bright sky for a pursuer, but it remained empty. I could not remember if I had followed a path when I came this way, and Dulcie was no help. I picked a direction and plunged into the bushes. My wings caught in the branches, shivering into pain as the sharp twigs scraped the sensitive membranes. My flight muscles burned in my torso, so worn out and sore that I could not keep my wings folded.

The unremitting struggle to fit my changed self through the thickets made the day long. I grew weary and weak with hunger. My feet dragged under the burden on my back. By afternoon I thought I was lost.

"Which way is L'din?" I asked Dulcie. But for once she refused to help me, and yearned toward the way we had come. At last she would go no farther, forcing me to choose between leaving her or carrying her. Raging, I tucked her ungently under my arm.

Eventually I came to a stone wall, with a harvested field on the other side, and a cluster of flat buildings within sight. I shied away, remembering Eia's warning about Walker bows and arrows. Somewhat later I spotted a black figure flying into the sun. With Dulcie in my hands I hid in the bushes.

A long time the flyer searched, moving in wide circles, but keeping away from the farmland. I lay down in my hiding place, but could not seem to find any rest. Not until sunset did my hunter head back toward the maze, flying slowly, as if id was weighed down in the sky.

Only one moon rose, the tiny moon Lla, bright as a polished jewel but too small to cast much light. Knowing that Aeyries cannot see well in the dark, I was less

cautious, leaving the dense vegetation of the wild countryside and coming to the road where traveling was
much easier. Even so, I was sick and stumbling with
exhaustion when I came into L'din.

The town was dark, and its streets were empty,
except for a few market-day drunks sleeping where
they had fallen. But as I came near my own house, I
saw that I was not the only one awake in this town.
Teksan stood at the doorway, amid the trailing, light-
diffusing plants with which I had filled the courtyard, a
long time ago it seemed now. The Rope which bound
us to each other reeled me in, like a waterwyth on a
fishing line. But even as I drew too close for escape,
that secret thing inside of me, that uncanniness which
Teksan did not know about, spoke within me: *I am a
prisoner*, it said. *So long as I remember that, I have
hope of being free.*

I walked past him through the door, and as I passed
him it was as if I passed into a mist, and entered from
one world into another. Now it was Eia and the glass
maze which seemed to have happened a long time
ago, to another person. This was my place; the place I
belonged. The dreaming was over.

The seer inside of me spoke again: *No*, it said. *No,
it is not over.*

I went down the hall to the kitchen. When I passed
through the mist I had not lost the new body which
certainly belonged in that other place, and I could not
sit on Walker furniture. I leaned my shoulder on the
wall, a piece of bread in one hand and a dipper of
water in the other. Teksan came in and looked at me.

"You must have known this was going to happen to
me," I said, my mouth full.

"Yes, I knew. You are an Aeyrie, did you guess?"

It was the seer in me who recalled and felt anew
what I had felt that first time, when Eia told me. I let
Teksan read it in my face: dismay mixed with reluctant

relief that at least I was not a monster. "Why did you not tell me?"

"For your own good. Your body is Aeyrie, but your heritage is Walker. It was to spare you what confusion I could, to let you be what you are and not what you felt you were supposed to be."

"Why so kind to one of a race you hate?"

His thin face gave away no secrets. His mouth was narrow and his eyes were like stones. "Perhaps I was curious. Perhaps I was thinking that it is not their race which makes Aeyries what they are, but only their heritage. Where have you been, these six days?"

"I thought I was dying. I wanted to be alone for it." I cut a chunk of cheese and scooped more water out of the pail. The cheese was dry and the water was stale. I felt as if I could eat all night. Teksan might well believe that I had taken no food for six days.

"Where?"

I looked at him. "What does it matter?"

"I tried to find you."

"I hid well. I didn't want to be found."

"You were in a place," he said in a flat voice, "Where my Mirror could not see."

I straightened, lifting my shoulder from the wall. "What?"

"Delan," he said softly, blocking my way through the doorway. "Someone has been in my room."

I told myself he could not know how afraid I was. But in fact I knew nothing of sorcery, and perhaps he was able to look right through me, as if I were a bowl of water. Certainly he seemed to, as he stared at me with his stone eyes. "Some knowledge is dangerous," he said.

"I am the one who was in your room."

"What did you see?"

"Books. Something else, that made me piddle on the floor. Was that the Mirror?"

"That was the Door."

There was silence. Then I heard my voice say, "Is there a way sorcery can make something into something else?"

"What do you mean?" (*Listen,* Delan the seer said inside of me. *Listen to his voice, how casual it is. Too casual.*)

"Can you make an Aeyrie into a Walker?" My voice was shaking, and the cup quivering in my hand. I set it down hastily.

"It might be possible."

I started toward him then, stopping myself only when I remembered that my wings would not let me drop carelessly to my knees. The breath hurt in my throat.

"You do not want to be an Aeyrie?" he asked softly.

"I am not an Aeyrie, I am nothing! All I want is to belong somewhere!"

"It would not be easy, Delan. And all sorcery must be bought. This one would take a high price."

"I wish I had died, then. What do I have before me? I belong not to both races but to neither!"

"There is something you might do," he said. "Not a small thing, but something the world would thank you for."

"If I did it, would you be able to make me into a Walker?"

"Yes."

"I will do it, then. Whatever you want."

The night was half over when I went up the narrow stairway and into my room. When I lay down on my cot, I felt so weary and wretched that I doubted I would never get up again. But my feelings contested with each other in my belly: anxiety and despair and exultation and a deep and terrible knowledge of my solitude. I did not sleep soon, or well.

* * *

Even if there was no one in L'din who knew that Aeyries were winged, I could no longer show myself. But I had lived on enemy territory my entire life, and if now I had to lurk in a dark house and hide in my room when Teksan had visitors, it seemed only inevitable. Afoot I was trapped, unable to take off from the ground and not designed for fleeing; in every way overpowered and outweighed and outnumbered by those who hated and feared me. I could think of no safety except in hiding, an uncertain safety at best. Perhaps all Aeyries felt like this in a Walker world, with their lightweight bodies and their vulnerability on the ground.

As for the Walker resentment which made life for my kind so dangerous in the first place, I still did not understand it. Without ever choosing it, I had been different from everyone else since before my egg sheath was slit. I could not imagine what it was like to hate and fear that which was not like me, when everyone I had ever met on earth was not like me, save one.

Of that one I thought constantly, wretchedly.

Teksan ceased spending his days at the tavern. It rained, steadily and drearily, day after day, until the gutters spilled over and the roads became rivers. Through the window of my room I watched the people of L'din preparing for winter hibernation: shuttering their windows, securing their food supplies, bringing in great quantities of stove fuel. Everything was wet. I brought my blankets down to the kitchen every morning to dry out by the stove. Dulcie grew short-tempered and mischievious with the confinement.

I did not try to go out, even at night when I lay wakeful and tormented on my rope bed. Something about the windows and doors of the house made my fur stand on end, something which let me know that Teksan did not entirely trust my compliance, and that if I even once rebelled, the spells he had laid across the exits would have let him know it. I awoke, day after day, to the sound of water dribbling off the roof, with depression lying in my belly like a stone. Bored and indifferent, I survived the day, and went to bed a little earlier each night, a little more deadened, a little more enslaved. And each night sleep evaded me.

One afternoon, five of Teksan's friends came up the walk and were admitted to the parlor. I watched them through the cracked shutter. The sound of their voices came up the stairwell: slow speaking, solid Walker voices, with anger in them.

Teksan called, "Delan, come down."

I got up from my stool. My only other choice was to dive out of the bedroom window, into the pouring rain. I told Dulcie to stay behind, and went hesitantly down the stairs and into the parlor.

I knew the visitors all by name: Caban the smithy, Lekur and Hapstn the merchants, Presle the land seller and Jandra the market manager. I had seen them often enough, going about their business. Their astounded stares confused me for a moment because I persisted in forgetting how changed was my appearance. They wore work clothes, with quilted vests against the cold, holding hot cups in chilled hands. Over the steam of their cups of tea, they examined me, eyes wide and disbelieving. Then, as one, they looked at Teksan, as if for the answer to a question already asked.

He hooked a stool over with his foot, and bid me sit. "All she has to do is tell the truth. That she was hatched from a misplaced egg, and only when she came into her wings did she know she was an Aeyrie. They will take her in, especially since it will be winter, and she will be grounded. They would do anything for their own, and never question her explanation."

"How do you know she will then let us in?" Presle

asked. In the cold, he had exchanged his eyeshade for a knitted hat, dyed berry-red.

"Delan will do as she is told, and be rewarded for it."

Unfriendly, untrusting eyes looked back at me, where I sat with my fingers twisted in the cloth of my shirt. "Yes," I said.

"The roads are impassible during the winter, I have heard."

"We will journey by another way, which will take us only moments. As I have already told you, Caban. You do not believe me yet?"

The smithy, a crabby woman whose overgrown muscles made her seem misshapen, grumbled into her cup, "I have heard much talk of sorcery, but I have yet to see any."

Teksan said, "Delan, fetch the mirror from my room."

I heard their voices pick up after I left. There was a feeling in my belly as if I had just survived something.

The lock on Teksan's bedroom door fell into my hand when I touched it. The Door still swirled in the center of his room. A mirror stood innocently atop a clothes chest, a small thing only two hands wide, small enough that I had never noticed it on my other visits. The face reflected there was closed and hostile, with challenging, angry gray eyes, half shielded by the tangle of a silver and charcoal mane. It scared me, that face, despite being mine. That face had a secret, a power and a rage that I kept hidden even from myself.

I stole a single sheet of blank paper from the desk, folded it up into a small package, and tucked it into my shoe. By the bookshelf, I hesitated, sensing there the tension of a set trap. Did Teksan suspect I could read?

I went back to the parlor, and gave Teksan the mirror. "Did you want me to lock the door again, sir?"

"Yes."

When I came back again, the Walkers were so crowded around the mirror that I could not see what they were looking at. Their faces were tense with hidden fear. I stood back indifferently until Teksan turned to me. "Come and look."

The others made room for me then, hastily, trying to avoid being touched even by my clothes.

The mirror no longer reflected my face. I was looking as if through extremely clear water at a distant scene. The Glass Mountains were already stripped bare by the winter wind. One peak was centered in the Mirror, a peak on the top of which was glued an eccentric tumble of towers and rooftops. Around this wild dwelling, a few flyers could be seen. It was utterly inaccessible; even a medog with its six prehensile feet could not have climbed that steep peak. Clouds swept through the sky, pushed by a fierce wind which occasionally threw the flyers off their courses. I saw one narrowly miss being tossed into the side of a tower.

Teksan was looking for a reaction. I said, "I doubt they do much flying in winter."

"One might say they are imprisoned by the wind for two months of the year."

"Once they accept me in, how am I supposed to give you access to it?"

"Not all Aeyries can fly, as you know, and they are extremely protective of their juveniles." He paused as the Walkers snorted and snickered at the notion of coddling children. "Therefore, there is a stairway inside the mountain for their escape in case of some mishap, but we would not easily find or open the entrance. If you come on foot, claiming you cannot fly, they will have to take you in that way."

"Why do you want to get in?"

I felt the others stiffen around me, but Teksan said

disinterestedly, "To take something which should be ours by right: knowledge. A few books."

I nodded, and the Walkers relaxed. "Does this place have a name?"

"Ula t'Fon the Aeyries call it, 'Nest of the Sun.' Traders call it Down Nest because it is farthest south of the three Aeyrie towns." Teksan was talking in his superior schoolteacher voice. I stood back, pretending boredom to cover my shock. Eia's town, with which id had spoken with such sadness and longing!

How was Teksan going to do this thing in the dead of winter when all Walkers including himself were hibernating? But this was one thing they did not tell me. Teksan turned to me abruptly and said, "You are excused now."

"Sir." I left.

In my own room I spread out the folded and crushed paper from my shoe, and found my store of charcoal, taken one bit at a time from the kitchen stove. I thought a long time before I began to write.

"Eia," I wrote, and suddenly my eyes were burning with tears. I rubbed my face on my sleeve, and wrote through the blur. "Teksan and his people intend to use me to gain access to Ula t'Fon. They say they will only steal some books, but they are angry and hateful people, and I know they mean your people harm. It will be done soon, and Teksan will use his sorcery to make the journey there short, and also to somehow prevent hibernation. I do not know if I can ride this hellwind. I am not asking you to help me, except to keep Dulcie safe. But I hope you can help your people. Delan."

I folded up the paper again, and tied it with a piece of string to one of Dulcie's front legs. "Go to Eia," I told her. "Do not come back to me."

"Delan," she protested, clinging to me. "Love you, Delan."

"I know. Go, Dulcie. There is danger here." In haste, for fear I might change my mind, I untangled her claws from my clothes and threw her out the window. The days had grown short, and it was near dark by then. The rain had stopped, but the clean streets remained empty. The light of Teksan's lamps scattered across the wet, narrow street. Dulcie crossed the light like a ghost. As I watched, she seemed to falter, so briefly that as soon as I noticed, I was telling myself it had been a trick of the light. She flew strongly into the shadows, and was gone.

Shortly afterward, Teksan's guests left in a muted group, walking together but not talking. Teksan called from the foot of the stairs, "I am going out. I am not certain when I will be back."

I said, "My onfrit went out before sunrise."

"So?"

"If you see her, would you tell her to come home?"

He did not bother to reply. I heard the door slam, and through my window watched him go down the street, in the same direction that the others had gone.

I lay down on my bed and stared into the shadows. Dulcie would awaken Eia in the middle of the night. Eia would read my note. Perhaps id would lie in bed, awake, thinking, thinking of some way to get a warning message to ids people. Maybe id would remember me and how it had been between us. Maybe, I thought, maybe id cared for me a little. Maybe id would not leave me abandoned and without recourse. Maybe id would help me.

Chapter 6

Teksan was not home when I awoke in the morning. Ill at ease and unable to do housework, I had been wandering the house for several hours before I finally heard him unlatching the door. "Did you see Dulcie?" I asked anxiously as he came in, to keep him from guessing what I had done.

His face was pale with weariness. I could see the first signs of hibernation on him: a languidness and heaviness of motion, a vagueness of eye. He snapped something at me and went into the kitchen. I kept out of his way. Eventually, he went to his room and I did not see him again for the rest of the day. It was a very long day.

In the evening the people began to come to him, people with strange expressions on their faces: grim and afraid and determined. I watched them coming from all directions, some of them walking singly. Some were strangers, riding farm drafs which would soon be set loose to fend for themselves in the winter countryside. Many of them were from L'din. I counted individuals: there were some hundred of them in all, who came into the parlor, and after a short time left again. I listened to the voices coming up the stairs. They cursed the Aeyries, over and over. But when they were not cursing, the people spoke in hushed voices.

They left as they had come, walking singly past shuttered windows.

By the end of the day I was desperately afraid. I awoke in the night with my heart in my throat, certain they had come to get me. But no one was there.

The next day, the neighbor's windows remained shuttered, and not one door opened. It was a cold day, becoming even colder when the wind stopped blowing. I sat by my window, shivering sometimes, watching the sky. Over the rooftops I saw bare treetops shifting in the wind, the only motion in the entire town. But of Eia I saw nothing, not even a message-carrying onfrit.

L'din had fallen asleep for the winter. I could not even remember what it had been like, to sleep like that, so deeply and for so long, coming out of it only occasionally to take care of personal matters, eating nothing and drinking little. And then to awaken and find that two months had passed. I wondered with dull dismay if I was to spend the entire winter a prisoner in this house, with nothing to occupy myself. I would go mad, surely.

In the late afternoon I heard Teksan in the kitchen. I went downstairs. He sat at the table with a cup of tea in his hand. I said, feigning surprise, "Everyone else is sleeping."

He snorted. "I have not hibernated in fifteen years. It is a carryover of a more savage time, before we learned to farm the land or to store food. Then it was the only way to survive the winter. Now it is unnecessary."

"I never thought of it like that," I said, for I was trying my best to make him believe I wanted to please him. "Why do you suppose I don't hibernate?"

Teksan looked at me with stone eyes. "Because you are an Aeyrie."

I looked at my feet. "I keep forgetting. What did all those people come here for?"

"Various things." He buttered a slice of stale bread. I had done no baking lately. I had developed a sudden violent hatred for cooking and housework. My precious potted plants, which I had brought in out of the cold, were now dying from neglect. Teksan did not seem to have noticed.

He said, "We are going tonight. Wear warm clothes."

"Yes, sir."

Though I was lonely and desperate with boredom and anxiety, and hungry as well, I could not endure being in the same room with him. I went back upstairs. I stared out my window as the sun set, trying to think of how things could have been different and still hoping despite myself for the sight of something moving in the sky. My windows tingled with Teksan's spell, but the shutters were not locked. Dulcie had made it out safely. Perhaps I could have leapt out as well, but it would have made no difference. My entire life I had been trapped, and I was still trapped. By what I did not clearly know.

When it was dark, Teksan called me and I came down the stairs. I had devised ways of adapting Walker clothes to my winged body, and like him was wearing the quilted jacket I rarely needed, and kipswool pants. I carried my glass knife, for no reason other than that it made me feel better. He looked at the sheath, but made no comment. He took me to his room, where he picked up his satchel and gripped me by the elbow. "Do not lose contact with me, or you will be lost in the Void."

Fear opened up like a wound in my belly. "No!"

He turned to me a disdaining face. And then my will was entirely gone, like the frail flame of an air lamp snuffed out for the night. Empty and dark within, step for step I walked with him, walking helplessly toward the swirling storm in the Door, until the wind sucked us in.

It was cold, cold beyond anything I had ever imagined. And it was empty, with nothing for my senses to hold onto for sanity. I saw nothing, neither darkness nor light. I heard nothing, not even the intangible ringing of silence. I felt nothing, not even the whisper of air on my fur. In the Void, there was only my own internal life, frozen and timeless, cut off from any other reference. I looked at myself because there was nothing else, and was unimpressed. All I could see was cowardice.

And then I was falling, falling, hitting something dry and crackling, using my wings instinctively and landing softly on my hands and knees. Near me, Teksan was still rolling. I sprawled myself hastily, lest he notice that I had landed too well for someone who did not know anything about flying. Only then I realized that my will was once again my own. I shivered with cold, but the bitter winter night seemed almost warm and friendly after the Void. I wanted to huddle there on the ground and never open my eyes again.

Teksan's steps crackled in the dry stems of the sucker plants. He toed me sharply with his boot. I got up awkwardly. Jagged mountain peaks lay against a black, star-hung sky. "How—?" I began stupidly. At the edge of my vision, I saw the swirling opening which was another Door.

Without a word, Teksan walked away. I followed him hastily. Until he snuffed that light in me, I had not truly known what helplessness was. I would have done almost anything to avoid having that happen to me again.

We followed a passage between mountain ridges. The wind shrieked across time-honed edges and howled in the hollows. Sometimes it forced me to struggle against it, jerking my wings askew. Sometimes it pushed me from behind, as if to hurry me impatiently forward, making me lose my footing in the darkness.

As we fought our way down the pass, three moons rose, one after the other, like a string of beads. The dark moon, Abki was full and in the lead, red and smoldering, a bad sign some would say. The lucky moon Ahbi trailed near the end, with its brightness tarnished and only partially visible and half of its body obscured in shadow.

I tripped in the dry tangle underfoot, and nearly fell into Teksan. He took me by the elbow, holding me too tightly for kindliness. He gestured into the impenetrable darkness. "A trader path lies ahead of us. Do you see it?"

"No."

"It is there. Follow it toward the west, and you will reach Down Nest by tomorrow afternoon if you do not linger too much."

"Tomorrow afternoon! I don't even have anything to eat!"

"They would expect you to arrive tired and hungry. It is six days' walk to the nearest Walker town, but you must make them believe you have come farther still, from the town of H'chan which is similar to L'din. Say you have been eight days on the road. You had better get your clothes dirty."

"Yes, sir," I said bleakly.

"Hold out your hand."

I held it out. I could not see it, but I could feel it shaking as Teksan took hold of my wrist. I did see starlight glittering on his knifeblade, just before it cut into one of my fingers, cold as ice. My arm muscles gave a shocked spasm. Still he held my wrist. I felt blood collect and begin to drip.

Then the thing that Teksan was holding in his other hand began to glow with a sickly, red light. I watched, paralyzed, as a drop of my blood spattered on it and then disappeared as if it had been consumed. The glow brightened. Another drop fell, and another, until the thing was glowing like an air lamp, but casting no light.

Teksan let go of my wrist at last, and tossed the thing into the air. It hung suspended. It was round as a fruit, and seemed featureless until it turned, and looked at me. It was an eye.

"Through the Eye I can both see and hear you," Teksan said. "But to everyone else it will be invisible. I would not want you to feel as if you were alone, Delan. It is a hard thing you are doing."

He seemed to expect me to thank him for his thoughtfulness. I could make no sound. I felt as if I was choking.

"Two nights from now. I will be waiting at the base of the Acyric Mountain. You will let us in."

I nodded. I still could not speak. He turned and walked away, until I could see him no longer. But the awful, glowing Eye remained with me, and with it the oppressive presence of overpowering evil.

It was a noisy night. The wind wailed its eerie song across the elemental glass. It buffeted my frail body like a rough-playing friend, making as if to knock me down or carry me off. I was too aware of how fragile I was, how easy it might be to crush the fine spokes across which my wing membranes were stretched, how sharp and heartless was the uncovered glass. The occult Eye followed behind me. I set one foot in front of the other, fighting the wind.

At first a wind blew within me as well, a whirlwind of plans and rebellions: I would not go to the Aeyrie town at all. I would go there, but tell them everything. I would find an enchanted place where Teksan could no longer see me. I would ask which of the Aeyries was a magician, and point out to him where the Eye was, so it could be destroyed. But soon I was too tired and cold and hungry for such thoughts, and all became hopeless and dead quiet within me.

Dawn was late coming, and still the sun delayed, as if hesitant to face the chill. The path crossed a narrow-channeled stream. I lay on my belly to drink the ice cold water. It made my teeth ache and my throat hurt. I found I could not move to get up again. I lay my head in my arms, too cold for rest, too weary for anything else.

A mountain peak exploded with light. And then another. In each of the peaks, the sun rose, again and again. Breathless with wonder, forgetting for a too-short moment how helpless and wretched I was, I watched the darkness take flight. Slowly, light dribbled toward me in rivulets down the mountainsides. But it would be a long time before it reached me, and even then it would have little warmth in it.

I got myself to my feet somehow, stiff with cold, and began to walk again. Six days to the nearest town, Teksan had said. I knew what chance there was of finding food in the mountains, even in midsummer. All my body fat had been transformed into wings, and I had already been over a day without food. I had no choice but to go to Down Nest and unknown Aeyrie hospitality, and worry then about Teksan and his people. It was either that or die, an option which, for all my misery, I did not consider seriously.

The sun hastened to its peak, and even more hastily started toward its setting. I had to lie down to rest again, on a bed of dried sucker plants which had soaked up a little of the sun's warmth. My dreadful satellite floated above me, a mere shimmering in the sunlight, which was fading too soon into nightfall again. I huddled, legs and arms drawn up under my wings, weak in all my muscles, with Down Nest not even in sight.

For an abrupt moment, I was in the dark, and chilled by the loss of the sun. Before I knew that it had been a shadow which crossed over me, the flyer

had landed, so softly the sucker plants scarcely crackled under id's feet. I turned my head and looked at
idre stupidly. Ids startling, bright red fur was tipped
with gold, with the mane bound in a hundred tiny
braids. Streaks of light quivered in ids gold-dyed astil
clothing. Ids wings, as amber as my Dulcie's, folded as
I watched. Frowning, the flyer said something in words
that sounded like the sound of water splashing, then
turned id's face to the sky and shouted.

I looked up and saw the other one hovering, black
as a stormcloud, challenging the gale arrogantly and
casually with each stroke of the wing. There was such
grace in that one that I thought at first that it must be
Eia. I struggled to get up. The stranger stepped forward to help me, and then supported me as I stood
swaying and scrubbing my sleeve on my wet cheek. Ids
body was hot with the exertion of flying. Id spoke
again, in that wild, sweet tongue that I would forever
think of as the language of lovemaking. It was H'ldat,
that which should have been my native tongue.

I said, "How far is it?"

The Aeyrie hesitated, but replied in the Walker
tongue, though id spoke with a soft, haunting accent.
"Is it Ula t'Fon you seek? Not so far, by air. Are you
walking because you are injured? Why are you alone?"

"I do not know how to fly. I have always been
alone."

A long time the Aeyrie looked at me, examining my
unkempt mane and Walker clothing. No doubt id felt
me shivering with weakness against the support of ids
arm. "Who are you?" id finally asked. "Where are
you from?"

I was hungry, and exhausted, and fearful of the
coming cold. If I told the truth, would I be given
shelter? I did not hesitate long. "Delan. From H'chin.
I thought I was a Walker."

"By the Great Mountain!" id said. Then, "How

long since you have eaten?" Not waiting for my reply, id tipped back ids head again and shouted.

The black Aeyrie landed, so softly that I had to look again to be certain it truly was not Eia. Id looked at me in puzzlement. "T'Cwa-dre? Ishta-dre?"

"From H'chin, id says."

"H'chin!"

" 'I thought I was a Walker,' id says. Id does not speak H'ldat."

Something exchanged between them that told me they were lovers, intimate in ways I had never even imagined. The Red said, "Id needs to eat; do you have anything left in your bag?"

While the Black rummaged in ids satchel, I asked, "What are Ishta-dre and t'Cwa-dre?"

"Hana was just speculating wildly about who you are. I am Gein—"

"Vida Orpha Gein," the other said.

"And this is Tefan Malal Hana, who will be successor to the Chieftainship of Ula t'Fon."

The Black muttered something fervently in the Aeyrie tongue. Gein translated it politely: "May the season of change come late."

While I stared in a daze, overwhelmed by too many names and realizations at once, Eia's sibling gave me food, a bar of something sweet and crunchy which melted to nothing in my mouth, and a transparent skin of something like milk except that it tasted of a rich and exotic nut. "Flight food," id said apologetically. "It will scarcely pause in your stomach."

I ate, and felt at once better and worse, for I stopped shivering and my muscles became strong enough to hold me up, but my awakened and cheated stomach growled in rebellion. "Will I be welcome in Ula t'Fon? Can I reach there before it is dark?"

"You will be welcome," Hana said. "We will walk with you."

So I had company for the last part of my journey, the two of them taking turns supporting me and fending off my apologies, asking more questions than they answered. I had not expected to find any Aeyries flying in this wind, but I did not question them on it, for it occurred to me that Teksan would be even more anxious to understand it than I. They both appeared to be serious flyers, broad-chested and bulging with flight muscles. I quieted my curiosity by concluding that they were athletes, and probably reckless besides.

It was sunset when Down Nest came into sight. The community appeared just as it had in Teksan's mirror: an eccentric, incredible construction, with windows and porches of all sizes jumbled in disorder along crooked, wildly angled walls. Hana, without much apparent effort, climbed the sheer side of a spire of glass, and then dove off it. Id struggled at first against the rising wind, but gracefully mastered it. Soon after, our arrival was announced with a sweet, faint horn call. Many shuttered windows drew open, and curious faces peered down at us, distant triangular Aeyrie faces, framed by manes clipped or braided or combed or as unkempt as mine, hooded behind by folded wings. I looked up until we were so close my neck ached from the tilt.

I wiped my blurring eyes and chilling face dry on my shoulder. Gein looked at me inquiringly.

"There are so many! I thought I was the only one. The only one like me in all the world."

"Well," said Gein, "Aren't you?"

But I was silent in shame, not at my tears but at my knowledge that I was an interloper and a danger to these people, Eia's people whom I wanted to also be mine. I hated the weakness in me which made me able to care only about warmth, a bed, and solid food. I had already lied for the sake of these things, and was certain I would be doing it again before the evening was much older.

Hana had achieved the height of the town, and landed there on a porch with no railings, where long streamers of bright cloth swam in the wind. Soon after, id reappeared again, to dive over the edge and glide down to us in extravagant swoops, with all the curious community still watching. "Show off," Gein said beside me, lovingly, rousing envy in me.

"I brought more food," Hana said when id landed. "They are opening the lower door, but it will be a dreary climb for you yet, Delan. You should hear what they are saying!"

Gein mimicked an excited voice: " 'A white winged silver! Young, and without a Companion!' You said it yourself, Hana, when we first saw id. You have a very unusual coloring, Delan."

Hana distributed more flight food from ids satchel. "How long since you were winged?"

I felt giddy with their fast, bright words. "Thirty days, maybe."

Gein's protective wing tucked around me. "Some might offer to bed you. Better to say no, for now, for your own sake. Do not be afraid to ask for advice."

Hana snorted, and crunched down on a bar. "Everyone will advise you, too. Worthless and self-important nonsense, most of it."

I leaned against Gein, welcoming id's solidity. *The Aeyries indeed are different from the Walkers,* I said to myself, utterly dismayed.

Chapter 7

At the top of a short pathway amid a rubble of broken glass, we waited near the sheer side of the mountain. In the depth of the mountain itself, a faint shadow moved against a blurred glow of light. Abruptly the thick door which was cut into the glass creaked open on heavy, strangely designed hinges, revealing an old and wizened flyer, with a withered wing and a mane gone gray with age.

Hana greeted idre and brought me forward. The old Aeyrie examined me with eyes too wise and seeing for comfort, but did not speak.

The door swung shut. I watched as the old Aeyrie latched the door. There were no keys, only knobs to be turned. I did notice that the door could not be opened at all from outside. We were in a narrow tunnel, with jagged walls indicating that the passageway through the mountain had not been painstakingly cut, but instead the glass had been shattered like ice before a thaw. Until now, I would have thought such a thing impossible.

The tiled floor whispered under my shoes. Air lamps scattered glittering light on the walls. Each lamp was unlike the next, even clinging to the wall in a different manner, as if the lamp crafter made it a policy to never repeat idreself. The mountain surrounded me with a great, still silence. I wondered that this rift within its belly did not make the mountain uneasy. Once I looked back, and saw that the Eye was still following me.

The tunnel led us to the bottom of a well. A narrow stairway cut into the glass wound around the inside of the great shaft, lit all along the way by lamps. Even though it was not very wide, it had no railing. Even with a railing, not many Walkers would have had the stomach for voluntarily climbing a height like that. A contraption like a cage rested on the floor, tethered somewhere far above with a multitude of thick ropes. This would be how supplies were raised to the town, I guessed, assuming that the hard work of raising it was done with human bodies and pullies. I wondered suddenly what they did for water, so high in the air. I learned, later, about cisterns and pipes and the pumps and engines which harness the power of the wind.

Gein said, "You can ride the lift, but I think you might prefer going on your own feet."

"Yes," I said, knowing I would regret it halfway up the stairs. And I did regret it, more than once.

The old Aeyrie stayed behind. I had spotted a rude bed near the foot of the stairs. I wondered that someone who was treated so respectfully lived so humbly. "It is by choice," Gein explained as we paused to catch our breaths. "Id is a Sh'man, a wise one."

Gein and Hana took turns half-carrying me the final few turns. At the top of the long stairway, the door was open, leaking the sound of many liquid voices which echoed eerily in the well. I walked through the door on my own two feet. Even Gein, as sensitive to my pride as id had been to my need for support, let go of me at the end.

A hush fell as we came through the door into a great, tapestried room crowded with comfortable, well used tables, and long-legged, low-backed chairs. Black and red and gold and brown, somewhat less than a hundred and a half Aeyries, glimmering with undecorated astil and hooded by translucent wings, stilled their spoons in their bowls at my entrance. Furred and maned and thin as starvelings, casually carrying their great burden of wings on their heavily muscled torsos, a weird, alien people greeted my Walker eyes. The intelligence of their curious or distrustful, smiling or expressionless faces was uncanny. Fear came over me like winter twilight: sudden and unannounced.

I turned my head, catching sight of my own pale wings, folded against rough Walker wool like flowers blooming among stones. I felt utterly disoriented. My rage against the ground-walking race lay disemboweled within me. When the Walkers looked at me, the entire structure of their Universe shook in its foundations. How could I blame them for distrusting me, or even, out of fear, maltreating me?

I am an Aeyrie, I said to myself. *This is my people. This is where I belong.* Yet I knew it was not true, and would never be true.

Gein's warm hand took my elbow. Perhaps id had seen my trembling. "Wingling," id said, muted and somber. "How can I help you?"

"Stay with me," I pleaded, like a child afraid of the darkness. Protect me, take care of me, make everything better.

"Of course." Id looked at me as if peering down my eyes into my soul. "Ride it out," id suggested. "Don't struggle; just keep your wings spread."

A Black stood up among the tables and made ids way to us. Hana stepped forward to present me to idre. "My parent, chieftain of Ula t'Fon, the taiseoch Tefan. This is—" id's mouth quirked with a half-sad smile that reminded me so of Eia that my throat closed shut. "This is Delan, who is alone and does not know ids parentage. A wind-drift."

The chieftain put out a hand that was wrinkled and gnarled with age, but firm of grip as it took hold of mine. There was nothing to distinguish idre from the rest of them, no trappings or symbols, only a heaviness of experiences on ids bowed shoulders, and a deliberation of speech that suggested the thought which went into each word. "Rest here," id said. "You are welcome. In the morning I will talk with you."

As I ate dinner, hungry despite myself, around me rose a confusion and interweaving of conversation the like of which I had never heard before. Even though I did not understand the words, the intensity of it unnerved me. Gein fended off the curious at the cost of ids own meal. Later id led me out in my exhausted daze, and showed me to the guest room, and I think even undressed me and put me to bed.

I awoke in the morning to the sound of the windmills whirring and singing on the rooftops as they were engaged. All my muscles ached, but the bed was soft and warm, and I lay a long time only half awake.

I turned my head, and looked by accident into the awful gaze of the Eye. I buried my face in the soft, crinkled blankets. But there was no hiding: I had eaten and rested and now it was time to decide what to do.

But I could not decide. Every plan I considered had a flaw, or an intolerable risk. I did not know and could not hope to guess at the extent of Teksan's powers. With not even the flick of a finger, he had quenched my will, leaving me for a moment more dead than if I were buried and disintegrating. Could he do it again, even over the distance which separated us? So long as the Eye was watching me and the Rope was binding me, was I within his power? One thing was certain: whatever thing I did in rebellion, it had to be decisive, and so sudden that my master had no chance to react.

Why had Teksan not simply emptied me out and used my disenfranchised husk to open the locked doors? My intact and willful self was a risk to him, and the traps he had set for me in his house showed how little he trusted me. The only answer to this question was a shred of hope as amorphous as mist. *Perhaps because he has limits*—I thought, and could go no farther.

I got up at last. I used the commode behind the painted screen, and fought open the window shutters. My room was high, overlooking several levels of roof-tops slanted to catch the rain and carry it to storage. A hundred spinning windmills were in sight. The big ones, though colorful, appeared utilitarian enough, but the smaller ones were whimsical toys. They flapped and spun and jiggled and danced, clattering and rattling and whirring in the wind. There were bells, also, tinkling and ringing and humming, and astil streamers writhing like waterwythes in a strong current. Surely these were a people who unabashedly loved the wind! I laughed with delight by my open window, but the feeling inside of me was a kind of weeping, and there were tears on my face.

Gein tapped on the door and came in as I was still wiping my eyes, and paused there, looking at me. "Ah Del, there is complexity in you."

I turned to the Red, forgetting again the occult Eye and the unclear ways which were before me, thinking for now only of the likeable, trustable, bright-furred Gein. "What do you do, Gein?"

"Most people can tell within a moment or two what I am. 'You must be a healer, Gein,' they say."

"Of course," I said, feeling stupid for not having recognized it. But Gein's impulse to ascertain and meet other people's needs had seemed to me too natural to be acquired. Walker-style healers are very intellectual people.

"The taiseoch has asked me to serve as your Companion for now, with your permission. I thought I was too young, but id thought that since we were already acquainted with each other and I am fluent in the Walker tongue—"

I had not even considered important the fact that I was not yet dressed, but now I reached overhastily for my clothes. When I turned back, Gein was smiling. "To interpret. And to explain. And to support if you need it, in my capacity as a trained empath. That is all."

I clutched wool and quilt to my chest. Embarrassment held me silent.

"Did the Walkers assume that you were female?" Gein asked gently.

I nodded.

"It must be very strange to grow up in a society where there are two sexes. To be forbidden to love someone because by some accident both of you can lay eggs, or cannot lay eggs. What a strange and arbitrary notion!"

When I thought about it that way, I smiled reluctantly. It did indeed seem rather ridiculous.

Gein took my hand, and took my clothes away and threw them onto the bed, and drew me away from the window, closing the shutters in passing. "Come to the baths with me. There are some new clothes being brought there for you, Aeyrie clothes, and it is a good place for talking."

The Aeyrie town was a warren, laid out by designers as mad and whimsical as those who made the whirligigs. I could not imagine how I would ever find my own way alone through its twisting hallways and unexpected stairways, but I was hungry to wander at my own pace, to look at the things which hung from the walls or hid in nooks: weavings and paintings and carvings, engine parts and toys and things I could not even name, the leavings of an eccentric and creative people. I hung back to examine this and that, until Gein, laughing, dragged me the last few steps. "One would think you were only going to be here a few hours. There will be time to look at everything!"

Reminded that it was all too possible that this would be my only day here, I was much muted as we came into the baths. In the plain dressing room, a few articles of clothing hung from hooks. "This must be yours," Gein said, touching a soft, white, shining thing that was folded on the bench. Gein hung ids golden garment on a hook, and we went into the next room, a warm, steamy, echoing place cut out within the mountain itself, with moisture dripping down the walls and lush plants in pots thriving in the damp half darkness. It was dimly lit by a few lamps protected within clear bulbs from the worst of the moisture. The occult Eye glowed in the mist, watching me.

It was unpeopled except for ourselves. We showered under streams of hot water, soaping ourselves all over and lathering each other's backs and wings. The water ran brown and grimy from my fur, for since I was winged I had not been able to bathe properly. Here there were no baths at all as a Walker would know them, no tubs or pools of water. "We sink," Gein explained. "Our wings make swimming impossible, and we have no fat to make us float."

"All my life I have been afraid of water."

"A wise fear."

I shook the water out of my wings, and toweled it out of my fur until I was merely damp. Gein led the way out, to another warm and dimly-lit place, but this one both hotter and drier than the last, and furnished with benches and tables where other people lay or sat, most of them solitary, some of them talking together. It was a mystery to me how sound was swallowed up in that place so that their voices were mere wordless murmurs. I had never imagined one could be so private in an open room.

Gein took up a bottle from a rack. "Lie down, Del, you are the guest." I lay on one of the tables, feeling very self-conscious until I realized that the others had not even glanced at us. Gein oiled my sensitive wings, and then perched on the table beside me, fluffing up my fur with ids hands as it dried. In a relaxed daze, I turned my head to look at idre. Gein had brought us here because it was a good place to talk, and both of us had scarcely spoken. My half-unfolded wings gleamed in the warm light. Beyond them, Gein's face was alive with secret thoughts. A pair of Aeyries left the room, fingers intertwined, wings touching.

The Eye was out of sight, somewhere behind and above me probably, keeping its arm's length away. I murmured, "Gein, pretend that I am not talking. Think of a reason to bring your head down to me."

Id continued absently fluffing my fur as before, not even turning ids face to me, so that even I wondered if id had heard me. But after a time, id looked down at me with a smile. The fluffing became a stroking, slow, and soft, and then ids hand came up to my mane and ids torso pressed against my arm. My breath caught, and for a moment I entirely forgot what I meant to do.

"Wingling, tell me what is troubling you."

I whispered words that were scarcely sound at all, "I have an Occult Eye on me, set there by a Walker sorcerer. Tonight I am to bring up danger through the lower door."

I sat up then, pulling the Red's body close to me, thinking to hide in our embrace whatever reaction id had, and even in my desperation worrying about what the others in the room must think of my behavior. Gein breathed something in H'ldat and startled me again by softly kissing my mouth before murmuring against my lips, "Be at peace, l'shil, it will be all right.

Thank you for telling me." And then, less quietly, "I am partnered, though I am sorely tempted to forget it—maybe you will consider taking Hana and me together. Shall I discuss it with idre? Do you like idre also?"

I was utterly flustered. But to the watching Teksan, my confusion certainly was not without apparent cause.

The Taiseoch's rooms were high in the community, at the top of a wide stairway. Id received me in a small, plain room, where the painted decorations on the wooden floor were rubbed away by the passage of many feet, and the furniture was worn as well, and many times mended. Id seemed to have no servants or attendants. It was Hana who brought in a tray of hot drinks and sweetbread, balanced on one hand as id managed the doors with the other. Id was not dressed, and had long streaks of dust and dirt in ids fur.

"Been mending a windmill?" asked Gein.

"A pump fitting broke."

"Those pump fittings always break," said Tefan absently.

"Someday someone will invent a metal that doesn't wear out, and Ula t'Fon will be rich." Hana handed out steaming cups of spicy tea and sweetbread crammed with nuts and cheese, and perched on a stool, vibrant and cheerful in the cold sunlight spilling through an open window. "Then we'll get too fat to fly, and loll in luxury, and hatch as many children as we want, and own more than one garment apiece even."

Gein smiled indulgently. "And wreck the world out of sheer boredom."

A pair of onfrits appeared on the windowsill, but waited to be invited in, when only crumbs were left. I was careful to spill nothing on my new clothes. Despite having spent most of my life producing astil, I had never actually worn anything made of it. When I had hesitated to put on something so beautiful and expensive, Gein had said gently, "We do not wear astil for the luxury of it, but for its light weight and its ability to cut the wind. Remember you are a flyer."

After we had eaten, the Taiseoch prompted me, and, with a few major omissions, I told idre about my life. The chieftain listened intently, turning occasionally to Gein for a translation.

"So I knew I had to be an Aeyrie," I concluded. "But I did not know you would welcome me—I am very grateful for it." I looked down at my hands, imagining what my life would be like if all the tale I had told were true, and how I would be feeling now with a new life ahead of me in this wonderful, rich place. Would I spend the rest of my life catching up with my peers? Could I learn how to do as I liked? Might I someday vibrate as Hana did with energy and creativity, or distribute affection and acceptance as generously as Gein?

Tefan asked me some questions, but did not tell me what I most wanted to know. I finally said, "Taiseoch Tefan, do you have any idea who my parents might be, or how I came to hatch among the Digan-lai?"

The chieftain stood up, shaking out stiff joints. "Only a mating of two Silvers will make a Silver child. There are only a handful of Silvers in the world. It should not be difficult to identify your parents. As for how your egg came to the Digan-lai, or why it was brought there, I do not know. But I am very curious to find out."

Gein said softly. "Hana, will you host Delan for a while? I need to make my rounds."

I left that place feeling both haunted and relieved by the notion that much had been withheld from me. I wondered, despairing, what the Taiseoch would think of me when Gein relayed my muttered message, as would surely happen as soon as the door was closed.

"You were carrying a weapon," Hana said. "Do you know how to use it?"

Suddenly I was embarrassed of the homemade knife, the possession of which had once caused such controversy. "It is just a glass shard, bound to a wooden handle. I have never done more than threaten rude children with it."

Hana grinned, and drew ids own blade. Blue glass it was, of a length with mine. "We always make our weapons out of glass. It is half the weight of metal, and stronger by far. Let's go look at yours."

We spent the rest of the day together. We went to one of the community's many workshops where a glassmaster helped me to shape my blade. Hana, who apparently dabbled in many crafts, helped me to bind an Aeyrie style handle to it, attaching it with metal screwed through two holes we had drilled in the glass with the help of a smoking chemical. The handle had a metal loop through which I could tether the knife to me. "So you won't have to land to retrieve it, if you lose it in the air," Hana explained.

Id was a careful and deliberate crafter. I could see why id was the one who had been called to repair the windmill. As far as I could ascertain, Hana had no regular duties, but dabbled in everything. I thought it was because of ids station, but Hana told me that many Aeyries had no defined role, and simply did whatever appealed to them. Some, on the other hand, were specialists, with a particular love or gift for one kind of work. Out of these a handful were sh'mans: teachers, or wise ones. But even they had to share in the common work of cooking, cleaning, and caring for the children.

"Are you Tefan's only offspring?" I asked, knowing the answer perfectly well.

"I have an elder l'frer," Hana said. "Even for an Aeyrie id is talented, very good at an impossible variety of things. A politician, a fighter, an artist, a scholar. But prone to unpopular stances and solitary ways. Id went over to the Triad, and my parent is ashamed and will no longer speak ids name. But I miss my l'frer. Too long it has been since there was word from idre. And frankly, id would make a far better taiseoch than I! I hope id will give up playing prophet someday and come home again."

"What about your other parent. Malal?"

"Id is dead," Hana said. "Walkers shot idre out of the sky." Ids face closed and I did not ask any more questions. But suddenly I understood why Tefan, who seemed a person of great restraint and reason, might not be at all reasonable on the subject of Walkers.

"Shall we go to the h'shal Quai-du?" suggested Hana.

I had learned that a h'shal was any common room of the Ula, one to which anyone had right of access. "Quai-du?"

"You will hear the suffix 'du' very frequently here: it indicates that the noun has to do with flight."

"And 'Quai?' "

"Ah, that is one of those Aeyrie words which doesn't easily translate. It means at the same time, 'fight' and 'dance.' "

"The room for fight-dance flying?" I translated.

"The place for study of the ancient martial art of Quai-du. I am a master—see, this is the mark." Id turned a wrist. Branded in ids flesh was the same triangle I had noticed on Eia's wrist, which I had assumed to be the symbol of the Triad.

Hana took me by the elbow. "Come with me and I'll show you."

The h'shal Quai-du was as big as the Common Hall but empty of any furnishings except for a ladder leading to a flight balcony. A line of windows, made of a nearly colorless glass cut in impossibly thin sheets, let in the pale winter light. The floor was of inlaid wood, but it was so smooth that I could not feel the joinings.

With my hand on ids shoulders for support, I stood on one foot so Hana could examine the sole of the other. Hana snorted. "Shoes!"

"So?" I said, for I was quickly growing weary of the Aeyries' habit of denigrating even the Walker's most mundane habits.

"You'll blister badly, your feet are so soft."

"Why not wear shoes then, so I won't get blisters?"

Hana found this suggestion hysterically funny. "Why don't Walkers go blindfolded on bright days when the sun hurts their eyes?" Id asked when id could talk again. "Draw your knife, l'shil. There is something you need to learn."

Anger made me reckless, and I drew my blade with a flourish.

The next few seconds were among the most hectic and frightening of my entire life. It ended mercifully quickly, with me crashed up against the wall with the breath knocked out of me, my blade somewhere on the other side of the room, and Hana's very sharp edge tickling the fur at my throat. "Well," Hana said, "You have it in you."

"What?" I gasped.

"Your first reaction was to defend yourself, and you did it well. Two things you did which are worth remembering. First, your feet: what did you do with them?"

Naturally I had no idea. My body was still shaking as Hana demonstrated slowly how I had reacted to ids attack. "You are still awkward, but beginning to get your balance. Someday you will not even remember your childhood clumsiness. You put your feet so, which made it very difficult for me to offset you. You had no idea what to do with your blade, of course, but you did know what to do with your wings, like this."

Crouched, with one foot well behind and apart from the other, Hana's wings lifted and flapped, propelling idre forward, knife leading, in a way which made me very glad that knife was not coming at me.

"You know the most important thing about Quai-du," Hana said. "Use your wings for momentum and power. That is a wise body you live in, Del. You will learn quickly."

I had been called wise twice that day. But it was a measure of Hana's skill that I was not injured that afternoon. I did quickly come to appreciate just how important it was that my feet be in direct contact with the ground.

Hana explained that the life-fire burned hot in me, and that keeping it fueled was a serious business, especially when flying. "To faint in the air is to never fly again. If you even survive." Id also instructed me on the care of my vulnerable wing membranes, which would not heal easily if damaged, almost inevitably requiring a healer's attention. I found myself wondering if the impulse to teach was hereditary in Eia's family.

Quai-du is as much an art of the air as of the ground, and after I had announced the end of my efforts by sprawling exhausted on the floor, Hana demonstrated some of the maneuvers of the air. Id hovered, turned with impossible swiftness, and dove for the floor, only to swoop upward, all with the knife glittering, slicing and stabbing at an invisible attacker. It was both beautiful and awful to watch. I was riveted not only by Hana's precision and power, but by a new respect for my own potential.

Although supper was a communal meal, Gein did not appear for it, which seemed to puzzle Hana as much as it disturbed me. Hana came grim from a private conference with ids parent to where I was trying to focus my attention on the bread and stew, which had been prepared by cooks who were far more skilled and inspired than I had ever been. "One of the children has taken seriously ill and Gein cannot leave idre. I am going to bring my partner some supper—will you be able to manage by yourself?"

"If I can find my room again," I said, smiling, for despite the terrifying afternoon I had learned to like Hana.

But Hana looked away from my smile. "I will ask someone to help you." Ids voice was cordial enough, but it had an undertone that left me dismayed. For appearance's sake, I finished my meal, but my appetite was gone.

Chapter 8

With the voice of Teksan, the Eye spoke: "Delan. It is time."

Despite the warm guest bed, my bones were ice. I had not been able to sleep.

"Delan," my master said.

I didn't move or reply. The wind sang across the mountain ridges, moaning in the hollows. My window shutters rattled.

The Eye spoke: "Do you remember this name? Eia," it said. "Eia."

I unscrewed an arm of the lamp and took it with me, the little flame flickering with my motion. I walked alone down empty, shadowy hallways. I passed a light glowing under a doorway, and for a few moments the murmuring and laughing of lovers haunted my way. A sculpture cast a black, winged shadow. It said in my memory, "I think you underestimate yourself, Delan."

"I'm sorry," I said. "I should have listened."

I walked on, driven like a kip before the Eye. The Common Hall swallowed up the whisper of my feet on the tiles. The tables were cleared, and the chairs tucked neatly under them. It was dark, and silent.

"I'm sorry," I said, shivering in the cold, hoping that someone was there hidden in the shadows, preferably a whole troop of Quai-du fighters with weapons at their sides. I worked the bolts to open the door to the stairwell, and drew it almost shut again behind me.

The darkness seemed to drop endlessly below me. I went down, turn after turn, until the stairway seemed something from a nightmare, a way I had no choice but to walk, infinitely, without hope of arriving anywhere. Then, bewildered and dazed, I was at the bottom, wondering if the Sh'man was awake in ids bed, watching me. I was so dizzy from the darkness that I wandered in circles before finally stumbling into the corridor. It was cold as the Void in that place. Shivering so I could hardly walk, I finally arrived at the lower door, and turned its three bolts by feel.

It was a dark night. Black clouds frayed across the stars. The wind moaned like a ghost in the ravines. It flung a handful of my hair across my eyes. Through the haze of hair I saw Teksan, leaning against the jagged stone.

"How do you know about Eia?" I asked.

The two who were hidden in the darkness on either side of the door grasped me by the arms, and there was a blade at my throat, cold metal, awfully cold. "Teksan!" I cried in rage, as if I were surprised.

He straightened from his slouch. "Your onfrit led us to the Black's cave, carrying your pathetic little note," he said. "But your paramour is still alive. Remember that, Delan."

My voice rang cold and empty in my ears. "Where is id?"

He stepped up to me. "Delan," he said, softly and mockingly. His fingers stroked my chin with an obscene gentleness. I cringed away from the touch, making him smile. "Delan, do you think I would trust an Aeyrie?" Then he was gone.

In the grips of my captors, I dully watched the Walkers pass, one or two at a time, through the door.

I counted: there were near a hundred of them, a great many people to steal only a few books. Every one of them was armed with a long knife. I could hear the sound of their reluctant footsteps as they climbed the long stairs. Single file they would be going up, hugging the wall in their fear of heights. Two by two at most, they would be going though the door at the top. Was a bloody battle being engaged up there?

I waited, a desperate long time. My two captors grumbled at having been left behind. I thought about the knife at my side, newly remade and deadly sharp. But each of my captors was twice my size, and escaping the cruel grip of even one of them would not be easy. I waited, thinking too late of all the things I could have done to prevent this disaster from happening.

I had violated Eia's safety and betrayed idre to the enemy, and I had done it out of selfishness, because I wanted idre to rescue me.

One of the Walkers said, "Someone coming back, is that Teksan?"

Footsteps came quickly across the tile. And then he was against me, sweat stinking and breathless with anger. "Someone must have noticed that the door was ajar, and latched it."

I began to shake in the arms that held me.

"You will come upstairs and pound on the door to waken whoever it is to let you in. You will tell them you were restless and wanted to—"

"No." I said, "I won't do it."

He hit me. His blow left me hanging in the grips of the Walkers, looking dazedly at a Teksan who blotted out the stars like a figure out of a nightmare. "No," I said again, tasting and feeling the word like blood in my mouth.

"For the Black's life."

"Why should I believe you? Do you think I would trust a Walker?"

Despite my bravado, I cowered when I saw his hand raise again. He stopped himself, probably remembering that it would be short-sighted to injure me so badly I could not climb the stairs. He said to his two followers, "Make it walk."

I said to his back, "I told Gein. They are ready for you."

"You what?"

My voice was shrill with terror, yet I could not stop myself. "The community will not let me in the door, they know better. Why don't you open it with sorcery, Teksan?"

After the shock of the blow came the awful, mock gentle caress. He turned my chin with his fingers so he could see my face, and then he hit me again. After he left to gather his people, the two who held me captive beat me as well. They were less dreadful, but more brutal. By the time he came back, I was only half conscious, puking from pain where I lay.

When I came to myself again, I hung upside down, slung over someone's shoulder. My head lolled on a broad farmer's back, my wings hanging around me like children's broken kites. My hands were tied behind my back. The Walkers cursed breathlessly and monotonously in the darkness around me. I wondered dully why they had not killed me yet, and wished they would get it over with. When I moved, vaguely thinking to ease one of many pains, the one who was carrying me set me down. I went to my knees. He jerked me to my feet. "Walk," he said.

I walked, and fell, and when I was pulled to my feet I walked some more. I realized that Dulcie was dead. I wondered if they had destroyed the book Eia had been writing. Then somehow we were in the Void.

"Eia is captive of some very angry Walkers," Teksan said. "Shall I take you and let you see what they are doing to it?"

He had worn out his anger at last. I lay trussed and unclothed on the bare floor of his cellar. He had gagged me, even though the entire town except for his followers was in hibernation. I found this puzzling. All I could think was that he feared that even his disciples would be offended or distressed by the sound of my screaming.

The sodden gag choked me. One of my eyes had swelled shut. I guessed hopefully at the number of days it would take for my hot life-fire to burn itself out without fuel. Surely it would not be long. My injuries and the desperate cold would certainly hurry me along.

Teksan stood over me, breathing heavily, smiling around his words. "You are doing this the hard way, Delan. In the end you will do anything, and beg me to let you do more. You can reach that point intact, or you can reach that point a cripple. It is entirely up to you."

I shut my eyes. I felt very tired. At last he went away.

Little had remained of the night by the time we returned to L'din. Teksan had given a speech to his followers and spent his energy until sunrise in boosting their morale and distributing ale from his cellar. I lay in the corner like an old rug awaiting the junker.

I would have expected the night's fiasco to be the end of Teksan's ambitions, but soon I realized it was not to be. Teksan claimed that the Aeyrie communities could not communicate with each other in winter. Therefore Out Nest and Up Nest would not be forewarned, and the Walkers of the world could still awaken from hibernation to discover that they were free of the Aeyrie tyranny. As for Ula t'Fon, Teksan had a plan, and I found it too easy to guess what it was. Surely Eia, natural heir to the taiseoch, would not be denied entrance there, however wary the t'Fon-dre became.

The Walkers seemed willing to continue to support

Teksan. Their other option was to feel like fools. The terrible thing was that I now knew that long air journeys were never taken in winter by the Aeyries, because the cold used so much energy that even the strongest of flyers could not carry enough food to support a long flight. Teksan was right: t'Han and t'Cwa would be his for the taking.

Teksan's people went away heartened. And Teksan took me down to his cellar, and taught me just how helpless I was.

Now it was full daylight, getting toward the noon of the brief, too-long winter day. Pale sunlight fanned out from the one vent, at ceiling level and smaller than a Walker child, with a grate fastened over it.

Something in me had changed: I cried, now that I was alone, but not for myself. I cried for the Walkers. Once they had wiped out the Aeyries, they would likely focus their resentment and hatred on the Mers. When they, too, were extinct, the Walkers would start destroying each other. I cried for the Aeyries, rich and proud in a culture that gave them everything but what they needed to survive. I cried for the mysterious Mers who were distant and safe in their watery land and did not concern themselves with the world under the sun.

I saw too much, and hoped too little. Finally my ravaged body insisted on sleep.

With rest and time, Teksan became subtle. Hope having already fled, dignity soon abandoned me as well. Not even my despair could survive his artful assault. By the end of the first day, I had promised to do whatever he wanted, if only he would stop. He looked down at me, smiling as always, where I was prostrate in dirt and sweat and blood and vomit and the sharp stink of urine. "No," he said softly. "Not yet."

By the third day, the sound of Teksan's hand turning the lock made me whimper with terror. His pleasure in my fear and pain taught me what perversion was.

Even in sleep, I found neither escape nor rest. Nightmares assaulted me, one after another, with moments of desperate wakefulness in between. Then there were horrible, vivid dreams of escape: My bonds fell from my hands, the door opened before me, I went out and saw Eia waiting for me. The awakening was so awful that I became convinced that Teksan was even torturing me with dreams.

The fourth or fifth night I dreamed the most vivid of these dreams. A scrabbling at the grate seemed to awaken me from sleep. "Onfrit," I said. My voice was hoarse and cracked with screaming, for Teksan had ungagged me when I became too weak to make much noise. "There is a latch," I croaked. One warm summer day, when I was out pulling weeds in the garden, I had opened the grate, trying to figure out why it had been designed to be opened in the first place.

I heard the struggle between small body and stiff latch. I heard the hinges squeak. An onfrit fluttered down from the dark ceiling. "Delan?" it said.

"Yes. Who are you?"

"Eia's Ch'ta."

"Ch'ta, you are a very smart onfrit."

"Yes," he said agreeably.

In better times, a conversation like this would have ended with me dizzy from trying to understand animal sentience and how it was different from mine. Now I only considered how amazingly lucky it was, that the one survivor of Eia's three onfrits was the most intelligent and experienced, whom Eia credited with abstract thought and a wide range of emotions, capable of reasoning through difficult and complicated tasks. Suddenly I realized that it was suspiciously lucky: this was certainly another dream, and it would have another unendurable ending. But I could not awaken from it. Apparently I had to dream it through to the end.

I decided to cooperate so it would be over quickly. I turned as far as I could, offering Ch'ta my bound wrists. "Chew through the rope." His sharp teeth tugged on my numb hands. Time seemed to keep its own pace. And then suddenly there was pain, and my own voice moaning and startling me into awareness as my arms and shoulder joints, so long immobilized, came unfrozen. I brought up one monstrously distorted hand before my eyes. The wrist was raw meat. The onfrit crawled over my side, tense with distress over my pain.

"Good, Ch'ta," I said through my tears. "Good work. Have you been a lonely onfrit?"

Ch'ta gave a low warble, an onfrit sound of sadness.

"I will be your friend."

Ch'ta huddled against my chest. I stroked him awkwardly with my swollen hand. "You did good work," I said again, when he seemed calmer. "There is another rope. Will you chew through that one, too?"

As Ch'ta worked on my ankles, my hands began to come alive. It was as brutal as any pain Teksan had so cleverly imposed on me. So as not to frighten the onfrit again, I endured it with my teeth clenched, distracting myself with thinking of a way to get through the locked cellar door. My brain seemed frozen in its works, like a clock left out in the rain. I could not even remember clearly what kind of lock the door had. Did it turn, or did it need a key? Could I pick it from inside?

When Ch'ta had my ankles free, I crawled across the floor and up the stairs to look at the door. I had come through it many times, to fetch things or bring things down, in a life idyllically predictable it seemed to me now, free of pain and above all free of responsibility. At last, the image of the lock came to mind. It was little more than a latch.

I sent Ch'ta out the vent to find a way into the kitchen and unlock the door. While he was gone, my feet came alive in the same way my hands had done. I was still gasping with it when I heard the bolt click. I grabbed the edge of the door with my fingernails and wrestled it open.

Except for the onfrit, the kitchen was empty. But surely it was time for the Dream Teksan to arrive, monstrous in the costume of my fear. Maybe, I said to myself, with the first shred of hope I had allowed myself in this nightmarishly slow and strangely logical dream escape, maybe Teksan had worn himself out with today's exertions, and was asleep, sound asleep.

I crawled back down the cellar stairs to the food store. I gave a whole winterfruit to Ch'ta, who seemed overwhelmed at my generosity. He peeled it neatly with his teeth, but I ate mine entire, seeds, tough peel and all, my first food since Ula t'Fon.

When I stood up, my legs bore me, although unwillingly. Wobble-kneed, I stumbled on swollen feet around the room, filling a basket with food. I told myself that this was no escape dream at all, but a warm spring day, and I and the onfrit were going on a picnic. I put Ch'ta, still occupied with his winterfruit, into the basket, slung it over my shoulder, and climbed the stairs.

In the parlor, I stole a rug that lay across the back of one of the chairs, a pretty kipswool weaving that I had gotten for a good price one lucky shopping day. I was heading for the back door when I missed my footing in the dark, and entirely by accident put my hand down on my knife and my astil clothes, which lay in a tangle of other stuff on the kitchen table. I was giggling hysterically when I went out the door and carefully shut it behind me. "Well, where are you?" I asked the Dream Teksan. But the street was empty.

When I awoke, the earth swayed and swung rhythmically beneath me. The back half of me was numb with cold, but the front half was warm. Under my belly, I felt the working of muscles and the shifting of bones in joints. I opened my eyes and saw the impenetrable black of a cloudy night. I was not dreaming.

The onfrit nestled between my shoulder and neck in a tight huddle. The beast beneath me had to be a draf. I tried to remember how I had acquired a mount, and could only think of what I must have done: stolen the draf from the stable. The draf had not been let loose for winter because his owners were among those not hibernating. I had a brief memory of myself, sobbing over the buckles and straps my fingers would not work, of Ch'ta's clever hands solving the problem.

I curled my arm around Ch'ta. My legs were hooked under a strap to keep me from falling off. I wondered vaguely where the draf was taking us.

When I awoke again, the sky was beginning to pale and the draf was grazing on an unappetizing tangle of dead plants. "Ch'ta?" I said hoarsely. The onfrit warbled overhead, and landed on my shoulder as I sat up, head throbbing. "Love you," I said. Ch'ta licked my neck and clung to me anxiously. I felt sick: giddy and still half dreaming, with my bones aching dully and the rest of me shuddering with cold.

"Where are we, Ch'ta?"

"Going home."

"How does the draf know where to go?"

Ch'ta blinked at me; the question seemed too much for him. "Draf knows."

"All right."

I gave him some more food out of the basket, and ate some myself. I was thirsty, but afraid to get down from my mount to look for water, for fear I would not be able to get up again. I petted the draf's neck, and when he turned his sad eyes to me I gave him a piece of winterfruit. He seemed to take this as a signal of impatience, and started walking again, chewing as he walked and rumbling to himself deep in his belly.

The next time I awoke, we had entered the maze. My astil garb magnified the insipid sun into warmth. Ch'ta flew high overhead, but came down when I called, in great, showy swoops that reminded me wrenchingly of Hana. I stroked him when he had settled on my shoulder. My hands were still swollen, but not so much, and had lost their purplish color.

"Are you showing the draf where to go?"

"Yes."

"You speak draf language?"

"Onfrit," Ch'ta said, as if that answered my question. For the first time I considered how strange it was that Ch'ta was speaking to me in the language I knew. Eia's onfrits had always spoken to idre in H'ldat.

"Onfrits speak all languages?"

Ch'ta licked his paw delicately, looking at me through bright eyes, as if to say disdainfully, "Of course. Doesn't everybody know that?"

The short winter day ended and the sun sank in the sky. We reached Eia's cave before nightfall. I did not need to ask Ch'ta to drop down the rope for me, for it hung against the cliffside. A sickness dizzied me as I realized that Eia must have left the rope down that night the Walkers came, left it down every night regardless of ids own safety, so that if I returned I would know beyond doubt that I was welcome to come in. So Teksan and his people had climbed that rope.

The cliffs glowed faintly. The little stream lay frozen in its bed. I did not want to climb up and go in, knowing that the place would be inhabited with ghosts, and perhaps even with dead bodies. But I was even less eager to spend the night in the sand with the draf, knowing that Teksan was certainly not far behind me.

I climbed the rope, dragging myself up one handspan

at a time. After the first day, Teksan had hurt me without actually injuring me, for even in his madness he had remembered that he wanted me to live. But I was exhausted, and unrecovered from the first brutal beating. It was a long way to the ledge. I dragged myself over at last, as the stars came out above me.

The cave was ravaged, the books scattered and shredded, the furniture broken up, the food rotting in the storage bins, the floor bloodstained. There were no corpses, but, on the onfrits' ledge, Ch'ta greeted and fussed over another, who hissed fiercely at me when I drew near. One of her wings hung at a stiff angle, broken and beyond repair. A piled store of dry food lay within her reach. I guessed by the droppings collected in the farthest corner that she had not gone outside in a long time. When I drew close, she frantically chattered her sharp teeth at me, but did not give ground. Injured and traumatized as she was, she was brooding over an egg.

She brooded over something else as well. It was Ch'ta who showed it to me, hidden under the leaves and rags piled on the ledge: Eia's manuscript, damaged and dirty, gathered page by page by the loyal Ch'ta and protected in the best way an onfrit could manage against the marauders who might come again.

Chapter 9

Lying in Eia's tumbled bed that night, I learned a new kind of loneliness. The blankets were fragrant with ids musk, and even the scent of my own body lingered faintly. I had never before been so weary, yet rest avoided me.

I awoke late. All my muscles hurt and my back throbbed as if the crude farmer's boot had kicked it only yesterday. My wrists and ankles had scabbed over, but the joints were stiff. I felt very tired. My wings drooped like old rags. I would have given much for a Companion: not a lover even, just someone to pat my shoulder sympathetically and brew me a cup of hot broth.

I knew that it was very important that I avoid thinking about what had happened to me in Teksan's cellar. I shut my burning eyes and considered my situation. This cave was as much a trap as a haven. Teksan and his people could not get to me so long as the rope was up, but neither could I escape. The cave's supply of usable food was small, and the water was going stale in the bucket. I was not safe here.

If I were a hero, I would have decided to return to L'din to rescue Eia. But when the mere thought of Teksan's footstep rustling on the floor was enough to make me wet myself, I could scarcely consider myself a hero. Even if my courage were not shattered, I could have done little. His sorcery would tell him when I drew near. Only his heavy sleep and my good luck had made escape possible.

I could not rescue Eia. I could bring ids manuscript and onfrits to a safe place, where perhaps there were others who could be ids champion. What I could do seemed insignificant to me, but to do it was far better than doing nothing at all.

I knew I was too weak to climb the rope more than once. I threw over the cliff edge the scented blankets, which could each be crumpled down to a bundle the size of my fist, a bag of flight food and hard bread and other dried foodstuff, and Eia's manuscript, tied in a bundle. The draf, who was wandering about in pale sunlight, started with surprise at the objects falling from the sky. He spotted me on the ledge, and rumbled complaint and hunger at me. I had nothing to feed him, and the sand was barren.

The broody onfrit, having lost mate, master, and the power of flight, lived only for her egg. I was claw marked and bloody before I succeeded in taking it from her. The egg sheath was much like my own wing membranes, soft and tough, giving without yielding. Under the bleak gaze of the onfrit, I laid the warm egg very carefully in the basket, which I had lined with nesting stuff, and stood back. But she cowered where I had put her, all the fight gone out of her.

"We have to all go to a safe place. Your egg, too."

The onfrit stared, blank-eyed. When I slipped my hands under her and picked her up, careful of her injured wing, she lay limp and unstruggling. I put her hastily in the basket. I was beginning to wonder if I would have to devise a way to incubate the egg myself, so long was it before she stirred to look under her belly. She settled herself at last, making anxious trilling noises.

She did not budge when I picked up the basket, or when it rolled from side to side on my back as I climbed down the cliff. Distracting the complaining draf with a winterfruit, I loaded him with my gear, packed into makeshift backbags, and hung the onfrit in her basket against his side. Ch'ta landed abruptly on my shoulder, ice from the upper regions of air shimmering in his fur.

I asked, "Did you see people coming?"

"No. No people."

"Have you decided where to go?" My muscles were trembling. But I was still ahead of Teksan.

"I know the way." Ch'ta patted me reassuringly with his miniature hands.

"All right. I trust you, Ch'ta."

With the woven rug I padded myself against the draf's hard bones, but even so, getting up onto his back was an agony. I lay down at last, my face against the coarse fur of his powerful shoulders, dizzy with effort. Ch'ta warbled. The draf began to move under me. I looked back at the confused depressions his feet left in the sand. But the helpful wind began to fill in the marks of our passage, one glittering handful of sand at a time.

The color of the glass and of the sand underfoot shifted gradually from blue to purple. The wind died. For a while I felt warm, until vanguard clouds extinguished the sun. By afternoon the sky had turned dull, sullen, and snow heavy. I indulged myself in the futility of trying to decide whether or not a storm would be in my favor.

The enigmatic maze surrounded me. Even looking at it from above, as Ch'ta was, surely it was a puzzle beyond solution. Yet the draf and I did whatever the wise onfrit told us to do, turning, climbing, sometimes seeming to be going in circles. After the sun disappeared behind clouds, I became hopelessly lost, having nothing on which to base my sense of direction. When we stopped to rest in the afternoon, I gave the draf a drink of water in a bowl, and a piece of fruit which he ate in one bite and then looked at me accusingly.

By nightfall it was snowing. Ch'ta and I and the draf and the broody onfrit all huddled together in a makeshift shelter constructed of a blanket and string tied into Aeyrie-made pins which, crammed into fissures in the glass wall, clung there as if by magic. I had neither fuel nor the means to light it. The onfrits and I lay together against the shaggy side of the draf, atop the rug and under the remaining blankets. The food supply, shared among so many, was rapidly shrinking. The hungry draf would have a struggle of it in the snow tomorrow. How long would the fragile tent and the tiny pins hold against the increasing weight of snow?

The survival of the animals and the manuscript depended on my safety, so I lied to myself that I was safe. My bruises and aches and deadness of heart had neither healed nor diminished. After only one day, my journey seemed impossibly long.

I could not help but think of Eia, lying in filth and pain and fear in somebody's cold cellar. I was not certain how much time had passed since the night I sent Dulcie to be death's guide through the maze. Ten days, at least. How long could Eia endure imprisonment? Now that I had escaped, what would happen to my betrayed Companion? The possibilities, now that I knew Teksan so well, were awful. I told myself not to think about it any more.

I will never get to sleep, I thought, staring open-eyed into darkness, where with hushed, muffled sounds the snow drifted. Ch'ta nuzzled closer into my chest and sighed.

My feet were numb, but the rest of me was warm. Pale, eerie light illuminated the shaggy edge of the draf, who lay like a weary monster with his head tucked under the blankets a handbreadth away from mine. Ch'ta stirred against me. "Good morning, onfrit friend."

He chirruped sleepily.

Getting moving was a torturous chore. I had no shoes. My tender feet felt the cold snow like burning knives. The draf's method of coping with snow was a form of hibernation, which he abandoned reluctantly only when I pounded on his ribs with my fists. The pins were frozen in their fissures, and my fingers froze in working them free. The broody onfrit snarled at me as I tied her basket to the side of the blinking, groggy draf. Ch'ta flew high, and came down to report that although he could see the edge of the maze, he was not at all certain he could get us out of it.

Shaking with cold and frustration and the blood-drinking parasite of depression, I wrapped myself in blankets atop the draf and swore at him until he finally began to follow the onfrit fluttering before us.

The short winter day dragged strangely. The sun was finally crawling down the side of the sky when, like a gigantic painting within a cliff-sized frame, a monochromatic countryside frosted with snow appeared, glittering in the exhausted sunlight. The draf, catching sight of dead leaves on snow-coated bushes, broke abruptly into a heavy trot, throwing clots of snow behind.

"Stop!" I shouted, hastily steadying the basket where the unstable onfrit shrieked with rage. But he did not even slow down until his mouth was full. Then it was equally impossible to convince him to travel as he chewed.

I finally gave up beating on his shoulder and slid to the ground.

Behind us a clear trail showed where we had crossed otherwise untouched snow. I leaned against the trunk of a stunted tree, which spitefully threw a handful of snow at me. Ch'ta landed on me, his experienced claws gripping my shoulder gently. "Ch'ta," I said automatically. "You got us out. You do good work. Thank you."

"Sad?" he asked.

"Tired. I am so tired."

"Delan," he warbled affectionately. "Long traveling."

"Too long."

He licked my fur, and I petted him. Slowly my cloud of misery faded in the warmth of sympathy. The shadows were getting long, but perhaps we would find a farmer's shed where we could shelter the night. Maybe I could even boil some water and have a cup of hot tea.

I cried out, jerking upright. With a startled shriek, Ch'ta flung himself off my shoulder. Snow dislodged by my motion showered around me. And then the Rope had me.

I fled on the draf down unmarked ways, through the scrub and the snow, leaving signs of my passage that a mere child could have followed. What did it matter? Teksan knew exactly where I was. How long would it take him to open a Door, I wondered? How long before he and his people came walking out of thin air to surround me?

I knew it was hopeless, and yet I fled.

We stumbled upon a road in the darkness. A little later we came to a farm, where a herd of drafs standing in the snow rumbled at us as we passed their haystack. The windows of the stick and mud farmhouse were boarded shut for winter, a Walker family sleeping peacefully within.

I unloaded the draf in the middle of the walkway,

and sent him to join the strange herd. I picked the lock of a storehouse crammed with equipment. In a sheltered place, shielded by wooden boxes and overhung by a torn tarp, I hid the onfrit in her basket. Beside her I laid Eia's manuscript, and all the food that remained. It was not much, but maybe it was enough to sustain one small onfrit through the winter.

"If you are very quiet they will not find you," I said. "Wait for Ch'ta. He will come back for you."

Ch'ta had told me, as well as an onfrit could, how to find the Community of the Triad. Fly east, he had said, until you get to the great water, and then north, many days, until there is golden glass and a high tower. It sounded like a long way to go, but the Triad was far closer than any of the Aeyrie Ulas. Now I knew I would never make it even that far.

Perhaps I had always known it. Before I ever left Eia's cave I had used ids pens and paper to write an account of what had happened to myself, and to Eia, and to Ula t'Fon. I tied it to Ch'ta's leg now, and bid him to go on without me, and to tell Eia's friends where ids manuscript and the injured onfrit were hidden. I watched him disappear into the twilight, in much the same way I had watched Dulcie disappear. But this time I knew the future all too well.

I felt very alone when he was gone.

Out of strips of blanket cut with my knife I fashioned myself some protection for my feet. Then I set about putting as much distance as I could between myself and the treasures over which the female onfrit brooded. For speed's sake, and because of my limited night vision, I followed the wagontrack. I still traveled northward, for part of me persisted in behaving as if the greater the distance between myself and my enemy's lair the safer I would be. A single moon ascended to mock me: the Walker's lucky moon. My wings became heavy behind me, dragging me down and a little backward with each forward step.

The cold night grew colder. I shivered in spasms. My feet felt as numb and heavy and shapeless as chunks of wood. I walked on, too tired to feel anything, too stubborn to give up. The road ran through a little wood, with the trees naked under their crust of snow. I passed several farms, and came to a bridge over a narrow river that ran in such silence that I feared to think of how deep it was.

"We sink like stones," Gein had said to me. But I was so obstinate that I crossed the bridge without pausing, holding in my mind a fearful image of myself going down fighting, with a bloody weapon in my hand.

The idea of actually hurting someone was so awful that it awakened my intellect and I pondered for a long time the curiosity of it. I had been raised by a pacifist people. Why did I carry a blade then? Why did I love it so? Of course, the weapon symbolized not violence, but my longing to have control over my own destiny. How could I have gone through life believing I wanted nothing more than to be left alone? It was not true at all. I wanted, oh I wanted many things, passionately, longingly.

When I fell down, I had already been stumbling in the ruts for some time.

"Aeyrie magic begins where Walker magic ends."

"Is this some kind of riddle? You monsters are all alike."

"Don't you deserve better than to be eaten alive by the Animavore?"

I could not breathe. The Rope choked the air in my lungs and the blood in my body. *Deserve?* I thought stupidly, as if I did not know the meaning of the word.

The internal voice insisted, "Don't you deserve better?"

"I—deserve—better."

And then I knew what to do. Aeyrie magic begins where Walker magic ends. With the maze through which Teksan could not see and the doors Teksan could not open.

I could scarcely move, so tightly did the Rope have me. In cold and ungiving darkness I lay, bound many times over. I knew he would come soon; I could sense his will bending the pathways of the Universe. And he would consume me this time. With his pain and his fear he would easily destroy me, take me beyond mere death, make me live on, but crippled beyond recovery.

"I deserve better!" I said. My voice whispered weakly in the snow-still night. Painfully I moved my arm. My entire body was heavy and nerveless. My limbs were scarcely more mobile than the limbs of a tree. Yet I moved. My hands had gone numb. I drew my glass knife but could not hold onto it. It fell into the snow.

I found the knife again, not by touch or sight, for neither of these senses served me any longer, but by some other way, sheer luck it seemed. Did I actually see the Rope? I felt it so vividly I seemed to see it, black and thick, pinning my wings, choking the breath in my throat, holding captive that precious, fading flame in me. Suddenly I knew my immobility for what it was: it was anger, vast and frozen anger.

Surely such great anger could be power.

I shouted aloud in my vision: "I am poor, I have always been poor, yet you would take the little I have! You will regret having ever met me, Teksan Lafall!"

I brought my knife down on the Rope, the Rope of his will. It shredded away like smoke in wind. And then I was myself, lying on my face in the snow. I was cold and tired, but not so that I could not get up again.

I stood up, swaying and dizzy. I stared at the knife in my hand. It glittered in the starlight. Suddenly my heart leapt with hope in my chest.

In the distance, I could see something, not light exactly, but the suggestion of it. It did not lie in the direction I had been going, but I left the road and headed toward it. Right there where I had been lying, Teksan would construct his Door. Perhaps he had been waiting for me to wear myself out in fleeing him. But he would not delay any longer, for he would have realized as quickly as I that I had cut my bindings.

Walking unsteadily on wobbly knees, I crossed rutted, icy fields. My feet could not feel the ground. I thought about each step I took. I hoped the ice would leave little sign of my passage for the hunters to follow.

The light I had seen originated in a farmstead, a big one, with a huge barn. I walked between dark, silent buildings: sheds and houses lying like abandoned ruins under their unbroken coating of snow. Behind me a line of footprints showed where I had come out of the field. I went to the house where the single air lamp burned through a window whose boarding was falling down. Nothing was moving. No doubt someone had lit the lamp while looking for food and then had neglected to put it out again. I found a door. As with most farmhouses, it was not locked. I went in and shut the door again behind me.

I found no relief from the cold, but it was food I wanted. I ate some winterfruit, and a single piece of hardbread. Resisting the temptation to eat more, or at least bring some with me, I went out again and stood very still, listening to the echoing emptiness of the night.

My ears rang with the silence and ached with cold. Faint as a whisper, the sound of a hushed voice floated across the field. Another responded, harsh and impatient. My stomach twisted: it was Teksan.

I forced myself to move slowly despite my panic. Even the snow crunching under my feet seemed loud. One step at a time I crossed the yard to the barn, and bit by bit cracked the door open enough to let me in. The barn was crammed with dark, ghostly shapes: plows and wagons, draf harnesses hanging on the walls. It was a ladder I needed, a long ladder. Shaking with cold and anxiety, I walked the length of the building, peering into the shadows and sometimes feeling with my hands. I finally found three fragile pickers' ladders, but I needed one which was longer and sturdier. How did the height sensitive Walkers get to the barn roof to repair it?

I went out the back door and listened again. I heard nothing. I walked on the bare ground under the eaves, leaving faint footprints as I circled the outer wall. There at last I found a way to go up, more a stairway than a ladder, built firmly into the wooden wall.

I climbed. My legs were weak and weary. By the time I reached the handholds at the top and dragged myself onto the roof, showering snow into the shadows, my knees quivered with fatigue and fear. Fortunately, the roof did not have much of a slope. I crawled on the crust of slippery ice to the edge facing the road.

The land glowed silver under faint moonlight. Shadows wandered on both sides of the road. Clearly Teksan rightly believed I was too weak to travel much farther. Even at this distance I saw the weirdness in the air which was the Door, shimmering faintly and writhing with storm.

I crept to the edge of the roof farthest from my hunters. With my knife, I dug out solid depressions for my feet, and then I unwrapped the strips of blanket that had been serving me for shoes and left them in a tangled pile on the snow to mystify whoever came up here to make the repairs in the spring. I already carried little: one of the blankets for warmth, a pocketful of attaching pins, and some twine. I left it all, keeping only my weightless astil garment and my knife tied down in its sheath.

I stood up on the edge of the roof. The ground seemed very far away. Eia's voice spoke patiently in my memory: "It is gaining altitude which uses your energy. But the higher you get, the longer you can glide. On a good day, you can stay in the air from sunrise to sunset."

"But I am afraid," I said silently to the Eia inside of me.

"I will count to five. If you haven't jumped by then, I will push you."

I jumped. And the wind lifted me up.

Chapter 10

I collapsed into landing near a remote farmhouse. When I opened my eyes, I lay where I had collapsed the second time, inside, on the floor, near the stove. I vaguely remembered the tinderstick dropping over and over again from my numb and lifeless fingers, and my hearth thundering with panic in my throat. Then, a lucky spark at last, catching in tinder with maddening reluctance as I sighed on it. Now the stove radiated warmth, the coals cracked softly in the silence, and I shivered in a huddle on the bare floor. A purloined winterfruit lay in the dust where I had dropped it. I reached for it, my shaking hand heavy on my strengthless arm. I ate it as a draf would: in two bites, frantic with hunger.

Later I was able to crawl to the stove and put in more fuel from the wood basket by the wall. I puffed into the firebox, and got a faceful of ashes. In the depth of the cooling stove the secret red of a coal's heart sent out a tentative tendril of flame.

I crawled to the kitchen, where I filled a bowl with fruit and hardbread. Then I crawled back to the stove, and ate until my stomach was a pain within me. I knew there were things I needed to do. But as the renewed warmth crept into my fur, and dug deep into my exhausted muscles, it made my very bones go limp in my body. I could do nothing; I could go no farther. I could not even care that my feet were still numb, or that the floor was not kind to bruises and worn out muscles throbbing with pain. I curled under my wings, and slept.

In the afternoon I took a few shaky steps. I had frostbite, of course. I could not tell yet how bad it was. I had done something to my right side which hurt abominably and made my wing droop. I bound the wing up with cloth, easing the pain somewhat. I ate, and lay down and slept again.

It was nearly evening before my anxiety bestirred itself again. Teksan would guess that I had taken to the air, and that I could not have flown very far. If I stayed long where I was, he would certainly find me. Perhaps even now he was drawing near.

I wanted to shovel out the ashes from the stove and fill the basket anew with fuel, to sweep up my crumbs and peelings and wash the bowl. But apologizing silently to the people who lived there, I left the mess as it was. Walking heavily to make my feet break through the frozen crust, I laid a false trail out to one of the fields. Then I wrapped my feet in stolen rags and backtracked a roundabout way, walking softly atop the crust, leaving only faint depressions for a trail.

I stole supplies from the household which involuntarily hosted me: a tinderstick, an armload of blankets from a storage cupboard, a worn pair of workshoes, and a basket of food. I imagined that the people who lived here were kind-hearted and honest folk, who would forgive my thievery when they realized that I had taken only things for survival. It was not just for the sake of my uneasy conscience that I imagined this. If I could not believe that fellowship and kindness survived in this indifferent and cold world, I could not have continued my journey.

Night fell, and with it the chill turned again to bitter, heart stopping cold. I headed for the woods.

I laid two more false trails among the trees, and had picked out a possible refuge: an upthrusting spike of glass which blacked out the stars on the horizon. The night was still young when I heard, in the crisp, echoing night, the sound of my pursuers' distant shouting voices. The sound wove among the saplings. At times they seemed eerily, impossibly close.

Despite the voices trailing me, I kept walking at my steady pace, eating as I traveled and keeping my eye on the red star which gave me direction. I came upon a trail beaten into snow by the feet of a woods creature as solitary and unsleeping as I. Welcoming the cover for my own tracks, I followed it. The five moons hung overhead, each of them a sliver the size of a fingernail. My footsteps crunched loudly in the snow.

I had not rested long enough. My brief energy burned itself out like dry grass in a stove. I stumbled as I walked. I dreamed awake. I was in the baths at Ula t'Fon, where it was warm, and soft, and dark. Someone was tending me, hands stroking slowly and softly through my fur. My wings were wet with oil. The hands touched them, reawakening the extraordinary sensitivity which after Teksan's subtleties I had feared forever lost. I turned onto my side and reached up to touch warm, fragrant fur, a thoughtful, fine-boned face with a haunting, crooked smile—

The gulf of my loneliness gaped open under my feet, and I fell.

I was on my knees in the snow with my face in my hands when I heard the Walkers coming, heard their voices muttering on the rising wind.

"There it is!"

"Kill the damned thing and be done with monsters, I say!"

I struggled to my feet with my blade in my hand.

There were two of them, dressed in thick jackets against the cold, running heavily out of the shadows, puffing white smoke out of their mouths. When they overran me, I was still untangling myself from the blankets I had wrapped around myself for warmth. I flung my little weight forward behind my knife, and jabbed, and met resistance. One of them yelped. Then my hand was empty, my glass blade was flying, and I was being wrestled, half fainting and crying out with pain from my outraged injuries, down to the ground.

I brought up my knee. It rammed into something, and in the haze a Walker grunted with pain and cursed furiously. Then ice cold metal scratched at my throat, and I went limp.

"Kill it!"

"Teksan said to—"

"We have the other one."

I said, "Dean. I saved your crunchfruit plants from suckbugs. Remember?"

There was silence, strange and explosive.

"I am a person. I am a person just like you. I'm cold and tired and scared and angry, just like you."

"Shut up!" Knuckles slammed into my mouth. And then—I did not understand what was happening. There were incoherent cries. The ice cold blade at my throat disappeared abruptly. The bruising grips on my arms disappeared as well. I scrabbled across snow, grabbed my blade in my hand again, and did not even look around myself until I was on my feet.

Something huge and black and six-legged was chasing the Walkers among the saplings. They were screaming.

I ran in the other direction, twisting between trees and leaping over frozen brooks. I ran until my breath was a pain in my chest, until my feet tangled in the star-bright snow and my breath sobbed in my burning throat. And still I ran, up a hillock and through a clinging thicket, until I came to an open, flat place where the snow lay smooth as the frosting on a teacake. I fell down. I knew I would die of cold if I lay long in the snow. I did not want to die, but I could not stand up. At last, I lost interest and struggled no more.

I heard the monster coming. Its six-footed progress made a rhythmic confusion of crisp noises as each step broke through the crust. It drew close. I heard a soft, musical rumble, like distant thunder.

My mouth tasted of blood. "Leave me alone. Please. Just leave me alone."

Breath whuffled against my shoulder. Somehow I found it in me to turn my head. The monster was big as a draf. Slanted eyes glowed yellow in the moonlight. Its breath steamed around it.

Inspired by the size of it, I raised my head further, offering it my throat. Its head came down, huge and shaggy, with white-tipped pointed ears standing out in the darkness. I thought I did not care, but I shuddered when it touched me.

A hot, rough tongue brushed my neck. "Brother," the monster said, in a distorted, growly, hesitant voice, almost shyly.

Cold air burned down my throat into aching lungs. I could no longer feel the cold of the snow. I said hoarsely, "Yes." This did not seem the time to try to explain to it that I was both brother and sister.

"Hurt?"

"Yes."

It lay down beside me, full length. Its breath steamed and burned on my face. The warmth of its body was a shock against my freezing flesh. "Ride me home."

"You will not hurt me?"

The monster seemed shocked. "Hurt you! No."

To move was agony. I struggled myself out of the mess I had made of the beautiful snow, and dragged myself onto the monster's narrow, muscular back. It had a mane like mine. I dug my numb hands into it, and wrapped my aching legs around its middle as it stood up, graceful despite my weight. It turned its head to look at me anxiously as if expecting me to fall off. "How far is it?" I asked.

"Far? Not far."

"All right." I rested my head against a lean, muscular shoulder. It shifted smoothly under me, moving as sinuously as water. Its feet crunched in the snow. Its warmth began to warm me. All around me, the night crackled with frost. I shut my eyes, and trusted. Why not?

He lived partway up the spike of glass where I had thought to find refuge. I had to climb the steep trail on my own very limited strength, but he clung behind me in impossible positions, helping me with his many limbs, of which he seemed to always have at least one spare, and encouraging me with musical growls that had no threat in them.

He inhabited a spot where the elemental crystal had split open, a cave like Eia's, only narrower and higher. He had closed off the opening with a crudely constructed twig and mud wall, and hung over the doorway a flap which had once been a farmer's tarp. Within, it was crowded with primitive twig baskets containing a winter store of food: nuts primarily, and dried fruit black as coal.

When I awoke from my first exhausted sleep, my blankets covered me, and my tinderstick lay beside me. The monster who had befriended me had apparently gone back before daybreak to recover my lost supplies. He (in the morning light I saw that he was male) was asleep next to me now, as warm as any fire. I was feverish and weak. But he awoke at the change in my breathing and delicately offered to help me outside so I could relieve myself.

His forepaws were short-fingered hands. He could rear up the front third of his body so his torso was as erect as any Walker's. If I had first seen him in this position I might have thought him a creature from legend: half Walker, half draf.

I stood on the narrow path with his forelimb around my waist to support me on my unsteady feet. My urine smoked in the bitter chill. Far below me, the gray and white wood cast stark, long shadows in the cold red sunset. Beyond the edge of the wood, brilliant cliffs broke through earth and aimed skyward, red glass burning under the red sky. The farmsteads were almost invisible under the smothering snow.

"What is your name?" I asked as he helped me back to shelter.

"Oorrrchth," he said.

"Och?"

His huge, dark green eyes sparked with amusement. "Yes," he said, though my attempt to repeat his guttural, musical growl had obviously been an utter failure. He lay me down and tucked the blankets around me, and brought me food from his stores, and water in a leaky bark bucket.

"I am Delan," I said with my mouth full.

"Oorrrchth bring wood. Make fire, make Delan warm."

"Do you eat meat?"

His expressive brows lifted. "Meat?"

"You have big teeth."

He bared them. The incisors were pointed, but the rest of them were flat as a draf's. "Bite enemy, no eat. Crack nuts. Sun-melon, apricocks."

His command of the Walker tongue was extremely limited, but I discovered that he spoke far more H'ldat than I. I was definitely not the first Aeyrie he had met. His own rumbly, musical language was entirely beyond me. I heard enough of it to figure out that his people might be primitive, but they were far from simple.

He washed his paws one by one in the bark bucket after he had eaten. "Why did you befriend me?" I asked sleepily.

"Delan brother," he replied, as if that explained everything.

"You chased the Walkers away, but you took me home."

"Walkers bad. Put people in cage. Other Delan in cage, too. You open door. You open Och's door. You say, Och is my friend. Be free."

I gathered that an Aeyrie had befriended him once, and therefore Och in turn had befriended me. "What happened to Other Delan?"

"Walkers come. Run, fly. Never see Other Delan again." He sighed. "Many seasons. Spring, summer, winter. Many, many."

"Where is your birth home?"

"Go over water, far away." He sighed again. "Want to go home again! Want other Och."

He fetched fuel as he had promised, but the fire he helped me build near the door did not generate much warmth. Och was nocturnal, and went out when it was full dark to check his territory. I huddled miserably by the open flames, too cold and anxious to sleep well, starting awake nervously every time the frost cracked or the wind whispered. Was that Teksan? Was he coming for me? But the only one who came was Och, and I heard him singing as he climbed the steep path, a sad tune in a minor key. He slid in gracefully, scarcely moving the tarp, shielding his eyes from the firelight. I put my arm around his huge head as he lay down beside me. His tangled, frosty mane grew wet as the ice thawed under my hand. I thawed in the warmth and safety of his presence, and slept deeply.

I awoke when the sun rose, throwing a pale glimmer of

light across the rough floor. Och's fur was the color of smoke. He rumbled with pleasure deep in his throat as I stroked his long, curved backbone.

He lifted his head to groom my fur with his tongue, as if I were the Other Och he longed for. But there was little we could do for each other's loneliness. He was Och, and I was Aeyrie; we were not enough like each other. All we could do was keep each other warm.

I slept through another day. When I awoke again, my fever was gone and my strength was returning. For the first time since Teksan's cellar, I felt resilient and hopeful. "I have to go in the morning," I said, as Och cracked open nuts with a rock and I picked out the meats for our evening meal.

Och crushed a nut as easily as if it were a crisp piece of hardbread. "Not stay?" His voice was very soft.

"Want Other Delan."

Och looked up at me, out of alien yet human eyes. "I know. I know."

"I will come back. I will find out where your home across the water is. I will come back, and tell you how to get there. I promise."

At daybreak, Och came home from his night-long wandering to report that he had encountered no one about in his woods. The Walkers who had been pursuing me had vanished, and had not come back. I hoped they assumed that I had been killed and carried off by the monster.

He gave me a ride to the edge of the trees. "Hurt," he said miserably as I hugged him good-bye. It was not easy to walk away from him. I turned back once. Half invisible in the shadows, he still watched me, though the rising sun must have pained his sensitive eyes.

Guideless and mapless, I followed the roads as well

as I could, using the sun to give me direction. East and north I went, walking a long, dreary, lonely way, on feet which never ceased to hurt, in a haze of weariness which never entirely lifted. I stole food and fuel, and used many a kitchen stove without permission. I might have been the only person alive in the world, so silent was it, so still, so empty. I welcomed the sight of a herd of drafs, huddled against the shelter of a barn wall. They were alive. Their breath and body heat laid mist over their shaggy backs. I did not even consider taking one with me, but the reassurance that I was not alone in the world made me glad.

As I lay down to rest that first night after leaving Och, on the wooden floor of yet another farmhouse filled with hibernating Walkers, I could not sleep. As soon as I closed my eyes, I knew that someone was following me. It was a knowledge beyond reason, a physical knowledge that throbbed in my blood. Tenaciously, heartlessly, tirelessly, someone was following me. My follower was not close, but was getting closer. How my follower knew where I was I could not begin to guess. How I knew that someone was on my trail was even more of a mystery. I scolded my active imagination. I told myself that it was my inheritance from Teksan, that because of him I was unable to believe in my own safety. But I could not sleep.

My certainty never left me; not that night and not in all the days and nights which followed. By the second night I was tired enough that it didn't matter. I slept anyway, but in a room with an exit, with my knife beside me. In the morning I panicked and took flight, walking at a grueling pace along a smooth road. My blood told me that my pursuer lost ground. But I had worn myself out, and so I lost my advantage in the afternoon when weariness slowed me down.

I decided to pretend that I was playing a game. All I had to do to win it was to keep ahead of the one

following me. I steadied my pace. I had a long way to
go.

By the fourth day, my anxiety was dulled by the
monotony of walking. My stolen shoes did not fit well,
and I had wonderfully painful blisters to distract me. I
slept soundly at night. Eventually I was laughing at
myself: how ridiculous this game was, this imaginary
pursuer and the strange compulsion to keep ahead of
him. But I did not stop walking, though I was footsore
and all my muscles hurt, though my torn flight muscle
throbbed miserably, though I had lost weight rapidly
until my ribs stood out sharply under my clothes and
fur.

In my imagination, I began to lose ground. I could
not go as far or cover as much distance as I had been
able to at the beginning. I thought of stealing a draf,
but could not bring myself to do it. I felt guilty enough
about the hardbread and winterfruit and coal, none of
which I had properly earned. Unwilling to trust the
certainty which, much like the wings on my back, had
sprung into existence unexpected and unexplained, I
heeded the advice of my guilt. It was a mistake I
probably could not have avoided, but I regretted it
soon enough.

Ahead of me, mountains appeared, distant and hazy
points on the horizon. The snow melted slowly. A
brief snow flurry dusted the ground again, and minis-
cule, perfect crystals hung suspended for long moments in my fur before suddenly being transformed to
drops of water. The sun came out. I hesitated at a
crossroad, trying to decide between a road which went
more or less northward, and one which went due east.
I had lost track of the days I had been walking; but it
did seem I should be getting near the ocean by now. If
so, the easterly road would be the one to take.

I stood there longer than I really needed to. I was
awfully tired.

That mysterious thing inside of me warned me to look back at the way I had come. The road I had been following stretched straight and flat behind me, overhung by a few barren trees.

Far away I saw a suggestion of motion. My heartbeat froze in my throat. Steady-paced, making no attempt to hide, my follower traveled down the middle of the road, walking step for step in my very tracks: the one I would not believe in, the one I had named a mere shadow.

I took the easterly road. The dusting of snow had melted, and I walked carefully on frozen places, to leave no mark. This was a stony land, with great chunks of red-orange glass lying in immense broken piles. I had passed an occasional kipsfold and attendant house, but otherwise the land was uninhabited. The night before, I had slept in the open, so exhausted that even the bitter cold had not kept me awake.

My heart pounded. At last, out of fear, I obeyed my internal prompting. I left the road abruptly. Knife-edge sharp boulders defied me to try to climb them. Growing up in the Glass Mountains had not prepared me for this: even the tough-skinned Digan-lai were too often injured or even killed by glass. I went slowly, thinking about each step, careful of my balance. Frost crunched in shadows where the sun had never shown.

Soon the road had disappeared behind me. I told myself I would cut across to the northerly road, and leave my tracker to assume I had continued east. But the seer within me told me he would not be fooled, for he, too, was guided from within, and needed no sign to follow.

The day was not much older before I was utterly disoriented, without landmarks to refer to, and without sensible shadows to tell me what direction the sun was going. I struggled onward, stopping only to wrap my hands for protection against the sharp edges, consoling myself with the certainty that my follower, if he was still behind me, was having as hard a time of it as I.

Suddenly, the sun was gone, and I was shivering with cold. The sky had filled abruptly with black clouds. Soon the first flakes of snow floated, white and dizzying in the darkening day, landing to cling like tufts of white fur to the barren glass.

I had no shelter, little food, and no fuel. I said out loud, as if the voice inside of me was not myself but a misguiding other, "Why have you led me into such dangerous land, into the teeth of the storm?"

The stranger within me replied calmly, *This way lies safety*.

I laughed harshly. But there was nothing to do but walk on, uselessly cursing weather and bad luck, trying not to heed the panic thundering in my throat. Silently, relentlessly, the snow fell. Behind me, the pursuer stalked, unmystified by the complex way I had taken, slowed somewhat but not as much as I.

Day sank into an early night. I edged around a deadly corner that I could scarcely even see, and gradually realized there were no more boulders ahead of me. My night blind eyes could not see what lay ahead, whether flat land or precipice. I remembered how the areas of broken boulders had lain in north-south lines across the land, like hedgerows, with strips of comparably opened spaces between. I turned left, with the nearly invisible broken glass at one side to give me direction. I brushed the snow out of my eyes, and kept walking.

The darkness moved with snow. When I became dizzy, I closed my eyes and made my way by feel, with my numbed hand dragging along glass and my numbed feet setting down carefully, step by step. Time slowed, and almost seemed to stop. I set down my foot, settled it firmly, and picked up the other. I slid my hand along the rough side of the glass boulder, beginning to shift my weight forward.

My hand slid into empty air. My foot set down on a smooth slope, and I was slipping in the snow, falling strangely slowly, gasping with pain as my injured wing struggled to save me. There seemed an infinity of time in which to think, to feel the muscle's ragged pain like an arrow in my side, to shout silently my helpless despair. And then the shuddering shock of glass sliced into my fragile flesh.

Chapter 11

A dark blotch spread across the white and glittering snow. Three half moons hovered in a patch of sky. A voice shouted, echoing and shattering in the brittle air: "Where are you? (Are you? Are you?)" Snow flurried across shadows. The moons again, ghostly behind shredding clouds. A lone Walker deliberately and implacably came through the snow, step by step.

My voice cried out hoarsely. The Walker multiplied into three. Why were they making me feel this pain? Why didn't they leave me alone and let me sleep?

Liquid fire burned in my throat. "Swallow," a voice ordered.

I cracked open my eyes, choking. My body was half lifted. My head rested against a padded shoulder. Above and beside me I saw a Walker face outlined by lamplight but hidden in darkness.

Cold metal rapped my teeth. "Swallow."

"Leave me alone," I mumbled feebly. But I swallowed. My body spasmed with terror and pain. I knew what Teksan would do to me! I spotted a shred of my sleeve, black and stiff with frozen blood. Why hadn't I hurt myself worse, and died?

The chest against which I lay moved in a deep breath. "Despair?" the person said. It was a soft chest, much too soft to be a man's. Someone else crouched over me, gripping my glass-sliced arm. That one spoke, liquid, questioning words. Someone near my feet also said something in H'ldat. Walkers, I protested to myself, do not speak H'ldat.

The Walker woman's fingers burned hot against my chilled skin. "Feili. Maybe id will trust an Aeyrie. Tell idre who we are."

"Delan, we are Eia's friends. We are from the Triad."

I turned my head to peer up at the speaker, stupid with bewilderment. The triangular face above me was outlined by lantern light. The gold mane flowed out from ids face, burning in the lantern light. Pale wings glowed against the black sky. Sharp bones; bright eyes, an Aeyrie constructed of flame.

"Ch'ta?" My voice was hoarse with cold.

"He is guiding the others," said the Walker who half lay beside me.

I turned my head again. "But—"

"Guesswork put us within your reach. But I knew when you were near, there was no need to search. Your spirit was like a beacon in darkness. And you turned your way toward us, as if you sensed our coming as clearly as I did yours."

I said, "I have a stranger in me, a person who knows . . ." But it took too much effort to try to explain when I did not myself understand it.

"Never mind," the woman said. "It is not important. We reached you in time. We can unpuzzle it later."

"There is someone following me."

The Aeyrie called Feili spoke, ids softly accented voice awakening the warmth of kinship in me. "The Stalker follows you no longer. Do not be concerned. You are truly safe."

I lay quiet. Something very strange had happened. Perhaps someday I would understand it. Right now I did not greatly care. The person who had spoken little chafed my feet with snow until I began to have some feeling in them, a pain which I recognized as far better than numbness. I asked suddenly, "Will I get to meet a Mer?"

The Walker woman's chest shuddered with kindly laughter. "Yes, child, I promise you. Already, she wants to meet you as well." The padded jacket against my cheek smelled of woodsmoke. I breathed it in, and shut my eyes. She smelled like a hearth, she felt like a home. She settled me more firmly in the crook of her arm, and held me close to her, like a very young child. I felt like I was about to cry, but instead I sank, suddenly and helplessly, into the oblivion of sleep.

Of the rest of that long night I remember nothing. I am told that the Triad-re carried me in a sling of blankets to their draf sleigh and alternated riding at the reins in the bitter wind and lying with me under the blankets, using their body warmth to thaw the ice out of my bones. It was after daybreak when we arrived at the community, but I did not open my eyes again until the day was nearly over. I was blanket-wrapped and propped on pillows, in a warm bed, in a small, plain room. I blinked groggily at the woman sitting in a chair beside me. She was gray haired, the age lines fanning out from her eyes and accenting her mouth. An old Walker, gentle as spring, strong as winter.

She said, "You are at the Triad. Do you remember?"

"What about Eia?" My voice sounded worn and frail.

"Two of the Aeyries have flown to L'din to deliver idre, two who can challenge Teksan himself if they must. How do you feel?"

My brain flapped within my limp and strengthless body, but remained earthbound. "There is something wrong with me."

"What do you mean?"

"I feel like—am I going to die?"

"Gracious, no. You are recovering very quickly, like the l'shil Aeyrie you are.

"I am?" The emptiness in me did not feel like recovery; far from it.

"You have been in shock, and are utterly worn out. The best thing you can do for yourself is to relax, and trust your body and mind's common sense. When it is time for you to feel alive and normal again, it will happen."

She leaned forward, with the warm light of a lamp burning on her weathered face. She wore a simple, rough-woven shirt that opened at the neck, revealing a necklace of translucent shells striped with pink. Her eyes were a deep, bright blue. "How is the level of your pain? I gave you something for it, but it was a cautious dose." Her hands were resting on her knees; the long-fingered, many-jointed hands of a Walker born to do delicate work.

"It hurts a little."

"Tell me if it gets worse or prevents you from sleeping. I or someone else will stay within call."

"I wasn't expecting to meet Walkers. Do you have sorcery, too, to keep you from hibernating?"

She laughed. "No sorcery. All it takes is a stimulating tea and a bright room for one or two days."

I sighed. For some reason, knowing that Teksan's sorcery was at least partly fakery made no difference to me. "How badly hurt am I?"

She turned down the covers and showed me. My fur had been shaved, baring the dusky skin beneath. The long gash down my upper arm was a crooked but neatly stitched seam, swollen and discolored, but clean.

"The frostbite—"

"—Would be disastrous if you were a Walker. Your

feet will hurt for a few days. Delan, be at ease. You truly are safe and healing."

When I met her gaze directly, I felt utterly disoriented, the way I felt when I looked into the Void, but without the fear. I looked into her eyes, and looked away, and yet looked at her again. She watched me steadily and thoughtfully.

I finally said, "Thank you for taking care of me—I do not even know your name."

"I am the healer Lian of Troyis. Lian Merfriend I am also called. I am the Triad Mer's herd substitute; her mind-partner."

I blinked, taken aback. "You are a—a telepath? Is that how you found me in the snow?"

"Pilgrim is a se'an, one who communicates in thought. I am an em'an, one who comprehends feeling. Between the two of us we know a great deal."

"The Aeyries would not want to believe in a Walker like you."

She laughed suddenly. "They do have difficulty with it. But not nearly as much difficulty as the Walkers have."

Her fingertips tentatively touched my tangled, grimy mane. "I am a monster in my way. Your acceptance of me is impressive. But there is an anxiety in you, enough to inhibit your healing. What are you afraid of?"

I was so accustomed to fear that I almost denied that I felt it. But Lian was right: my skin crawled with tension, my ears ached with listening for that one step, the one that meant degradation and pain. I said, "Teksan will find me again. He always does."

"We found your Stalker as we searched for you. It was not really a person, but a thing of sorcery, though it used to be a man. Now it is dead."

"Dead?" A sadness, sudden and unexpected as the piercing of a thorn, panged me.

"Outside of actual magic, the only way to get rid of

a Stalker is to put yourself into deadly danger. Because of its nature, it must share your danger. When you fell, your Stalker, too, had to fall. But its injury and the cold killed it."

"Why did he die, and I did not?"

"Maybe because you are an Aeyrie, and better able to survive the cold. Maybe because you wanted desperately to survive, but all his capacity for desire was burned out of him."

"It is not right! It was his only life!"

Somewhere in the room there was a stove. I heard it crackle and I heard the lamp flame flutter. I heard the healer breathe, slowly and deeply. When she finally spoke, her voice was hushed as if she hesitated to interrupt the stillness. "No, it is not right. Who is Teksan Lafall, to think he is justified in using and abusing and wasting people?"

Something shuddered in me. Lian looked down at me. "Just the sound of his name does this to you."

"When I heard him coming . . ." My voice was shaking. "I could not fight, or run, there was nothing I could do. And every time he came, he stayed for hours."

"What did he do to you?"

"He hurt me. Eia warned me—"

"Did he rape you?"

The gentleness in her made it possible to answer, to remember something I had felt it necessary to forget. "It was—a kind of rape."

"Did he penetrate you with objects? Did he masturbate?" I did not have to answer. She said quietly, "I did not examine you thoroughly while you slept, but it would be best if I do it now, with your permission. If for nothing else, for your reassurance."

Despite being a Walker, she knew Aeyrie bodies. I expected pain or shame, but experienced little of either. Afterward, she cuddled me against her, as I wanted her to do. She told me I was scarred, but not so it would make any difference either in lovemaking or in egg laying.

"The scars on your spirit are more worrisome."

Of course, I knew that: that sex would never be the same; that Teksan had carved his mark into me like initials in the side of a tree, permanently. I rested my head against her soft shoulder, tempted by despair.

I was caught unawares in what seemed a gust of wind, but it was a wind of alien thought, containing not words, but currents of energy and emotion, moving like water, enveloping and encompassing and expanding. . . . Then I was myself again, dizzy and disoriented and strangely aroused.

"Please pardon us. We have learned that to give advance warning does more harm than good."

I felt it then, how the tight strings of fear had snapped and were disintegrating within me as the memory of a nightmare does in the light of morning. My eyelids were heavy. "I know who you are," I said sleepily. "You are the one, the one Eai—"

"The one who regrets that she could not return Eia's love."

I looked into those tranquil, disorienting eyes.

"Pilgrim and I have a special pool," she said, answering a question I had no right to even be wondering.

"I—"

"There are several Walker-Aeyrie pairs also. We can't cross-breed with each other, but once it came out that, despite being different races and the same sex, Pilgim and I are lovers, the gulf between air and earth ceased to seem so great."

It was not shock which made me unable to speak. It was amazement.

I slept for two days. For two more days I remained disinclined to move, incurious and enervated, weary and sometimes depressed. I got to know the walls of the room very well. I got to know the rhythms of the community as well: the flurry of activity in the morning, cheerful voices and hurrying footsteps in the hallway; settling down to busy silence until the sunlight took on a reddish hue. The evening seemed full of the voices of children. Once, remotely, I heard the sound of a stringed instrument. I listened until my ears ached, but I had no desire to get up and find the musician.

Lian brought me a H'ldat grammar printed on the Triad Press. I was content with leafing through it, seeking out the Aeyrie words for which there were no Walker equivalents, and practicing their pronunciation under her tutelage. By the time I was on my feet I had acquired a limited, eclectic H'ldat vocabulary. I had learned the words like l'shil, sh'man, and l'frer which described people without implying gender. I had also memorized a multitude of words for wind and the experience of flying, with subtle shadings in definition that were beyond my experience and comprehension.

I thought I was merely following a whim in my eccentric approach to the language. It was Lian who pointed out to me that I could not think of myself as an Aeyrie until I knew the words in which to contain the concepts. I was not studying a language at all; I was studying myself.

Weariness lay over my spirits like smoke palling the sky. But, on the fifth day, Lian came in to find me standing shakily at the window with one of the shutters opened. I was looking out at a neat garden, bedded down for winter, bordered by a tumbledown stone wall. Beyond the wall stretched a flat, snowy expanse of land, scattered with white hummocks that might be bushes or bunches of tall grass. The land ended abruptly, as if sliced away by some monstrous knife. Beyond that edge, the emptiness was filled with mist.

I shivered as Lian came up to me. "What is it? Is that where the world ends?"

"It is the edge of the cliffs, and beyond that lies the ocean. Perhaps the mist will burn off, and you will be able to see the water."

"It moves as if it were breathing."

Lian put her hand on my shoulder. She was smiling. "You see differently from most of us. It is an important difference."

My knees wobbled under me. Her arm slid around my waist to support me. "Riddles," I said.

Lian closed the shutter. "It's time for you to sit down."

I sat obediently on a stool, but at once I was itchy to be up again. "I want to meet Pilgrim. I want to see the printing press."

"Hold still." She studied my wounded arm. I fell anxiously silent, but she seemed satisfied with what she saw. "Breakfast. A bath. And the press. But to meet Pilgrim you have to get down to sea level, and I don't think you're up to the climb yet. You do appear to be feeling better."

There had been no nightmares, no ghost at my window, no imaginary prowlers at my door. Even as I felt the despair of knowing I would forever be afraid of Teksan, it had ceased to be true. Out of the shell of my tiredness, I had hatched as eager and curious as an onfrit.

I could not trust my recovery. It was unnatural. "How did it happen?"

Lian stood back. Her eyes were like lake water, always changing their color. She said, "Even when you were a mere embryo, others interfered with you, displaced you to a hostile, loveless environment, deprived you of every kind of nourishment, treated you indifferently at best, though you are no stranger to cruelty either. You do not need to learn yet again that you can overcome and recover and survive. Haven't you done it every day of your life?

"Pilgrim and I do not interfere like this lightly. But the chance to thrive for once, that was a gift we thought it safe to give you."

"To thrive!" I said it as if I had never heard the word before, in mock horror.

Lian's face was sober. "Delan. Now you are afraid."

I had not realized how large was the building in which my room was just one niche. Its regular shape and straight walls testified to Walker architecure, but the Aeyrie influence had transformed its dull utilitarian construction. Windows of colored glass glowed despite the misty morning. Rugs or straw mats which felt good under my bare feet covered the cold stone floors. Once we were outside, I saw that the building we had just exited would have seemed unspeakably eccentric to a conventional Walker. On one corner a round flight tower pointed skyward, and along its unheard-of second floor, balconies crowded, with streamers and whirligigs clattering and hissing in the wind.

"Walkers on the first floor and Aeyries on the second."

"That was the idea when we built the building. But things have not been nearly so neat or simple. Motivated Walkers can overcome their fear of heights."

We walked on a cleared pathway edged by piles of dirty snow. The bathhouse was a separate building, with smoking stovepipes and no windows. The roof was covered with black pipes, but the sun-heating system did not work in the winter mist, and the water was heated by coal. "It will be crowded," Lian warned me. "We only have hot water once a day in winter."

The drying room was jammed with energetic children supervised by four tolerant adults, all of them naked, races and sexes mixed indiscriminately among mounds of wet towels. But nonetheless I was unprepared for the bathing room. Aeyries and naked Walkers of both sexes sat on stools, washing themselves with sponges dipped in buckets, and talking energetically in languages equally mixed together. Standing in shallow tubs along one wall, a Walker male emptied a bucketful of water over the head of an Aeyrie Red. The Aeyrie shook water out of ids eyes and laughed. A few air lamps glowed fitfully.

If not for Lian's grip on my elbow, I would have fled.

"Let's find you a private spot, Del—I always forget how overwhelming this place is to newcomers. We couldn't divide bathing time according to sex, you Aeyries just make it too complicated."

Dumb with panic, I followed her through the steaming, noisy crowd. She sat me on a long-legged stool behind the artificial shelter of a fragile woven screen. A familiar Gold appeared behind her, wet fur plastered across ids muscular terrain, counterbalancing with one partially spread wing the weight of a bucket of water in the other hand. Each step id took was a kind of a graceful, terribly controlled dance.

The Aeyrie said, "Do you remember me?"

Lian stepped aside for idre. I said, "Of course, you are Feili. You must be a Quai-du master."

"By the summer sun, what makes you say that?"

"You walk like one."

Grinning, id turned ids wrist so I could see the mark. "You unnerve me. We had better take care of this one, Lian."

Lian looked offended. "And what have I been doing these five days?"

"Do you trust me to help the l'shil?"

"Will you be all right, Del? Do not get your arm wet."

Feili was already asking as she walked away, "Do you like our bath?"

My panic was only beginning to quiet. "No."

"Me neither. I always thought that if the Walkers had fur it would be a great improvement."

"Or if the Aeyries didn't."

"But then we would look as funny as they do!"

I looked up sharply. Feili was grinning. Suddenly I felt much better.

I could not bend over very far because of the lingering stiffness of my torn muscle, and so I needed a great deal of help with the water and soap. Feili radiated cheer and energy, and loved to talk. Id had hatched in t'Han, and not only knew Gein before id moved to t'Fon, but had been ids lover for a time. I had not realized until then just how small was the Aeyrie world. Limited to three small communities, the entire Aeyrie population totaled no more than four hundred, including the twenty-three at the Triad. For any one Aeyrie to at least be acquainted with all of the others in the world was not unusual. It was even more common for one person to have strong connections in every Ula: lovers, ex-lovers, friends and kin.

Feili briskly sluiced me down in the tub as I protected my injured arm from the cooling water. The worst of the crowd dispersed to breakfast, and soon we had the drying room to ourselves. Many of the Aeyries had gone out still damp and undressed, but Feili assured me that Lian would be profoundly displeased if I did the same. We oiled each other's wings, and sat a long time in the drying room.

Feili talked about Eia. They had been Quai-du shadrals, sparring partners. Feili said, "Of course I have met ids l'frer and l'per, also. And the t'Fon taiseoch-dre are all killers. The last time I visited t'Fon, it had been two years since Gein and I parted ways, but every time I spoke to idre, Hana looked ready to challenge me to a blood battle. It was not a restful business either, being Eia's shadral. Id is a ruthless fighter. But it was certainly good for my style."

I remembered the hushed voice, the hesitant, gentle, playful fingers. "I do not think we are discussing the same Eia."

"Of course not. The killer—that personality Eia kept in the storage closet. I would wager you never knew id carried a black blade."

"Black blade?"

"There are only ten in the world. The Aeyries who carry them won them in personal combat, at the Games that are held every five years. But you knew Eia the healer, since id saw you through the winging. And the lover, too? If so, I envy you. Or did the master of discipline find even a l'shil resistible?"

Suddenly I was irritated. "What is so irresistible about a l'shil?"

"The wonder, mainly. And the—the Walkers do not have a word for it. The *c'lol-fe*, the wildness which comes after the confinement of winter."

The coals cracked in the warming stoves. A few of my hairs had stuck to my fingertips. I held one up to the lamplight. The individual hair had its own coat of fur, which trapped a fuzzy aura of smoky light. No wonder I was so much warmer than the Walkers. I said, "Well, Eia found me irresistible. I like to think it was not just because I am young."

'You are as touchy as a Walker," Feili said mildly. "Why did you leave Eia and go back to Teksan?"

"You think I went back to him because I wanted to? I left because I did not want to know Eia was exploiting me."

"And yet you say you never knew Eia was ruthless!"

"Eia is the only one, the only one in my entire life, who ever cared about me, even just a little. Maybe I did not want to know."

I had never meant to say so much. I turned my head after a while. Feili's bright hair had dried, and now floated arounds ids face like a cloud at sunset. "I'm sorry to hear that." Ids mouth quirked up at the corners. "However, it is not true. Lian will understand why Eia concealed ids motives from you. But I am certain of this: Whatever Eia was trying to accomplish, to have to use you for a tool toward some end would have made idre miserable. I have known Eia a long time, Del, and never once have I know idre to care just a little."

"No you don't." Id glided earthward, bumping slightly

Chapter 12

Lian eventually emerged from the center of a huddle
of people, to join Feili and me at the end of one long
table in the dining room. A few late rising Walkers,
and one red-eyed, tousled Aeyrie who appeared to
have never made it to bed, lingered sleepily over their
breakfasts. Within hearing, dishes were being washed.
An old Walker slowly swept the red tile floor with a
reed broom.

Lian seemed tired and harassed. Someone set a cup
near her hand. She breathed in the spicy steam as we
recounted our recent conversation to her. Then she let
out her breath in sigh. "Yes, I do understand what Eia
was trying to accomplish. Though it hurts to think of
it. Eia told me that when a child, id met Teksan, and
was certain even then that he was dangerous to the
Aeyries. Last spring, when by accident id spotted him
from the air, id followed him to the Digan-lai community. Id knew, as you would if you thought of it, that
there is no imaginable reason for Teksan to go to the
Digan-lai: he is no astil trader, and the community is
not exactly on a beaten path."

I swallowed. "Except to fetch me."

"That's right, Del, it was no accident that he found
you. Now let me tell you something that is so com-
monly known that I am surprised no one has told it to

you before. Some twenty years ago, three fertile Aeyrie eggs disappeared from their nests. The Aeyries do not lay fertile eggs lightly, knowing that twenty years of difficult nurturing lie before them! So you may imagine the furor. And one of them was the egg of a white winged Silver, Gina Theli Ishta, the taiseoch t'Cwa."

My mouth was full this time, and I choked.

Feili pounded me on the back hard enough to start my arm throbbing. Ids sweet, loud voice turned heads in the room. "Ishta never hatched an egg! Id reluctantly named a cousin taiseoch-dre! And your other parent must be Mairli. Many years id wintered in the taiseoch's bed. Great Winds, Del, you're a taiseoch-dre!"

Lian said absently, "Mairli the inventor? Id used to visit us all the time, being Pehtal's close friend. Id was an exhausting person, a brilliant eccentric, the inventor of the air lamps, among other things: grab-pins, hollow needles, various new kinds of vegetable . . . Id's apparently dead now. Id was a loner and a wanderer; maybe a hellwind got idre. L'shil, are you all right?"

I had stopped coughing, but I felt rather dizzy. I said hoarsely, "What happened to the other two eggs?"

"I am surprised that even one survived. An Aeyrie could easily be killed by normal Walker childrearing. Aeyrie hatchlings die from boredom or lack of affection, and they cannot take solid food until the middle of their second year. There must have been someone, some Walker woman who loved you and nursed you for a second year, and embarrassed herself with 'coddling' you, as her fellows would call it."

I remembered the elder who had never been unkind to me, who had advised me the day I was sold. "You have never belonged here," she had said, as if her eyes had been on me from the beginning; as if there was a sympathy and sadness in her that she thought it best to keep hidden.

She had never told me.

After a long silence, I said to Lian, "So Teksan stole the eggs?"

"I believe he was at t'Cwa that year. The t'Cwa-dre considered Teksan a true rarity, an unbigoted Walker who valued knowledge. Of course they did not know he was practicing sorcery. He wintered at the University many years in succession, studying—what was it, Feili?"

Feili shrugged. "Everything and nothing, from what I hear."

"Eia thought he was hoping to uncover the Aeyries 'secret' store of magical books and lore. There are usually several mages at t'Cwa, but Teksan apparently didn't know it, or wouldn't believe it, or wouldn't believe what they had to tell him. . . ."

"And you think Eia knew all of this? Even who I was?"

"Id would certainly have deduced all of it, same as we did."

"But in a matter of seconds rather than days of discussion," Feili added.

Lian smiled suddenly, and just as suddenly the smile was wiped away.

I said, with stale bitterness, "Then why did id not tell me?"

"Why did you not trust idre?"

I stared at her. I had learned to expect more gentleness from her. But Lian reached across the table to pat my arm. "Del, you had no reason to trust anyone, and no experience with it. And you had every reason for suspicion. But Eia would not have been quick to trust you either. What reason did id have to believe that you would not rush to Teksan with everything you knew?"

"Id knew I was an Aeyrie!"

Beside me, Feili gave a humorless snort. I recognized my own simplicity almost at once, but Lian at least did not laugh. "You were a Walker in an Aeyrie body, with no reason for loyalty to any species. Even so, Eia's first impulse would certainly have been to rescue you, regardless of all other concerns, simply because you are ids own kind. Yet id decided to subvert you instead."

I looked up sharply. Lian's eyes were unfocused. She looked elsewhere: she saw the warm and aloof, tortured and serene Eia. It put sadness into her voice, and a depth of love which shamed me. She said, "Id decided to be kind to you, so you could know what kindness was and be equipped to see through Teksan's false kindness. To give you an onfrit so you would be less lonely, therefore less vulnerable—and also so Eia could use her as a spy in Teksan's household. To make certain that at your winging, that important time of transition and bonding, it was Eia who Companioned you rather than Teksan. To do all these things, knowing that id was cheating you of the right to your heritage, knowing that id was wrongly manipulating you, and certainly despising idreself for it."

"But why?"

"To find out and undermine Teksan's plans."

Feili burst out, "Of all the egotistical, foolhardy—"

But I sat in silence, thinking of the desperate solitude with which Eia must have acted, attaching ids own strings to me, until I was like a puppet with two puppeteers. It did not make me angry anymore. I had learned what the difference was between evil and mere error.

I remembered how I had seen Eia as a rescuer, a god, something better than myself. I realized suddenly that if we saw each other again it would not be the same. To understand Eia was to kill my bitterness. But the glamour also would be gone, and in its place—I did not know.

Still I wondered at the choices Eia had made, wondered above all why id had chosen to be alone, when the forces of kinship, friendship, race, and ideology could have been all standing behind idre.

Lian said softly, "No, Del, Eia has always been alone. Alone, id foresaw the extermination of the Aeyries. Alone, id recounted that awful vision, only to have ids own people see idre as a renegade, a doomsayer, even a traitor. But it was here at the Triad that id finally despaired of finding someone, anyone, to take the vision seriously enough to act on it. Do you remember when id finally stopped talking about it, Feili? I do. I was relieved."

Feili, who had heard Lian out with scarcely less agitation than myself, abruptly turned ids wonderful, sun bright eyes on her. "Now that is hardly fair. The Triad-re listened, we agreed on the danger—"

"And yet we insisted that there was nothing we could do, that it was using all of our resources merely to survive—"

"And it is still true."

"No. The truth is that we are afraid of risk."

Feili looked down at ids branded wrist, opened ids mouth to protest, but shut it again. I wondered in disbelief how a community of rebels, people who had voluntarily turned against the bedrock truths of home and kin, could be afraid of risk.

I was not too surprised when Lian again answered my unspoken question. "We are no longer a bunch of wild-eyed idealists with nothing to lose. We are a thriving community. We fear to sacrifice all the hard work we have put into building this house, this farm, into revising our understanding of each other and ourselves, into raising our children. For the same reason Eia was unpopular in t'Fon, id was unpopular here. Because ids prophetic voice challenged our contentment. Mine, too, as much as anyone else's."

For a long time none of us said anything. I looked at the pile of crumbs on my plate, and realized that it must have been my anxious fingers which had reduced the remains of my sweetbread to this mess. How simple it had been, when all I had to do was to flee my enemy until I had found haven. But now I understood that it was not merely Teksan who was the enemy, and Triad was no haven but a participant in the problem, and matters were not simple at all. I felt very tired. "What is going to happen?"

Lian's many-jointed fingers closed firmly around mine. "Right now, nothing. We all have to think, and wait for A'bel and Pehtal to return. You have to rest and regain your strength. Maybe Feili will show you the printing press. And then I want you to go back to bed."

By the time Feili and I started back to the house from the press, I no longer thought Lian had been amusingly overprotective of me. I was tired, but the arm Feili put around me was not really necessary for my support. The Aeyries were always touching each other, I reminded myself.

The Aeyrie lithographer and Walker craftsman who were in charge of the printing press had been willing enough to answer my questions. They had been in the middle of an argument as we walked in, but when we left they were holding hands somewhat absentmindedly, studying anew the disputed proof-sheet where it was pinned to a tabletop. "They have children?" I said to Feili in disbelief.

"One of each. By other partners, of course. If crossbreeding were possible, we would know it by now, believe me."

"Do Aeyries prefer males or females?"

Feili laughed. "Don't start thinking about it. It'll drive you mad."

"Have you made love with a Walker?"

"Well—yes."

"And?"

"And I prefer Aeyries, you nosy creature."

Id came into my room with me, still talking vigorously. But when the door shut, it seemed to cut off the flow of words as well. The room was still cold from the chill I had let in earlier through the window. Feili preoccupied idreself with starting a fire in the stove.

I sat heavily on the stool. "I think Lian was right. I need to rest some more."

"Lian is always right." Feili turned to me brushing a smear of soot out of ids burning bright fur. "How tired are you?"

Something in ids eyes made me avoid looking directly into them, something which tried to be playful and lighthearted and did not succeed very well. The friendship I wanted, wanted badly, was being taken heartlessly out of my grasp. This gulf of reluctance and fear opening up in my belly was destined to become a familiar of mine. I understood too much.

Feili's hand touched my arm tentatively. Too hastily I took it by the wrist and lifted it away. "Very tired," I said, standing up.

"Del—"

"Thank you for your time with me." By the time I had shut the door firmly against ids irritated and startled face, I was trembling. In solitude, I lay down on the bed and stared at the wall.

Feili was not very friendly after that. The rest of the Triad-re treated me like an honored guest: showing me around, stopping their work to answer my questions, and watching benignly as I played with their children. The children, Walker and Aeyrie alike, were few and well beloved, for the Walkers had adopted Aeyrie ways of nurturing. The children did little work, but I was envious of the schooling of which they complained so energetically.

I knew I should have felt lucky to be here, but I seemed to have developed an aversion to contentment. I felt restless and miserable. I went from bakery to workshop to kitchen to library, admiring the busyness and good cheer of the people, and feeling entirely separate from it.

The third morning I was on my feet, I rode a draf out across the frozen fields in the company of a farmer. The fields were edged by lines of tall trees, barelimbed in winter, guardians to protect the crops from the unceasing wind. I was told that only the cooperation of Aeyrie ingenuity and Walker experience had made it possible to grow crops in this desolate, notoriously infertile place. Now, the farmer said proudly, the yield doubled every few years as their methods and the soil were constantly improved.

When we returned, I found Lian in the common room. I had been told that, in the warm months, the Triad was hectic with sick strangers desperate enough to seek healing even in this forbidden place. But the winter hibernation did not seem to afford Lian much respite. I had rarely seen her without someone beside her, in need of her attention.

She was alone now, eating a solitary late breakfast. I hesitated to interrupt her, but she smiled up at me standing in the doorway. "Come sit. I am going to spend the afternoon with Pilgrim. Do you want to come down with me?"

"Yes."

"What's the matter, Del?"

"I feel like something is going to happen,"

She nodded, and turned back to her meal. I sat, glad to be in her restful presence, and watched her eat.

Afterward, we went together out a back door, and down a path from which the night's snowfall had not yet been cleared. My bare feet left a faint imprint in the snow, but Lian's tracks were deep. She wore a pair of soft boots made of cleata skin, a tough, water resistant stuff which the giant sea lizards shed on the rocks every summer. The sun glittered cold overhead. Our breath steamed around us. Lian jammed her hands into her jacket pockets.

To my right, I could see a strip of the green ocean, with faint suggestions of colored reflections below the surface of the water, where lay the deadly reefs. There, twenty-five years ago, Lian had sailed her coracle in choppy water, in the wake of a fierce storm. Her sensitivity to the emotions of others had made her take flight from pain, to live alone and isolated, in a solitary cottage on the edge of the cliff. Yet, in the night's storm, another's pain had reached deep into her sleep, dragging her awake to lie all night long, listening to the howling wind. At daybreak she had gone out, and found the Mer on the reef, injured and trapped among the razor-sharp edges.

"I knew, before I even went out, that my life would never be the same," she had said when she told me the story.

A cluster of trees had rooted here near the cliff's edge. The wind had distorted them into a weird grove of trunks growing nearly parallel to the ground, branches all reaching landward. Their tiny, tough leaves were crusted with frost. The path wove between them, among black shadows and out into sunlight again. Then we came upon an unexpected gash in the earth, into which the sea slid, far below, among the shattered golden glass. Lian squinted against the glare of light as she fumbled a pair of smoked lenses out of her pocket. The path had become a narrow, twisting walkway dropping down the cliffside, shining with slick ice and bordered with railings, at times suspended out over empty air.

I doubted there were many Walkers willing to come this way, even in the Triad where most of them had desensitized themselves to heights. But Lian attached the lenses before her eyes and started forward eagerly.

It was a long way down. At the bottom, the board-walk twisted over and around great chunks of glass. Soon we were walking over pools of still water. White and blue mineral deposits decorated the glass. In my nostrils lingered the sharp, sour smell of the sea.

From a small building, a long dock stretched across the water, pointing at a pair of boats tethered off shore. The water shimmered in the light, still and yet moving with that slow swelling which seemed like breathing. Light patterns twisted and broke and re-formed hypnotically across the surface.

"There," Lian said.

A form broke water in a spray of light, leaping exuberantly skyward, only to turn and slide into the water again, leaving scarcely a ripple.

I let my breath out in a sigh. I think until that moment I had not truly believed in the Mer.

We walked silently to the wooden dockhouse, where on the leeward side small boats were racked with their oars. A single windmill spun wildly on the roof, disengaged. Inside, long-handled seaweed forks and caricha nets hung on one whitewashed wall. In the center, a round hole cut in the floor gave access to a deep, tiled pool. I could not see the bottom of it, but its water level swelled and sank, telling me of its direct link to the sea. I put my hand in. The water was not frigid, but it was far from warm.

"Is this the pool where you took her, and took care of her?"

"Yes. I camped right where I'm standing, in my boat which I dragged onto the rocks every night. I went out every morning to gather seaweed for her—she can only eat it fresh. I ate nothing but seaweed, too. There was nothing else. But I cooked mine."

Another hollow immediately adjacent to the pool was no deeper than my knees. It was tiled like a bathtub. A valve ended a narrow pipe that ran down the wall, clamped against the stovepipe to warm the water. Lian laid a fire in the stove, and lit it with a tinderstick. A complicated switch in the ceiling engaged the windmill.

For a Walker to be a Mer's lover was no simple business! Just to make an environment acceptable to both of them required more than a little Aeyrie technology.

Lian laughed, overhearing my thought. "Of course! I sent to all the Ulas, asking the Aeyries to design this building in return for a chance to meet a Mer. A pair of them were intrigued enough to do it. A few months later, they came back. That is how the Triad began, right here in this building."

I dipped my hand into the water again. In the dark deep of the pool, another hand touched it.

She came up from the darkness, a gliding shadow that slowly took form in the light: long and sleek, with her flat, noseless face breaking water first in a hot spray of expelled air. She was six limbed and furred like me, but practically legless, with oars instead of feet. One set of arms had hands, though much different from mine. The other set were little more than rudders. She looked at me from wide-pupiled eyes, gripping my hand gently. Despite the cold water, her hand was as warm as mine.

I looked into deep, disorienting eyes. "Hello, Pilgrim."

"She welcomes you," Lian said.

"She will not speak to me?"

"Mer brains apparently have no facility for speech. Within the herd, there is no need for it. There is nothing one member of a herd knows that they all do not know. They sing, though."

"Did the herd abandon her because she was injured?"

"If they had found her, they would have killed her, out of mercy and to protect themselves from the experience of her pain. But the herd had been scattered by the storm, and she had lost contact with them. It was the first time in her life that she was alone, and could think of herself as an individual. The Mers have live births—and even in the womb the infants already are telepathically linked with the herd. For Pilgrim to be separated from them was a death. And a birth."

The Mer's hands were almost frighteningly strong. She reached above water to brush my dry fur with her fingers, and then sank back into that cold embrace, until only her eyes were above water. Unblinking, she studied me. I wondered what it was like, to live through another's life, as she was doing with Lian. Did she see both worlds at once, the sea and the land? Did she love only Lian, or did she love through Lian as well? Was she lonely, or did she share in Lian's extensive connections? Did joining with Lian limit her, or did it expand her?

I asked, "Why did you not go back to your people when you were healed?"

Lian said softly, "To love was to change and be changed. To return would be to change the herd.

Perhaps I would not be accepted. Perhaps I would lose and forget what I have learned and become. A thing I do not regret and do not wish to lose or forget."

"I do not regret. I do not wish to lose or forget." These words contained a world of answers.

"What is it like underwater?"

She sank away, until even her fingers were no longer touching mine. And then she showed me.

I turned and dove into darkness that was not dark. Sound resonated round me; the sound of my own voice murmuring back at me from the walls. A hollowness: time to turn. A thin ringing: time to twist around a sharp edge. I was surrounded by the vibration of my voice across dangerous, broken edges of glass. The way was narrow and twisting, but I never touched anything but water.

Then: light, green and shimmering, smoky with debris. Long, subtly moving stalks of seaweed, stretching like bronze ropes toward the brightness above, exploding suddenly with long, flat leaves. My body glided, knowing and trusting my element.

"Ah," my host sang, and the sound echoed back, altered. I scattered a crowd of translucent shellfish; I twisted among the seaweed and though a garden of carichas floating on their fragile tethers. Up I looked, at the mysterious surface, light-reflecting, overlaid by foam containing distorted pieces of sky. And then I pushed, pushed my body subtly against the water, upward, wildly upward, through the pull and tug of the surface currents, upward, and then I was breaking through.

I walked back alone, leaving behind me the Walker and the Mer in their heated pool. After the weightless flowing of swimming, I felt strange and loose in my body, and each step I took seemed heavy and jarring. The open sky awoke hunger in me. The climb up the cliff had been almost too much for me. How long would it be before I was strong enough to fly again?

"Delan," someone chirruped. "Delan!" A bundle of brown and amber fur plummeted around the corner of the path, into my arms.

"Ch'ta!" He was dusty and damp. His frail bones stood out under his skin. He panted in my arms, chirping incoherently with gladness. I hugged him to my chest, "Ch'ta, did you find Eia?"

But even before he spoke, somehow I knew the answer.

Chapter 13

Two strange Aeyries sat in the common room. Their loose manes tangled around their faces, wind woven. They wore flight clothes, astil to cut the bitter wind, and quilted vests to guard against hypothermia. A muted group of Triad-dre surrounded them as they ate with concentration from steaming bowls of stew. Eia's manuscript lay on the table.

With Ch'ta on my shoulder, I slipped in through the side door to join the group quietly and wait until the two travelers were ready to speak. But one of them, a Red with ids vivid color beginning to soften with age, lifted ids head sharply.

I froze in my tracks. I heard a roaring in my ears, as if I were standing under an avalanche. My knees gave way under me. And then strong hands caught me and a fierce, hushed voice said, "Hellwinds!"

My vision cleared slowly. I trembled in the arms of the red stranger. Ch'ta, knocked partway down my back, scrambled up to my shoulder again, scolding the stranger in onfrit language. "You must be Delan," the Red said. "Please pardon me— You have a shadow of sorcery on you and I assumed you were dangerous."

"I do?" I looked up, dismayed, into eyes like green glass. Id was as unlike Teksan as a waterwyth is unlike an onfrit. Yet I sensed the power in ids hands, in ids voice, power in ids very decision to hold back from hurting me. I knew this was a mage.

Id said, "But underneath the shadow you are bright. Very bright." The Aeyrie stood back somewhat, the better to examine me from head to toe. When the startling eyes lifted again, there was something more in the narrow age-marked face: gentleness, warmth, welcome, even a kind of protectiveness. And I did not even know who this person was.

I shook my head, utterly flustered.

"L'shil, Ishta is written on you, in your fur and your wings."

"You know Ishta?"

"I am a native of t'Cwa," id said. "I am Beta L'hem Pehtal. Come and sit with us."

The Aeyrie took me by the elbow and walked with me. At the table, the strange Brown had scarcely missed a mouthful of stew. "My partner, A'bel, a sun and wind crafter. A'bel, this is Delan. Ishta Mairli Delan, it seems."

The Brown nodded. "And you scared idre out ids wits. Very good."

"I am absolutely mortified."

I put my hand on the manuscript, still bundled roughly, with its bindings inexpertly knotted by my own fingers. "The hurt onfrit—" I said.

Pehtal sat on the bench, gesturing for me to sit also. "She is in the onfrit house now, with her hatchling. When she has her strength back, perhaps Lian will be able to repair her wing."

I sat down jerkily. Ch'ta chirruped excitedly at the smell of food. "Ch'ta told me you couldn't find Eia."

"All of the Teksan-dre are gone from L'din, and Eia with them. Here, Ch'ta." Pehtal offered some bread, which the onfrit accepted with delight. "Delan, do you know what they mean to do with Eia?"

"What they did with me. Use idre for entry through a door Teksan cannot open himself."

"How?"

"He uses his sorcery to make pain, and the pain to make more sorcery. He will—" This time I could not shudder away from the thought of Eia in Teksan's hands. Nor could I reassure myself any more with the knowledge that help was on the way to idre. My throat closed shut.

Pehtal did not press me, but bent to the business of eating. Days of flying had worn both the Aeyries down to sharp bones. After a long time, having searched my limited vocabulary for an appropriate title, I said, "Sh'man, Teksan will destroy Eia. I have an obligation to help idre. Even if I have to do it alone. Will you help me figure out what to do?"

The mage glanced up at me, a hard face, eyes glittering with an anger which I was relieved to realize was not directed at me. "Yes, I will do whatever I can. But you will not need to be acting alone."

The sun had set before Lian came up from the Gap, with the look of the otherworld in her eyes. She hugged Pehtal and A'bel in way I would not have dared. The three of them spent the time remaining until dinner talking in a warm alcove, holding each others' hands. A'bel and Pehtal surely were the two who had traveled here long ago out of curiosity, only to return and stay. I had met their children, who had hatched at Triad, and now were nearly grown: A Red who would be winged next year, but who even in pudgy immaturity moved like flame, and a pensive solitary Brown who at the age of seventeen was writing a novel.

After supper, the people remained for a council. A few who, for one reason or another had missed the meal, were fetched from whatever craft or study held them so absorbed. Eventually, all of the adults and older children were there.

It was Pehtal who opened the meeting. They used few titles in that place, and I had assumed that Lian was the Triad's version of taiseoch. But as Pehtal stood up to speak, Lian sat at her ease with her eyes half shut, looking as relieved and exhausted as a draf when the spring plowing is finally done.

Pehtal said, "All of you know Delan's story, and of our decision to go to L'din. But Eia was no longer there, nor any of ids captors. Either they have already gone to attack another Ula, or the disappearance of Delan made them decide to move away for the sake of caution. Therefore we are once again faced with a decision: what should we do now?"

Sitting through the discussion that followed was not easy for me. To my astonishment, the Triad-re immediately raised issues of cost and backlash and did not even mention issues of right and wrong. Just as with every Walker I had ever met, most of what was said began with the words "We can't afford . . ." Every time I heard those words, a shock of anger clenched my fists and set my heart pounding in my throat.

Pehtal finally looked up from the piece of brown paper on which id had occasionally been scribbling. "I gather the Aeyries do not think there is anything to discuss." Throughout the discussion, the Aeyries had all sat like me, listening grimly, with their arms folded on their hairy chests.

I found myself on my feet. "Is the Triad just another farm and the sole reason it exists to raise food and children? I thought the people of the Triad were different from other people. I thought you were all living together because you want to change things, not just because Walkers and Aeyries working together can grow more vegetables and corn than anyone else."

As soon as I sat down, I began to shake. But I was

not the only one who was angry. Several others spoke. A Walker and an Aeyrie exchanged subtle insults, only half in jest. Feili stood up, "If we do not act as Triad-re; then as members of a race threatened with extinction, we, the Aeyries, would have to act alone. Whether we do something or not is not even the issue. The issue is whether we do it with the support of our Walker kin, or without it. I cannot help but wonder, if it were the lives of four hundred Walkers that were threatened, would you Walkers still be arguing to do nothing?"

The room abruptly filled with an uproar of shouting. I cringed in my seat, doubting that the truce in this community was as strong as the Triad-re like to believe. But Pehtal calmly jotted notes like a scholar at a lecture. Once id turned to Lian to ask a question, and she smiled broadly and held out her hand in a reassuring gesture.

The uproar gradually died down. Some of the Walkers who had not spoken earlier spoke in support of action. Others recanted on previous statements. Somehow, however uncertain and troubled, unity hatched anew from the egg of dissention. The Triad agreed to send a group of people, Walker and Aeyrie together, to each of the Ulas, to warn of what was coming and, if asked, to participate in the outcome.

When the meeting was declared over, the Triad-re gathered in mixed groups, arms and wings around each other, making peace. But I drifted to the edge of the room, taking no part in the reconciliation, preoccupied with thoughts of Eia. All this activity would do idre no good. Depressed, I leaned against the wall. These people belonged with each other. But I belonged with no one.

When I spotted A'bel and Pehtal heading out the door, I gave in to my need and followed them. Behind me in the common room there was an explosion of laughter. Ahead of me, the pair clasped hands as they walked, and the sound of their voices murmured back at me. The lamp flame blurred in my vision as Pehtal ruffled A'bel's mane with a gentle hand.

I hesitated at the corner when they started up the stairs. Why was I following them? The afternoon had been so hectic for them that they had not even been able to go up to their room and change their clothes. Surely they had left the common room prematurely because they were worn out and wanted to rest. I called myself a selfish creature, and my chest ached as I watched them go.

Pausing between one step and the next, Pehtal turned ids head and looked down at me. Id did not seem surprised or displeased, but touched A'bel and said something softly. They both turned and came back down the stairs.

"You should have spoken, Delan, we didn't see you."

"Come up with us."

I protested feebly. But they put their arms around me, blanketing me generously in warm wings, enveloping me in the sharp-sweet scent of Aeyrie musk and sweat. I walked with them, as I had wanted so desperately to do.

"Lian tells me you and I have a friend in common," A'bel said.

"Who?"

"The Orchth."

I stopped short in my amazement. "Brother Och?"

They pulled me forward again, A'bel laughing softly. "Six legs, big teeth, loves to sing . . ."

"You're the Aeyrie who was in the menagerie?"

"Yes, unfortunately. Is he well? I always wondered what became of him."

"He has a cave in a wood, with baskets of nuts and fruit for the winter. He is lonely. He didn't want me to leave him. I told him I would try to find a way to get him home again. He saved my life. Because you saved his once, he said."

"Only after he saved my sanity. You will have to show me on a map where he lives."

We paused at a bedroom door. I began to protest again, but Pehtal gently hushed me. A'bel opened the door and drew me in.

It was a comfortable, cluttered room, full of bright weavings and books and mechanical drawings of windmills. It contained none of the bottles and vials and bowls and measurers that I had come to associate with sorcery.

"Well, no faerie has been here to clean up the mess."

"Somebody changed the sheets for us."

"Sh'man Lian, of course."

The two of them moved about softly, taking off their vests to reveal sweatstained flightsuits, hanging their knife belts from hooks. I went to a square chunk of blue glass mounted on a stand. Its sides seemed frosted over, but the top was smooth and polished. Lamplight glimmered on its surface. Leaning over it, I seemed to see something moving within, like the swirling of clouds in storm. I drew back hastily.

"Did you see something in the Glass?"

I turned to find Pehtal watching me. "I—thought I saw the Void."

In the periphery of my vision, I saw A'bel straighten into a profound stillness. Pehtal came over to me with ids garment half undone.

"I imagined it," I said, made nervous by A'bel's tension and Pehtal's overdone casualness.

"No, you probably saw something." The magician put ids hand on my shoulder. "Look again."

Clouds swirled within the Element, as if caged there. I felt very strange and light-headed. From a distance

Pehtal's voice said quietly, "You are sorely troubled by a question for which you have no answer. What is it?"

"How can I help Eia?"

"Now the clouds clear." Even as id spoke, the swirling dispersed into a whiteness and a shimmering of starlight. I was looking at a spire of glass, winter bare and white with snow. I saw a rudely walled cave. Was Och there? Scarcely had the thought come to me before I was within the cave. He lay on the cold floor, listlessly eating a handful of dried fruit. I heard the air in his lungs. I heard his claws scrape the floor.

I said, "Brother Och."

His head jerked up and his nostrils flared. "Where?"

"It's Delan. I'm talking to you from far away. I miss you, Och."

His staring eyes softened. What he did not understand, he could nonetheless accept. "Brother? Find Other Delan?"

"Not yet, but I'm safe. I found your friend A'bel."

He leapt to his feet. "A'bel! Miss you, brother."

"A'bel wants to see you again, too."

And then I looked at the Void again. Pehtal pressed against my back between my wings, arms wrapped around me, warm and solid against my dizziness. Id murmured, "So the Orchth is part of the answer? Wish again, Del."

I wished. As the swirling in the Glass cleared, I swallowed a cry of panic. Teksan looked out of the Glass. But his expression did not change: he was unaware of me. He spoke to someone I could not see. My heart thundering, I held myself very still.

"Up Nest," he said firmly.

I heard a vague murmur, someone protesting diffidently.

"No," Teksan said. "The Black is native to Down Nest. I have other plans for Out Nest."

The other spoke again. An ugly, awful look came

into Teksan's face. He was laughing. "It cannot lie to me! It is mine."

The Void wiped him away, like chalk from a slate.

Pehtal stood steady against my trembling. "So it is to be t'Han! That is useful news. Wish one last time."

"No!" I knew, oh too well, what I would see this time.

"Three times, or you will not know the answer."

The clouds swirled, faster and faster. From the center a point of black spread until I looked into darkness. It was a heavy, sticky darkness. I could hear, somewhere within that darkness, the sound of someone breathing.

I could not see. I thought, I need a flame, a little light. Something flared within me. I watched its glow spread, fighting back the shadows.

Eia sprawled on the floor in chains, Id was still, awfully still. Ids wings had a broken, crumpled look to them. Rib and hip bones stood out under dull fur. A painful breath heaved through ids chest, and then id lay still again.

"Eia," I whispered.

Id lifted a hand, and clenched it. Chain rattled on stone. The hand dropped to the floor again, open palmed.

Eia, open your eyes."

They opened. I saw my light flickering in the black depth of them, like a lampflame. A long time id looked at me, face expressionless. "What are you?" Ids sweet voice had hoarsened to a whisper. I knew too well why.

"It's Del."

The voice remained joyless and flat. "Del?"

"I know you think this is one of Teksan's dreams, but it's not. I got away. I'm safe from him. Ch'ta is safe, and so is your manuscript. Can you tell me where you are?"

Id stared into my flame. Finally id took in a breath, and let it out. "No," id sighed. "We went through the Void. Are you certain you're safe?"

"Yes."

"Good." Eia's hand clenched again, fisting around the shadows. "I hoped you might find Triad. No, don't tell me, or I'll tell him. Del, you have to warn the Ulas about him."

"I am doing that. But tell me how to help you."

"You can't. I am dead."

"No!"

"I cannot fight him anymore." Ids worn voice neither rang with conviction nor grew husky with emotion. I heard only emptiness.

I looked at the furred skeleton of Eia, thinking of the inner flame which Teksan loved to snuff out. I thought of it, and felt afraid. A wish made me able to see it. Within Eia's ravaged body it smoldered with a red that was nearly black. It still burned, but somehow I knew that when it was extinguished there would be no recovery.

"Give your Self into my safekeeping. He will think he has won. He will take care of you then, because you will be valuable to him. He will not hurt you any more."

The chains rattled. "Del—" Tears shone faintly on ids cheeks. I thought I could not bear it.

"Yes. I trust you. I give my Self. Into your care."

I reached out, not with my hand but with some other part of myself, to take the smoldering flame out of Eia's heart. Ids voice cried out, wild and despairing, raw pain dying to hollow silence. I cried out in response, as a ravenous burning and a primitive heaviness clutched as frantically as a found child within my shelter. And then I saw only the Void.

"What did I do?" I cried. "Pehtal! Oh, what did I do?"

* * *

I jerked awake in the night with Eia's despairing, deathly cry still echoing in my ears. I tried to hold myself very still, but Pehtal shifted beside me on the big bed, and reached a hand to my shoulder. "Delan?"

"I'm sorry."

"Why do you think I made you stay with me? Bad dreams?"

I nodded. I had not wanted to awaken idre, but I was glad now that id was awake, just as I had not wanted to stay the night with them, but had been relieved when Pehtal would not hear of me going to my solitary bed.

Pehtal said, "Scrying is a thing that happens at the dream level, which is why you need to tell someone about it right away, or write down what you see. Otherwise you forget. And afterward, sometimes, the nightmares." The mage's arm had pulled me close. At my other side A'bel stirred and sighed and then lay still again.

I said, "Then you must go through this all the time—"

"Too often, anyway. My partner is a good counter-weight: a realist, a scientist. Sometimes the thing I fear most is that id will grow sick and tired of coping with me, after all these years."

When I had first met Pehtal that afternoon, I would never have even suspected that id suffered from fear. But I had seen much more since then.

"Why did you want me to look in the Glass rather than yourself?"

"Because your personal involvement meant you could see more than I. Because love made you able to do something that my respect and affection would not be enough for."

"Love!" There was a bitterness in finally saying the word. "Better to have killed idre!"

"Maybe Eia will live to thank you for it. But to carry another's soul is hard work. And it will grow harder."

The heavy, smoldering fire in me was no burden. I cherished it, even as I was bewildered by its presence. How had this happened? I did not understand, and yet I did understand, as if in a dream, where logic follows its own strange ways, and draws its own incoherent, but sensible conclusions. I said, "It's not what I have to carry that makes me afraid."

"It's what you are that is frightening?"

I shivered. Now that I had said the word "love," there was a new word I did not want to say.

"To be a mage is not to be a sorcerer. The gifts which are called magic are just ordinary Aeyrie talents brought to their logical extreme. The ability to envision, to anticipate the future, to create, to tame natural laws. Often the very talented Aeyries seem like mages to me. Often my gifts of planning and building and protecting look very commonplace. The one thing which clearly distinguishes a mage is the ability to scry glass."

"You helped," I protested.

Pehtal's hand touched my sensitive wing. I lay very still, babbling silently to myself, id is just being kind, you do not feel this feeling, you do not.

Touching my rigid back, Pehtal hesitated. Ids voice was soft as the whispering of the bedsheets, warmed by kind amusement. "If you are going to spend time with Aeyries you will have to learn to say 'no' outright. We are, as the Walkers say, a shockingly promiscuous people."

My voice wavered, thin as a child's. "Teksan raped me."

"Yes, I know. The gentle healer warned me earlier that if I hurt you she would have me for a fur rug. Expect as much Walker as Aeyrie, she said. Expect you to be accustomed to being punished for honesty.

So how am I to know if I'm hurting you? Are you going to be able to tell me?"

Ids fingers drew fire on my wing. I shuddered and reached out a hand. Age lines were deep creases under my fingertips. Pehtal's mouth touched one of my fingers, soft and warm and wet. "Del?"

"You're not hurting me."

"But you're shaking."

"I'm afraid. I'm always afraid. Teksan dug a canyon in me. It's a long way down."

Pehtal pulled me into the curve of ids arm, against thick fur and hard, bulging flight muscles. Ids wide wing curved over me. I had witnessed Aeyrie children, held like this against warm fur, under a spread wing. I seemed to remember, not that it had ever happended to me, but that this was safety, this was what safety felt like. In that safety, I discovered that I had it in me to cross the gulf.

After a while A'bel's sleepy voice shocked me back into self-consciouness. "Pehtal, you nest robber."

Pehtal murmured, half under me, "It's all right, Del, don't go."

"Don't go." A'bels lean body tucked, not so much between us as beside us both.

Aeyries are uniquely adequate for such tangled arrangements. In the end, I could not distinguish between them.

The Walker part of me was shocked speechless, of course. But, in the morning, as the two of them made haste to beat the crowd to the bathhouse, they were kindly agreeable to pretending that nothing unusual had happened. I sought out Lian.

She managed to refrain from laughing. "Within the Aeyrie culture, joining a threesome is just about as shocking and unusual as eating breakfast in the morning. Aeyries often partner in threes and raise children

in threes. Even the Quai-du of war is fought in triad.
Established couples are rarely strictly monogamous.
Pehtal and A'bel have taken occasional thirds for as
long as I've known them. Remember what you learned
from your H'ldat dictionary? The Aeyries have no
word for 'family.' They are a fundamentally communal
people.''

"Oh," I said. In the course of Lian's short lecture I
had gone from distressed and embarrassed to irritable.
I hated being found amusing.

Lian said delicately, "I have heard that their partners do not usually have any regrets. That the two of
them have a gift for welcoming and setting at ease and
making their open-heartedness known."

"You arranged it, didn't you?"

Lian raised her eyebrows. "I? Your concerns are
Pehtal's business. When I realized how taken with you
id was, I told idre what I thought would be to your
benefit. Was I wrong?"

"No," I said reluctantly. In truth, it had been a very
sweet night.

She let me be, taking me by the arm and saying
something about how it was time for the stitches in my
arm to be removed. Two days it had been since I was
last aware of pain, even though my wound had been a
deep one. "You Aeyries and your high metabolisms,"
she said in mock disgust.

She did her work quickly as I watched in fascination. I kept waiting for pain, but I scarcely even felt
the tug of the thread pulling out. As she finished, she
said, "Now this business of scrying the Glass, on the
other hand—"

I answered too quickly, "Well, Pehtal is a mage
after all."

"Del, you know perfectly well that it was not Pehtal
who scried the Glass last night."

"Pehtal helped," I said desperately.

"Who helped you to guide the onfrit to where you were imprisoned so you could be freed? Or to cut yourself free from the Rope called Despair? Who helped you to know in advance when he was about to open a Door, or that a Follower had been set on your trail? How did you know what direction to turn to find help? Did Pehtal help you with all of these things?"

I startled both of us by bursting into tears. I had not even become accustomed yet to having wings. I still believed firmly that I was ugly and stupid and clumsy. I found it difficult to accept that I might be the off-spring of a taiseoch and an inventive genius. To have to admit that I was a mage as well was just too much.

At breakfast Pehtal told the Triad-re about the scrying. Assuming the vision had been Pehtal's, the people were quick to agree to go only to Ula t'Han, Up Nest, the Nest of the Wind. However, the three who did know that the seer had been I, also knew without question what I had seen. I was the only one who asked Pehtal worriedly, "But what if the Teksan-dre go to Ula t'Cwa?"

"They won't." And that was the entire discussion.

Many of the Walker females and half the Aeyries were pregnant. Since a pregnant Aeyrie was vulnerable, being too heavy to fly, none of them were to make the journey, even though few bore fertile eggs. I had not even considered before now that I might be fertile. I went to Lian in another panic.

It's too late in the season," she said. "L'shils don't lay anyway. There are precautions you can take, which you have an obligation to learn before next autumn. But most of us, Walker and Aeyrie alike, simply abstain from intercourse in season. It's only one month out of the year."

We were to leave the next day. Only seven Aeyries

were among the travelers, besides the one swift and enduring flyer who had already left the day before. All but I were skilled in Quai-du. Ten Walkers, Lian among them, and Pilgrim present in awareness, would also make the journey. Most also carried weapons, though there were far too few of us to stand against Teksan's numbers. With the help of Pilgrim, we hoped to avoid him.

At daybreak I walked with Pehtal through the chaotic yard, where children ran loose and drafs milled. The Walkers, bundled in winter wool, worked awkwardly beside the unencumbered, barefoot Aeyries. Pehtal caught one of the shoulders in passing. "Feili."

The Gold turned, attentive and polite. "Yes, Sh'man." Id was dressed for flight, with ids blade tied down to ids thigh.

"You are the best teacher we have. Would you instruct Delan in flight and Quai-du while we travel?"

Feili looked at me then, a swift, angry glance, as if to ask if this stupid idea was mine. The silence stretched out awkwardly.

"Why don't you two discuss it." Pehtal's tone was mild, but I knew an order when I heard one. Id walked away to where A'bel was being dictator over the final organization of the supply wagon.

"It's not as if there was something wrong with me," Feili said.

I said stiffly, "I like you. I wish you would be my teacher. I hate feeling so stupid."

"That's not what I mean."

"I know."

Feili sighed.

"It's Eia—"

"Great Winds, Del, every l'shil loves ids Companion! Besides, I doubt you ever said that to Pehtal or A'bel these last two nights."

Everybody knew about the affair, this being a small

community, and to my enormous relief actually seemed to approve of it. I said, struggling to be tactful, "If I decided to go somewhere else, they would just wish me well."

"Oh." Feili half turned ids back to me, pale wings tense and hunched in their folds.

"Feili—" I said unhappily. But I was tired of feeling guilty about something which really wasn't my fault. Feili was the one offering me hunger when what I needed was generosity.

The flyers were starting for the Tower. There was an uproar of leavetaking.

I finally said, "I'm sorry. I—I could have been nicer about it."

"You could have." Id turned ids face back to me, more troubled than angry. "But that's no reason for me to be so offended. It's not as if I haven't been turned down before, and survived it. Do you have a flight vest? Why don't you climb the Tower with me, and show me what I have to work with."

Chapter 14

The wind blew us inland. The swelling sea disappeared into haze. Below, the gray land lay, the ponds dull as unpolished metal, the trees black tangles against the shimmering snow. The frigid air felt firm as water under my wings. Like a boat on a swift current, I rode the wind. Below and behind me, small as children's toys, the Walkers plodded on drafback, dragging the supply wagon behind them.

I learned: wind and counter-wind, up-draft and down-draft, what the clouds mean and how to fly against the current. I learned the names of the ever-changing layers of air, and how to identify them by the way they feel: firm and solid, tingling, unsteady, unpredictable. My H'ldat vocabulary of wind words suddenly acquired a meaning for me.

Feili tested my new knowledge repeatedly, until frustration made my voice shrill. "Let's go down again," id said, for what seemed the hundredth time.

"How many times?" I shouted. It seemed very quiet there in that high place, but the sneak-thief wind snatched the words out of our mouths and carried them off.

"Until you know," Feili said.

"I know!" I shrieked.

"No you don't." Id glided earthward, bumping slightly in an invisible disturbance.

I shouted the wind-names at Feili's back as we sank downward. Through a wisp of cloud, a layer of chill, a layer of warm, many other layers as well, each speaking its personality against my wide wings.

"Better," Feili said.

"I didn't make one mistake."

"That's not the point."

By midmorning, weariness made flight no longer effortless. I flew beyond irritation and boredom, into an internal silence, a stillness and clarity of attention which was altogether empty of thought. Only two things existed: my wings and the wind which related to them.

Feili startled me out of it. "Del. Del!"

I turned my head. Id flew directly above me, synchronizing wingstrokes with mine so that we would not knock each other awry. "What?" I said stupidly, feeling as if I had been awakened from sleep.

"Now you know," Feili said.

I stared blankly at the bright Gold, bewildered. I could vaguely remember shouting wind-names at Feili, yet again, but shouting them without thinking, letting the knowledge of my wings speak directly to my teacher.

Feili handed me a flight bar out of ids thigh pouch. "We'll land."

The rush of energy overlaid my dull weariness like a last glow of sunlight on a twilit sky. Despite the flight bar I landed badly: My wings simply did not have the strength to sustain the stall. After scraping through a tree branch, I hugged the snow at last. Cold clawed into me.

Feili dragged me up, beating the snow out of my fur, pulling me roughly to ids chest, cupping me inside ids wings. I put my head on ids shoulder, weary beyond surprise. "S'olel," Feili said.

"What?"

"S'olel, the knowing which is feeling. The single most important thing. The one thing I cannot teach. Trust it, Del. It can save your life."

We stood there until Pehtal came to take me up behind on ids draf.

The Aeyries chose the place to stop for the night; a young wood where the snow was not deep, with a good sized hill nearby for the flyers to use for a flight tower. The evening's meal of bread and cheese and crunchy vegetables and foamy ale seemed a feast.

The cold day became a raw night. All of us slept in groups, in nests banked by snow and sheltered by tarps, with the chilled Walkers complaining only half in jest when Pehtal and A'bel and I slept with each other and there were not enough warm Aeyries to go around. Feili found idreself to be very popular that night.

It seemed a passage of moments from the time that Lian's liniment first began to burn in my muscles until the time that I opened my eyes to see the drafs huddled together and steaming in the pale light of sunrise. I tried to move, and groaned.

Feili's taut, bright body appeared suddenly around the edge of the tarp. I nestled closer into A'bel's hot fur under Pehtal's red wing and hastily tried to pretend I was asleep.

"Get up, onfritling."

"Can't," I mumbled.

"Fine. I'll just tell Pehtal you don't have the discipline for Quai-du, and should have been left at home."

Somehow I extricated myself from the embraces and blankets. My bedfriends nestled closer together without awakening. Stiff as a jointed puppet I straightened up, and stretched my wings one at a time. All down my sides and up the center of my back, pain burned. I groaned again.

Feili appeared unimpressed. "Bring your knife."

I limped after idre to a place where the drafs had trampled down the snow. Lian found us there later when breakfast was ready. Feili had ruthlessly drilled me in motions that had appeared simple and easy when id did them. I did not even ride drafback that morning, but curled up and slept in the supply wagon, atop boxes of hardbread, among cloth covered baskets of cheese and fruit. In the evening, when everyone else was setting up camp and cooking dinner, Pehtal took me out to an open space where we drilled together again, until the sun had fallen abruptly below the horizon and I felt my sweat trying to turn to ice in my fur.

Two more days passed like this. My endurance and patience increased, but Feili was impossible to please. Id constantly corrected the way I gripped my blade, the angle of my motion, the degree of bend in one or another of my joints, and above all the way I was using my wings. I hurt all the time, not only in my muscles, but in my brain as well. Having realized by then that I actually enjoyed this grueling work, I doubted my sanity.

"Spar with me," my teacher finally said one evening.

When I looked up at Feili, my heart stopped dead in my chest. Ids face was expressionless with concentration. Ids body was utterly still, yet the power and control in that stillness was terrifying. The friendly, importunate Gold that I had first met might never have lived. Reminded of Hana, I wondered what it was like when two masters met in battle. Then Feili moved, and I thought no more.

Afterward, we joined the others at the fire, and toweled the sweat out of each other's fur. The smell of bean soup made my mouth water and my belly hurt. "You did pretty good," said Feili.

A hard earned compliment from Feili the teacher

affected me more than all of ids earlier flattering. I could not even reply to it.

"You're trembling. Aren't you eating enough?"

"Still scared," I said.

Id laughed, and hugged me. "Do you know what Lian would do to me if I hurt you? Or Pehtal, for that matter?"

"A fur rug," I guessed. "A very pretty one."

"Why thank you. But I'll keep it attached if possible. Think of how good it will feel, when you can replace that brashness of yours with genuine confidence."

"Confidence?" I dragged my fingers absently through my sticky hair. "Whose idea was it for me to learn Quai-du?"

"Lian's, I think."

That the idea for the fighting lessons had originated with the same Lian who fussed and fretted over me and my pains and little injuries, and listened to me talk, hour after hour, was not as surprising as it might be. She coddled me shamefully by Walker standards, but she pushed me forward with one hand even as the other embraced me.

I said to her that night, "I feel like I have four Companions, with you in charge." As I sprawled on my stomach in my bed nest, her hands on my muscles made me gasp. "Do you have meetings about me?"

"Of course we talk about you, wingling. You are important to us."

She had leaned most of the air out of my lungs, and for a while I couldn't speak. "I like it," I finally said, utterly confused.

"Just remember that the role of Companion is to get you airborne and then let you go to choose your own wind. Del, I can hardly feel your bones anymore, you've got so much muscle on you, after only four days! Eia won't recognize you."

"Do you think so? I hope id gets the chance." I lay quiet a long time. The warm heaviness of Eia's soul throbbed in my awareness like a heartbeat.

The mountains sprang up before us, a bank of knives pointing at the sky. One heavy, sullen day, sunless and threatening snow, I flung myself off a rock at first light, to begin my study of precision flying. Before the morning was out I had nearly killed myself in a bad fall. I landed in snow and was not hurt much, but I lay stunned, with the wind knocked out of me, staring in horror at the blade-edged boulder that lay within arm's reach of me. Feili shouted from the air, "Del, are you hurt or what?"

I waved an arm weakly at id, got up, and climbed a hill to get myself airborne again. But it was a long time before my heart ceased to thunder in my head.

We ate in the air, ate often, and I could watch my energy burning off again, floating away from me in clouds of vaporized sweat. This kind of flying needed no clothes to cut the cold, though, as soon as I landed to rest, Lian handed me a blanket and I huddled inside it, shivering crazily. I mounted behind her on her draf. She handed me her supply bag without being asked. I had been eating all morning, but I was ravenous.

"Having you behind me is like having my own private stove."

"Mmm," I mumbled around a mouthful of crumbs. I luxuriated in the end of effort, and in the pride of having satisfied my demanding instructor. Feili remained in the air, a bright spot in the dull sky, swooping wildly and hovering incredibly as id sparred with one of the other Aeyries.

Lian winced when their wings collided and they both tumbled earthward. Their recoveries were at once so beautiful and terrible that it made my throat hurt.

"It's amazing they don't get hurt more often," Lian said. "Sometimes I can't bear to watch them."

By afternoon, we were in the mountains. The glass was blue here, cold and stripped bare, and the wind poured down the pass like a bitterly cold torrent of water. Feili put on clothes and vest, and took to the air again, with ids hands tucked into ids armpits to keep ids fingers from freezing. The rest of us hung our heads and bundled our wings, and the Walkers put on all the clothes they had, and still they shivered. I rode in front of Lian to cut the wind for her. She huddled against me with her face between my wings and her hands warm between her chest and my back. The draf sighed and moaned beneath us, but walked on steadily enough.

I looked up to see the sun, pale behind clouds, sitting atop a mountain ridge. Feili was out of sight, scouting ahead for a campspot. Even as I looked, a flyer appeared over the edge of a ridge. And then another, flying behind the first. Finally, from an entirely different direction, a third.

"Pehtal!" I shouted over the shrieking wind, and pointed.

Id frowned at the sky.

As the three Aeyries drew closer to us and to each other I could distinguish their colors in the fading light: the lone Gold, Feili, and a Red, and a Black. They met in the air over our heads, where they swooped and hovered on the back of the wild wind. Faintly I heard the sound of them shouting.

The Black was an extraordinary flyer. Suddenly shivering, I urged my draf closer to Pehtal's. "I know who they are. The taseoch-dre t'Fon, Hana, Eia's l'frer. And ids partner, Gein."

"A taiseoch-dre, out in this wind? What could they be doing here?"

"Hana is a Quai-du fighter, a good one," I said nervously.

"So is Feili. But Hana would be foolish to attack anyone under these circumstances. Id needs shelter and safety, just as we do."

Feili swooped down as if to land, but instead hovered immediately overhead, tossed about like a leaf by the wind, recovering, over and over, without even losing track of ids shouted, mixed language sentence. "I know them. They are on their way to t'Han, representing the taiseoch t'Fon."

"Have you found a place for us to camp?" Pehtal shouted.

"Just ahead."

"Invite them to join us."

"They seem nervous."

"It would be good for them."

"Give me some flight food. They're out."

Pehtal held out a satchel which Feili snatched up in passing. Id struggled upward with the satchel swinging.

"Those two won't be glad to see me," I said to Pehtal.

"They'll be glad to see our food supply. It's a long way from t'Fon in this kind of weather."

When we reached the campsite, the three of them were waiting for us, huddled together in a place out of the wind. Pehtal went over to them with an armload of blankets, but only to greet the newcomers quickly and then turn away to supervise setting up the camp. I unloaded and wiped down the draf, trying to keep out of sight. A cookfire flared under a big pot, and was immediately so surrounded by people holding out their hands to its warmth that the cooks had to shoo them off so they could do their work.

My draf wandered away, following an Aeyrie with an armload of hay. Lian limped up to me, stiff from the long riding. "Let's go relieve Feili at host duty, you and I."

"But—"

"You can't hide from them all night."

I sighed, and went with her, and then in an excess of bravado put my wing around her. Shivering with cold, she hugged close to me. "Will you share my bed tonight, wingling? For purely chaste purposes."

I was still giggling nervously when we drew up to the three blanket-wrapped Aeyries leaning against the side of the mountain. Hana nibbled a sweet bar, watching the camp warily. Id froze with the bar at ids lips when we drew near, staring at me in disbelief. Gein turned sharply, but at least retained ids self-posession, though id forgot at first that I didn't speak H'ldat. I had memorized a polite phrase explaining my language deficiency, and said it with reasonable facility.

Gein switched languages and said again, "Delan, is it really you?"

I said stiffly, "Yes. Is everyone at t'Fon all right?"

"Other than being frightened, yes, we are well enough."

Lian's nudge reminded me of my manners. "I am pleased to present the healer Lian Merfriend of Triad. Lian, these are the t'Fon taiseoch-dre Tefan Malal Hana, and the healer Vida Orpha Gein."

Greeting them in what I had been assured was flawless H'ldat, Lian put out her hand. Hana managed to be looking the other direction, but Gein took her hand, exclaiming.

"Yes." Lian said, "I am that Lian."

"Eia wrote to me about you."

"I hear you arranged your correspondence so ids parent wouldn't know about it."

"The taiseoch is a person of very strong opinions," Gein said carefully. "But I missed Eia very much, and Hana missed idre even more."

"So do I," Lian and I both said.

Hana abruptly turned id's pointed face to look at me out of night-black eyes. "You know my l'frer? What else did you fail to tell us?"

The Delan who had been facing down a Quai-du master for six days now astonished me by saying quietly, "I did not tell you a great deal, since I had Teksan's Eye on me. I was trying to protect Eia; I thought he didn't know about idre."

"Suppose you tell me why you didn't simply destroy the Eye?"

I felt, for a very long moment, as if I was all alone in this cold place, with the angry wind pulling at my wings and the sharp glass all around me. "How? I didn't know I could."

Lian moved slightly against me. "You expect a great deal of an uneducated l'shil. How was id to know that glass could be a weapon against sorcery?"

Hana's face turned cold as the wind, but Gein said, "Of course Delan could not know! But there was too much blind prejudice and too little wisdom in force that night."

"You did not have to come," Hana said shortly, shifting abruptly into some other, unfinished argument. But Gein did not respond, not even to turn to look at Hana.

Their shoulders had been turned to each other even before we walked up to them. Gein's face was sad and weary. Had id taken the opportunity to leave t'Fon, not intending to return there? And Hana refused still to accept the truth. Yet only a little time ago, they had loved each other; they had delighted in each other!

Gein said, "Delan, I am sorry we locked you out of the Ula that night. It was none of my doing. The taiseoch set a guard on my door or I would have interfered despite the consequences. You did not deserve to be treated so badly."

Perhaps the guard on Gein's door had been Hana idreself? I said helplessly, "I'm sorry, too. I kept thinking there was something I should be able to do, but—"

"It is as the sh'man Lian says: even if there was, it was wrong for us to expect you to do it, without any help at all from us. At least you managed to warn us, a fact which only I seem to appreciate. I told them that you hoped we would rescue you somehow. But they decided it was more convenient to believe that you were in collusion with the Walkers, and therefore they were merely giving you back to them."

"The hostile Walkers," Lian corrected.

Gein bowed neatly and said sincerely, "I beg your pardon." But Hana frowned into the distance, the muscles tight under the fur of ids jawline, seeming to pretend that id was elsewhere.

"So what happened to you? I am glad to see you are with friends now."

I had only just begun to be able to talk with Lian about what it had been like to be Teksan's victim, and what it had done to me. I could not respond to Gein's question, but my silence seemed to speak for me.

"Hellwinds, it was bad, wasn't it?"

Lian said softly, "You are an empath, Gein?"

They looked at each other, and I watched a little of the pain fade from Gein's face. "Sh'man—" Hana jerked angrily, jealous, it seemed, even of a despised Walker.

Lian said, "Feili, don't you think Hana should meet Pehtal properly?"

Feili who had seemed relaxed and even bored, said in a voice as smooth as kipsbutter, "It does look as if our taiseoch is finally going to sit down. Hana, you have heard of idre—'

Hana knew perfectly well that id was being politely sent away. But, having been put in a position where to refuse would be to insult ids host, id gave in with little grace. Lian sagged slightly against me as the two Quai-du masters walked away. Gein shut ids eyes, and there was a long silence. "That is an exhausting anger," Lian finally said. "The t'Fon taiseoch-dre are a passionate people."

Gein rubbed ids eyes wearily. "For good or for ill."

I abruptly let go of Lian to embrace Gein. Particles of ice scattered on ids clothes burned and then melted in my heat. Shivering in brief, controlled tremors, Gein hugged me tightly.

In the confusion and fear of my visit to t'Fon, I had been unaware of my growing affection for this gentle one. It was strange, to have lived my life in such solitude, and now suddenly to feel bound to so many. It gave me a tight feeling in my chest, as if my inner seams were straining like my garment was over my expanding muscles.

Gein said against my neck, "You are much richer than you were last time I saw you, l'shil. And bigger, too. Have you found a Companion? I hope so."

"Four of them. A healer, a mage, a crafter, and a Quai-du master."

Behind me Lian said, "And Delan is wearing us all out."

"And Eia?"

"Id winged me. I loved idre."

"Then you are indeed fortunate. But where is id now? Hana always listened to idre . . ."

Lian began to speak, but I interrupted her. "Lian, we should sit down somewhere, by a fire maybe. And get some more blankets for Gein, and food."

Gein shut ids eyes again. "If Eia is dead, don't tell Hana. Not yet."

"Not dead," said Lian.

"All right. Let's sit down, and you can tell me what has happended. Delan, don't let go of me. You're the only thing keeping me on my feet. Sh'man—"

"Lian."

"Would you whisper in Feili's ear to be ready to catch Hana when id collapses? I would hate for id to tear ids wings or fall into a fire."

Lian turned a bemused face. "Why not just tell idre to sit down?"

Gein shook ids head. "Go ahead if you want to. I know better."

Shortly after we had settled by a fire behind a wind bellied tarp, Hana fainted. Gein watched with an expressionless face as Feili caught the Black gracefully and eased idre softly to the ground where id lay, small and crumpled looking, surrounded by exclaiming Triad-re. Feili shouted at us in exasperation, and Lian got reluctantly from under my wing. During all the time she was gone tending Hana, neither Gein nor I said anything at all.

The three of us shared a nest that night, and the next day we arrived at t'Han.

Chapter 15

Snow fell during the night. When we dug out from under the powder in the morning, it was still falling. The fires had been protected with tarps, but their smoky coals did little to ease the chill. We packed up and moved out quickly, lest the weather trap us where we were.

I studied no lessons that day. Even Feili would not fly in such weather. Id walked patiently before the draf which carried Hana and Gein, neither of whom had ever ridden an animal before. That was a tense and discomforted group, and I kept my distance from them.

T'Han never did come into sight, not even as we followed the twisting, snow-choked path to the base of the t'Han mountain. The village over our heads remained hidden in snow and clouds. But the lower door opened for us when we pounded it. Our scout, the flyer we had sent ahead, stood on the other side. Other than idre, the entryway was empty.

"They would let you in out of the snow, they said. But the upper door is locked. They say they have no means of knowing friend from foe in this weather. Bring in the drafs—there is hay for them."

Hana, near the head of our group, said in outrage, "Where are the people to greet us?"

The Aeyrie shrugged. "No one is ever overjoyed to see the Triad-re."

Having an angry and proud taiseoch-dre in our company had not seemed much of an asset until then, but now it turned to our advantage. Id climbed the spiraling stairs in a cold fury, and the sound of ids voice shouting and ids blade hilt thumping on the glass echoed to the bottom of the well. We settled our drafs in near darkness, giving them grain and hay and places to rest. Our supply wagon we also brought into shelter. Well before we were done, some Aeyries of the Ula came hastily down the stairs to light more lamps and warily help us with the work. The t'Han taiseoch-dre also arrived. Id politely greeted Pehtal and Lian in both languages, and apologized for the cold welcome. "It is not always easy to walk the line between caution and cowardice," id said. "Please do not take offense."

Id was a quiet-spoken, self-possessed person, but something about idre drew my attention; a disruption beneath the quiet.

Feili came forward, hair glowing in the lamplight. "Hello, C'la."

For a moment the taiseoch-dre's weariness and tension were revealed under ids control like bones under flesh. Then id spoke, in H'ldat, softly but so slowly that I could understand it. "Fire-fur, I am so glad to see you I might almost forgive you for going away." Like a reflection of Feili's sudden smile, id also smiled. "Welcome home."

"Tell me what happened to the taiseoch."

"A flight accident damaged ids spinal cord four months ago. Id nearly died, but is recovering, other than being unable leave ids bed."

"We had not heard of it yet. I'm sorry."

The Bronze taiseoch-dre said nothing, but the rest of us, Aeyrie and Walker alike, relaxed abruptly. Perhaps the Aeyrie's muted sorrow reminded us that we were not figures in some summer drama, but real people, feeling real pain. Then Lian stepped forward to say, "I may be able to help the taiseoch. If you will trust a Walker."

Ula t'Han was organized more self-consciously than t'Fon. Instead of eccentric disorder, t'Han had elegant, well tended beauty. Around its many windows, exotic plants clustered. In each room, rug, curtain, and upholstery blended beautiful, quiet colors. Even the work rooms were beautiful. On the looms rare cloths were woven, with subtly dyed yarns hanging in bundles from the ceiling. The seamsters sat by their bright windows, embroidering for rich Walkers while one of them read out loud from a book of poetry. In the small theater a trio of actors rehearsed a drama for the summer festival. My explorations finally brought me to four huge greenhouses, watched over by gregarious gardeners.

None of them spoke my language. I followed them about, learning from them the vocabulary with which to ask my questions. They repeated themselves for me, corrected my pronunciation, and reassured me that I was not in the way. "You are very patient," I said, as we sipped steaming tea, sitting around one of the greenhouse stoves. The windows were so steamy it was nearly impossible to see out. Snow lay on the outside ledges, and, hanging from the eaves, icicles shivered in the wind.

"Of course. How else could we garden?"

"A cold winter," another said worriedly.

I saw very little of any of my friends or Companions. Feili was making peace with ids parents, from whom id had parted in anger three years ago. Pehtal and A'bel engaged in the business of politics: lengthy, wearisome discussions with the two taiseoch-dre. Lian and Gein were both closeted with the injured taiseoch. It had been agreed that Lian would be permitted to work with the taiseoch if always accompanied by a trusted Aeyrie. Gein, native to that town and a healer idreself, had volunteered, not so much out of duty as out of desire to remain in Lian's presence. What they were doing no one knew. Even I, in all my unschooled ignorance, knew perfectly well that there was nothing to be done for a damaged spine.

I encountered two other l'shils, and was more than a little startled to discover that I knew much more of the world than they. Their booklearning was impressive enough, but neither one of them had ever left the Ula except for some short flights before the winter weather set in. They were both training in Quai-du. Feili, after watching them at practice, refused me permission to train with them. They were not motivated the way I was. I was not advanced enough to be able to keep from hurting them.

At night, I slept in the big room where all of the Triad-re were housed, and where the Walkers, despite having been welcomed to the Ula, had segregated themselves from the community. But I spent the rest of my time elsewhere. I was falling in love with t'Han.

Early in the morning of our third day there, I sat alone in a deserted, dark greenhouse, smelling rich, wet earth and listening to the plants whisper their mysteries to each other. In an explosion of light the sun rose, blazing on the mountains, glowing on the inviolate snow.

I missed breakfast. I wandered in a daze, vaguely aware of the tugging of guilt: no doubt someone was wondering what happened to me. I came eventually to a big, empty room on the outer edge of the Ula. The door gaped open, so I went in. I crossed a tiled floor crusted with random globs and streaks of paint. The skylights let in a soft, pure light that made the standing easels and drawing tables, and the clusters of supplies on the cabinet, stand out in relief. On one of the easels an uncovered painting stood, a dark, pensive portrait of an old Aeyrie looking out a window at a bright summer land. There was sorrow in the somber colors, sharply contrasted to the promise and warmth of the land beyond the window.

I went to the counter and picked up a paintbrush. Bottles of vivid pigments cluttered the shelves, marked in the beautiful Aeyrie script which I could not read. I touched them, wondering how anyone could even dare to choose their colors, mix their paint, and put it on canvas for everyone to see, to come out like the painting on the easel, intimate, moving, rich with meaning, laying bare the hope and sadness of the painter.

I turned, hearing a soft sound at the door. A t'Han Aeyrie stood there, studying me. I set down the paintbrush hastily, saying in my imperfect H'ldat, "Pardon, I hope I have not done wrong." It was a phrase I had used often during the last two days when my curiosity had repeatedly led me to places I had no permission to be. Fortunately, being a curiosity myself, the t'Handre were usually quick to figure out who I was. Like the gardeners, they seemed to delight in answering my foolish questions.

The Aeyrie bowed slightly. "The h'ta h'shal belongs to everyone."

"I was brought up a Walker. I do not speak H'ldat very well. Please be patient."

"You must be Delan."

"Yes, sh'man." I was acquiring, I do not know how, the ability to distinguish the teachers and leaders and craftmasters who were to be given the title of honor.

"I am the sh'man h'ta. My name is Sardon Ande Stotla. Do you want to paint?"

I swallowed, taken aback. "Me? I know nothing of art."

"I have been watching you. I think you do." The art master came over and picked up the brush I had laid down so hastily, and put it back in my hand.

I missed lunch. I missed my scheduled Quai-du practice session. Feili appeared abruptly at my elbow and spoke to me. "Go away," I said.

"Id should not forget to eat," Feili said to Stotla, who was working on the pensive Aeyrie painting, and occasionally supervising me.

"There is food in here somewhere."

Feili found it and harassed me until I ate it, then id went away again. The light had begun to fade when Gein appeared and firmly took the paintbrush out of my hand. I stared blankly at idre, as if I had awakened abruptly from an intense dream. "Dinner," Gein said. "The h'ta h'shal will still be here in the morning."

Stotla was cleaning ids brushes. Gein bowed to idre. "Sh'man, Forvel has asked for you."

We were halfway to the common room before I realized how hungry I was, and that the bones of my body ached from standing so long, and that my hand was cramped. "Gein, something happened to me."

"Something good?"

"I don't know." I wiggled my shoulders and shook my wings, trying to wake up and organize myself.

"You don't know?"

"Is it good to be gone so far away? You could all have died, and I wouldn't have cared."

"Better answer that question for yourself."

"How is the taiseoch?"

"Much better. And so am I. I want to remain with Lian. I am thinking of joining Triad."

We walked the rest of the way arm-in-arm, but when we arrived at the common room, Gein left me, and sat with Feili. The Triad-dre were still segregated at their own table, an arrangement that, other than Gein, no one seemed able to violate. I sat down and replied absently to a question from Lian, and then sank into my daze again. After a while someone sat down next to me, and I heard the sound of a cane being laid on the floor. There was a stirring and whispering in the room. I came to myself enough to swallow a mouthful of soup, and turned my head to discover that Stotla's painting had come to life beside me: an aging, pensive Aeyrie, with lines drawn deep in ids face, fur thinning and frosting over. Probably feeling me jerk with surprise, id turned his head. "So, Delan, do you like t'Fon?"

I said sincerely, "Yes. Very much."

"My partner is excited by this day with you. Perhaps you will consider staying with us."

I had spent the entire day mixing colors and dabbing them on a canvas to see how they looked, which surely was not an exciting business to anyone but myself. I could see some of the colors in my bowl of soup now, bright highlights and swirling streaks of gold and brown. The Aeyrie turned away to greet a t'Han-dre who had come up hesitantly and stood with ids wings in tense bundles. The t'Han-dre said, "Forvel, is it truly you?"

The old Aeyrie laughed, slow and deep, and held out a hand for the other to take. At my other side, Lian pretended interest only in her dinner, but the entire side of her face crinkled up with laugh lines. I whispered, "Is this the taiseoch?" But I knew the answer.

Forvel would never walk without the cane, but the chances were quite good that id could fly as if nothing had ever happened. Pilgrim and Lian had done something to the channels in ids nervous system so that ids organs could function normally again, and were able to restore at least a portion of muscular control to ids lower body.

It was, as Pehtal put it cheerfully, by far the most important thing that happened since our arrival. Throughout the meal, the bewildered t'Han-dre kept coming up to the Triad table and touching idre. Some of them actually sat at the table, and even attempted some stiff conversation with the Walkers. I was privileged to see it happen, when one Aeyrie smiled for the first time in ids life at a feared and distrusted Walker.

Eventually Forvel turned back to me. "They tell me that none of the Walkers are making free of the Ula. They do not use the baths or the practice rooms. They do not visit the gardens. They have not gone to the library."

"They are trying to be sensitive to the fears of the t'Han-dre."

"Perhaps if they went accompanied by their Aeyrie l'frer, that would be sensitivity enough. And did not bear blades except in the practice room, as is our custom."

"Perhaps they might do this, taiseoch. But why are you telling me? Lian, or Pehtal—"

"Everyone knows you are both Aeyrie and Walker. Who better to act as interpreter between our peoples? Here then, look not so frightened. You remind me of C'la the first time I asked idre to represent me." Ids hand patted my shoulder lightly, but I swallowed painfully, unreassured. Id continued, "I have sent to Ishta, in the hope that the three Ulas might act in concert with each other. I told idre that you are here."

"I do not want to be a taiseoch-dre!"

Lian, who on the other side of me half listened to

three conversations at once, seemed as surprised by my outburst as I was. But she said calmly, "Then don't be one, child. Haven't you already spent too long trying to fit yourself into the wrong-size clothing?"

"They tell me," said Forvel, "that you are a mage."

Lian said sharply, "Let the child grow accustomed to ids wings in peace."

"Sh'man," said the taiseoch humbly, "and Delan. I beg your pardon."

I went to bed with Pehtal alone that night, but it was not lovemaking I wanted. Pehtal held me tightly, and did not speak, and did not request anything of me. Soon the sound of deep breathing filled the room, and yet I lay awake with my heart pounding in my chest, and Pehtal also lay awake, stroking ids fingers slowly through my fur. I finally said, "What is happening to me?"

"All your life you thought you were nothing. And now you have reason to fear yourself. Maybe you wish you were back to being nothing again."

"I spent all day in the art room—"

"Forvel came to me, seeking your Companion to tell id what had happened. It was something important, that ability to be so engrossed."

"I was just mixing colors."

"What did it feel like?"

"Like it was too big for me. Like it was going to consume me."

I stopped, feeling foolish, but Pehtal's head nodded against my shoulder. "It was important. I recognize that you are afraid. But you have to find your own way to uncover your own answers; there is no one else to do it for you."

We lay still a long time, until Pehtal said, "Do you think it would make me ashamed of you if you cried? I am proud of you, Del. Nothing will change that."

I buried my face in ids fur.

The rest of my life I would be struggling for balance, trying to know what I did and did not want, weighing my choices and fighting to keep myself intact as the desires of others pulled at me, the responsibility of power tied me down, and the compulsion of art closed me in even as it opened me up. Too soon I was no longer a l'shil. My life would never be simple again.

When I awoke, it was late and I was as exhausted as if I had not slept at all. The wind wailed, wild and lonely, rattling the windowshutters. A plate of sweetbread and a cup of milk waited beside the bed. I ate and drank, and then went out shakily in search of Feili. I was more than a little surprised to find idre talking soberly with Gein in one of the greenhouses. Their arms around each other's waist held each other very close.

"Well," Feili began as I walked up to them, in a tone of voice that told me id had been offended by my forgetfulness of yesterday.

"Feili, I don't feel good. Just say you'll come to the practice room with me, or say you won't."

"Of course I'll come."

Gein turned ids gaze away from the stark view of the mountains and the tumbling, boiling clouds. "I wish you used fake blades in training."

Feili snorted in derision, but as they parted their fingers linked and let go only reluctantly. I looked at Feili, wide-eyed, but id only smiled.

The practice room at t'Han was almost identical to the one in t'Fon, except that the walls were decorated with a painted border. Feili and I stripped off our garments and jumped off the platform to practice precision flying. Only when I bumbled into the walls in my tiredness did we go to work on the less demanding foot fighting. Morning slipped over into afternoon, and gradually I felt better.

"Enough!" Rubbery kneed, I rubbed sweat out of my stinging eyes.

Feili smiled at me. "Why don't you take a break, and give me a chance to work with my peers before I am completely worn out, too."

I noticed Stotla in a corner, half hidden behind a sketchbook. I came up beside idre, to watch Feili being detailed on paper as id talked to one of the other Quai-du-dre who had come in: the relaxed stance belied the power in the bulging muscles, nipples pointed with the excitement of fighting, wings hovered open to disperse body heat, blade dangled casually from one hand.

Stotla turned the page. A ferocious young Aeyrie hovered in mid-flight, wings wide and cupped around the still air, blade held in attack, mane flying out wildly around ids head. I blinked. "Do I really look like that?"

"Sometimes."

"Sh'man, I decided not to come to you in the art room today."

Id worked again on the drawing of Feili, soft pencil moving quickly across the coarse paper. Id did not speak, but I sensed ids attention.

"I was not so sure I want to love something that much."

The art master looked up at me. My stomach clenched with anxiety, but id only said mildly, "Come back when you are sure."

"Tommorrow I'll be there," I said. It was in that moment that I first knew I would not be returning to Triad. Like Gein, I had found the teacher I sought, at last.

The door crashed open. Hana rushed into the room, like a wild cloud riding a tumult of wind. For a moment id froze, poised and tense, with the shape of Eia in ids bones, wrenching my heart. "Feili!" id shouted.

Feili turned swiftly, wings bunching up, knees bending, fingers tightening on the hilt of ids blade.

I started forward, but too slowly. What happened was beautiful to see, beautiful and terrible. The jerk and tuck of the wings, the soft, light touch of foot on floor, the awful, brief, unbelievably fast chiming encounter of blade on blade. They slipped past each other. I watched Hana's blade slide close to the fragile membrane of Feili's pale wing. I watched Feili dance aside, counterattack, and be parried away, the blade edges slashing a scarce finger's width away from the Black's ribs.

Like me, others had started forward, and then had abruptly held themselves back. I clenched my arms across my chest over my pounding heart, and watched. Part of my brain babbled appreciation of their style: How neat that stroke was. How good Feili was at following up, attacking the wings when Hana was using them for momentum or balance. How impossibly fast they both moved, and how softly. Then there was blood in golden fur, bright and red.

"No." I shouted. "No, no, no!" I rushed between them, bare-handed and shouting. The stormcloud's blade shone clear in the lamplight, sky blue and overlaid with light. I caught Hana's wrist, and flung myself forward, using my weight to drop id to one knee. But id shook me off, like a draf would a biting insect, dumping me aside and getting afoot again in one powerful motion, face slack with concentration, scarcely aware of me.

Feili's blade hit the floor. Where was Feili? I struggled up from my sprawl, only to feel a strong hand

grip my shoulder. "No, don't move. Stand still, Del."
Feili panted heavily, but ids voice was terribly quiet.
"Someone go for a healer," id said.

I looked around anxiously for Hana. The Black
stood as if turned to glass. Feili had dropped ids blade,
and despite ids rage Hana would not attack someone
who was unarmed.

"Stand still, Del! My blade slashed your wing. Your
right wing. Hold it very still."

I felt the pain then, like a flame held to my flesh.
Feili's arm went around me. I leaned on idre. Ids hard
body trembled with tension against me. "It didn't go
all the way through, I don't think. But don't move, or
you might tear it. Del, I'm sorry, I tried to stop."

"Lian is going to—"

"Disembowel me," said Feili faintly. "Slowly. Using
something dull and rusty."

"She wouldn't spoil her fur rug like that. You're
hurt, too. Your blood is getting all over me."

Feili laughed nervously. "It'll wash off."

By the time Lian arrived, Hana was sitting down,
head resting on one hand, looking bleached and utterly exhausted. Over Feili's shoulder I stared at idre
rudely, hoping that by focusing on ids pain I would
become less aware of mine. The Aeyrie healer sewed
through my wing membrane with careful, awfully slow
stitches. If Feili had not been holding me up, I would
long since have collapsed.

"What happened, Del?" Lian asked mildly.

I replied incoherently. She listened in silence.

"Gein must have told Hana that id is joining the
Triad," Feili said when I was done.

"Id has decided so quickly? But why would Hana
blame you when it is I who. . . ?"

"We spent the night with each other."

"Oh," Lian said. Then she looked sharply at Feili,

as if struck by something surprising and unexpected. "Oh," she said again, very gently this time.

I realized that the healer had finished ids work and was packing ids bag. I moved my wing cautiously. Feili eased ids grip on me. Blood had glued our chests together, but Feili had stopped bleeding and it did not seem a dangerous wound. We both sat down on a bench before Lian, in a great deal of trepidation.

But she regarded us as remotely as a farmer assessing a draf. "A lone Aeyrie has been spotted on the western path," she said. "A Black."

Chapter 16

The injured Black limped slowly into the room. Aloof and upright, id looked at the taiseoch out of empty, dark-shadowed eyes. Forvel said, "I am the taiseoch. Welcome to t'Han."

"I am Malal Tefan Eia. Thank you for taking me in."

"Please sit down, a healer is coming. Do you need to eat?"

"Thank you, I was given some food at the door." This was a dead person, speaking in a dead voice and looking out of dead eyes. Id sat slowly and stiffly, as if id were a hundred years old. Ids face was a mask, skin stretched over bones, inset with dull stones in the eyeholes.

The satellite floating above ids head came into my view: An Eye, dead white, turning slowly to scan the room. Pehtal had warned me that it probably would not be invisible to me.

I shut my eyes tightly. I had promised I would not cry; I had sworn I would keep perfectly still, if only they would let me in the same room with Eia for a little while. Only it was not Eia. Pehtal's grip across my shoulders tightened as we lay on the floor behind a pile of furniture which had been moved as if for waxing the floor.

My burden lay hot and weighty in my heart. But I did not know what to do with it. "You have to trust yourself," Pehtal had said. "Remember that you knew how to take it away. Trust that you will also know how to give it back."

"You have some Walkers hibernating here?" Eia said.

"No," said Forvel. "Why do you think that?"

"You have drafs in your stairwell."

"Oh yes, they belong to some traders who wanted to start the spring with their animals in good condition. They paid us well to take care of them. Tell me what happened, Eia. Why are you traveling alone in the dead of winter?"

"I always travel alone, taiseoch, no matter what the season."

"Shall we notify your parent that you are here?"

I saw life then, a flash of rage in the dull eyes. Anger had survived when all else was gone, anger without any controls set upon it, as with Hana only much worse. Eia said softly, "My parent does not care where I am, taiseoch."

Brisk and quick moving, C'la entered the room. "Eia! It is good to see you again!"

Eia moved as if to rise politely, but C'la held out ids hands to stop idre from moving. Eia's thigh was wrapped in strips of ragged cloth, through which red blood seeped. "The healer?" C'la said to Forvel.

"Here id is now."

It was the same healer who had stitched my wing only a little while ago, now with an apprentice at ids side. "What happened?"

"I hurt myself in a fall," Eia said. "It happened yesterday. I have been walking all night."

The wound was a bad one, deep and dirty and uncared for. Eia's feet were frostbitten also, by the snow. But, for the skeletal thinness and the emptiness of heart, no explanation was offered. I watched the healer's face grow tight and angry. Id did not have to be told that an evil had been working here, a thing which consumed and destroyed and took great joy in watching hope die.

Eventually, they carried Eia away on a stretcher, the healer following behind, frowning with worry and anger.

"You're sweating," Pehtal said when the door was closed.

"You tried to warn me."

"Yes. But it is good that you know."

Eia was only the advance scout: we knew the Walkers were coming. Those Aeyries who were able to fly were readying themselves for battle, checking their gear and snatching what sleep they could in expectation of a long night. I remembered the red blood in Feili's fur, and the rage that had come over me, rage at the sheer stupidity of bloodshed. Now there would be more stupid violence, perhaps a great deal of it. Many people would say afterward that the Walkers deserved pain and death, and that the Aeyries who ambushed them had acted as they had a right to act. I would not be among them.

"Keep out of it," Pehtal had said to me. "The fight is the business of the taiseoch. Concern yourself only with Eia, just as I mean to concentrate on Teksan and his acts of magic."

"Are the people of the Triad going to join the fight?" I had asked.

"We have to talk about it, but I know we will not stand back and watch."

"Then the fight will be your business, too."

"Yes, as much as I detest it." Pehtal abrubtly looked very tired. "But it is too late for anything else. Our races have gone too long, blaming everything on the other. I mean to spend what it takes to keep this from happening again. But it is too late to stop it."

"Will the Triad Walkers kill other Walkers? How do they like being part of this?"

"Del," id reproved me gently, and I was silent.

I knew this feeling all too well, the haunting sensation that there was something I ought to do, but that I did not know what it was, or how to do it. Pehtal was helping me up from the floor now. Taiseoch Forvel watched us soberly. "I have never met Eia, but I have heard enough about idre to know that this Teksan Lafall, he is a destroyer, an obscenity. I am no longer uncertain about this."

I could say nothing. It was I, not Teksan, who had committed the final act of destruction on Eia. I could not regret it, and I could not forgive myself for it. This was what it was to be a mage.

The healer told us that Eia was very ill, utterly worn out, with ids bodily needs too long neglected, running a fever from the infected wound. Id had refused a sleeping potion, which seemed to confirm that the attack would be happening tonight. Perhaps Teksan feared that his puppet's strength would not last much longer than that. Asked if Eia could be a danger to the Ula, the healer had laughed in disbelief at the idea. But everyone who knew Eia had fiercely disagreed. A guard was set on ids door.

I did not even try to sleep. I went to the art room and made drawings of spheres and cubes. I drew them balancing on top of each other. I changed their shapes so that the spheres were flat on one side or the cubes concave on one side, and they could fit into or against each other. I could not come up with any way to do it without deforming the shapes. I was feeling very tired when I went in to dinner, but I was not the only one.

Pehtal was not there. A'bel told me where id was, and I brought a plate of food to the greenhouse. The mage sat quietly in the darkness beneath vines clinging overhead. The windows were misted over, but id had wiped a spot clear, and through icy crystal stars on the glass I saw blurry, distorted stars in the sky.

I gave Pehtal the plate and sat beside idre on the bench. "Won't I know, too, when the Door is open?"

"I might not even feel it. It depends on how close they make entry."

"How can you fly safely in the dark?"

"S'olel. I will let my wings do my seeing for me, like the blind Aeyries do."

After id had eaten, Pehtal spread a wing for me to huddle under. "I'm afraid, too," id said.

A long time we sat, unspeaking. A blossom opened somewhere, to haunt us with sweet perfume. The wind rushed like water against the stronghold. Within the greenhouse, it was spring. Out there, it was a bitter, stormy night, the kind of night that stripped the mountains and tattered the Ula's bright flags.

Out there in the storm, the Universe convoluted to a man's will and opened the rift in infinity.

"Well," Pehtal said, "I guess you felt it." I was on my feet. I could hear my shocked voice still crying out in the echoing, chiming glass windows. "They're coming in pretty close. They don't want to wear themselves out fighting the storm, I would guess." Pehtal was already wrapping the quilted vest between ids wings. I fastened it for idre, and tested it to make certain it would not come unhooked under stress. Pehtal stood up, saying, "Go tell the taiseoch, it will save me time. And be careful, Del; don't show yourself too soon. Remember that magic is like flying: all you have to do is jump off."

I kissed id quickly, and fled, knowing that perhaps I would never see idre again.

* * *

"The Door is open. The Teksan-dre are coming. Pehtal has already gone."

Those Aeyries who were pregnant, or who were single parents of young children, gathered to guard the entry. Those who could not fight at all stayed with the children in a secure room, armed with weapons that it was hoped they would never have to try to use. The rest of them, roused by messengers going softly from room to room, put on their flight clothes and vests, tied their weapons by long tethers to their wrists, and strapped pouches full of c'duni bars to one thigh. Each of them carried a roll of wide, sticky tape, like the stuff which reinforced the stitching in my damaged wing. I watched them gather in the common room.

Even those who were not going out into the bitter wind were carrying pouches of food. I took one up in passing and strapped it to my leg. I wandered anxiously through the crowd, my stomach churning with anxiety.

"Delan," someone said, "Surely you are not going to fight!"

It was a Triad-dre, a Walker. "No. I have something to do here at the Ula. Are you?"

"Not to fight," he said. "We have been with Lian all afternoon, Aeyrie and Walker alike, learning how to aid the wounded. It does not matter who they are, we decided, Teksan-dre or t'Han-dre, we will help them."

"How are the t'Han-dre to distinguish between you and Teksan's people?"

He showed me: a strip of pale astil tied around his forehead, another around his arm, and a mark on the pack of medical supplies he carried.

I felt somewhat better then. I found a quiet place by a window, where I could sit and wait. The sky was clouding over, extinguishing the stars one by one. I concentrated on my breathing, making it be slow and deep. I considered the sphere and cube problem, and realized finally that with people it was not so simple. We can compromise without ceasing to be ourselves. We can be one thing and the other at the same time.

After a long wait, dark shapes flew past the window, the scouts returning, buffeted and tossed like leaves on the wind. In the common room they landed on the platforms outside the windows. The voices of the gathered people swelled and subsided. There was no laughter.

I heard a step, light and soft on the tile. Warm hands rested on my shoulders. "Feili," I said. "Are you going to fight?"

"Only if I must, Del, to protect the Triad Walkers. Are you all right?"

"I think so."

"The scouts say the Teksan-dre are very close. We are about to fly out. The healers and the Walkers have already left. Isn't it time for you to go?"

"If Teksan knows about me too soon, he'll just guess the trap and escape. Pehtal hasn't closed the Door yet." But even as I spoke, I felt the terrible stress of the twisting abruptly release, like a sigh, as the rent Universe was mended. The enemy's escape route was closed. I leapt to my feet. "Pehtal succeeded. Tell the taiseoch!" I ran.

Except for the common room, the Ula was dark and empty, with only a few lamps lit so that the Teksan-dre (never, never would they get this far!) would be confused by darkness in a strange place. I ran in a panic. Feili and Hana had both warned me not to try to fight Eia. Id was ruthless, ruthless and deadly. Perhaps id would not even remember who I was. And they had not risked taking away ids blade, because of what that would tell Teksan.

The guard at Eia's door still sat casually on a bench, reading a book by the light of a single lampflame, knife hidden behind a cushion, I whispered, "Please wait here and come if I call for you."

Id gestured assent, and calmly turned a page of the book. I was panting, my heart thundering in my throat. Pehtal had told me I could do this. Was Pehtal always right? I turned the doorknob gently and eased open the door.

A band of faint light from the guard's lamp flickered across the floor. My shadow obliterated it. I closed the door behind me and stood very still, listening. The sound of my heart was the only thing I heard. I groped until my hand encountered the spoke of an air lamp, with a tinderstick dangling from it by a chain. I made the tinderstick spark, and one of the flame sockets sputtered into flame.

The Eye stared at me. It floated only an arm's length away. Once an Eye like that had made a traitor of me.

"Hello, Teksan," I said softly. "Remember me?" My glass blade flared, cold and bright with lampflame, as something also flared within me, heady and powerful: rage.

Soft, soft, use those wings, Del! The Eye tried to move away, but I was fast, shooting from the muscles of my own torso like an arrow from the bowstring. I pierced the Eye through. The brightness of my red blade was quenched in the black of old blood. Like a mist in a burning sun, the Eye dissolved in a mere moment. The room stank of something foul and rotten. Bile came into my throat.

"That was stupid," a voice said.

Id came out of the darkness, a dark, dangerous thing of muscle and bone and stretched astil wings, with lightless caves where ids eyes were sunk in a skeletal face.

"Eia," I said. The power drained out of me. My bones seemed to dissolve.

"That was very stupid," id hissed.

"Do you remember," I whispered. "Do you remember loving me?"

Id laughed, a cold, terrible laugh. "Yes. So?" Ids blade was already drawn: black it was, rare black, a blade that could only be won in battle, one of only ten like it in all the earth. I put my own fouled blade into its sheath. Do not try to fight the ruthless and deadly, the cornered and wounded. Do not try to fight the heartless.

"I remember it, too." Soft and husky, my voice vibrated as my body trembled. "How I lay down under you. How you shouted. Come here, Eia."

Id stood like stone. I pressed my hand to my heart and felt the double life burning there. "Come here," I said though I was dizzy with terror. "Let me touch you again, one more time."

As if I pulled on a string, Eia stepped forward, and again, awkward on one leg. Then id stopped, and I saw ids body shaking. "You have something—"

"It is something you want."

"Yes . . ."

I saw it happen: the gathering up, the lift and the release. It was beautiful, beautiful! There was nothing I could do against the beauty. I fell, fell beyond fear, sobbing as my wounded wing hit the floor, gasping as the black blade drove at my throat, twisting my head sideways, feeling the glass slash through my fur, through my flesh, then hearing it ring on the tile.

Before I even knew I was still alive I heard my voice shouting, "Kill me and you kill us both!"

"No! I will not do it, I will not!" Eia was weeping, in dry and hollow sobs that wrenched out of idre like blood from an artery. Yet, ids arm raised again.

An alien, crystalline quiet came over me. *Id will not miss twice.* I thought calmly. I felt Eia's enduring iron strength holding me to the floor. But I had a fire in me. I saw flames rising from my chest to Eia's, warming cold flesh and lightening the night's darkness, slowly, so slowly.

Eia jerked back from my fire, crying out. I had heard that cry before; it wrenched like a blade in flesh. The weight lifted from my chest, even as ids voice cried with hunger, desperate to remain, to take idreself back, to live again. Eia leapt to ids feet and fled into darkness. The window catches rang and clattered, and then the shutters crashed open. The wind snuffed the lampflame. Wide wings spread like black clouds across the few remaining stars, and then Eia had leapt into the night, and was gone.

The guard fought open the door. "I heard a cry—"

But I was already halfway across the room, shouting, "Tell Pehtal, tell idre—" What was there to say, that I had failed, that I had leapt in obstinate stupidity into the bitter wind, flying on a wounded wing, certain to perish? What was there worth saying? That I was out of my head with love? I ran to the window, afraid the guard would have the sense to stop me, and I jumped off the mountain, onto the unbroken back of the wild wind.

Trust the knowing that is feeling.

I closed my eyes. The wind tossed me back at the walls of the Ula. The mountain's bulky presence turned the wind back upon itself in a wild turmoil. My wings sensed where danger was. My wings knew how to turn me away. I struggled, stroke by stroke. Suddenly I was free of the hellwind. The air merely bucked under me like an untamed draf. I rode it, as I had been born to do, laughing briefly in surprise at my skill.

Night blinded me, yet I could see Eia before me, darker than the darkness, a hollow, cold emptiness which joylessly mastered the wind. I tucked my hands into my armpits and followed idre. The cold sucked away the warmth from within my fur.

Voices shouted below me, thin and harsh in the wailing of the wind. I opened my eyes. Far below me, garishly lit by white light, in confusion and turmoil, Aeyrie battled Walker. The sparkling lightwands in the hands of the Aeyries burned with terrible brightness, so bright that I doubted the Walkers could look directly at their attackers without being blinded. Working in groups of three, the Aeyries swooped and hovered, recovered, and prepared to attack again.

I heard someone scream: Walker or Aeyrie. A wing membrane tattered as an iron blade jerked through it, red blood spraying in the awful white light. Even as the Aeyrie fell, ids two partners and two other threesomes swooped to secure their save-lines and to carry idre to safety. At the edge of the battle, in a secure spot, red lightwands burned against a mountainside, marking the location of the supply wagon where the healers waited with their Triad helpers and guards. I remembered how Lian had winced as she watched Aeyries only playing at battle. I could imagine her now, pressed against Gein for shelter from the cold, face hidden. My eyes burned with tears. I shut them tightly.

In time, the rhythm of flight and the numbing of cold loosened the clenching of horror in my belly. With each stroke my right wing gave a sharp pain where healer's thread and wing tape reinforced it. I flew out of sight or hearing of the battlefield. Eia gradually lost altitude ahead of me. I had gained on idre. Ids feverish strength seemed to be burning itself out. I opened my eyes again. Overhead, the cloud cover crawled away from the stars. "Eat before you are hungry," a memory said in the voice of Feili. I pulled a c'duni bar out of the pouch strapped to my thigh.

I watched Eia's black shadow, overlaid by starlight, swoop downward. A person on the ground turned to meet idre, pointing upward and shouting. A hard, sharp lump of food crawled slowly down my throat. It was Teksan. He must have abandoned his followers as soon as the battle was engaged. "Coward," I said out loud. "Teksan Lafall is a coward." I forced myself to keep eating.

Shuddering in the turmoil of the ground turbulence, Eia struggled upward again. I hovered above idre, tethering my weapon to my wrist by a loop of spun astil. Perhaps this astil on which my life depended had been gathered by my own hands and spun by Crila, long ago. It was a comforting thought, for despite our misery, we had always done good work, Crila and I.

The blade in my hand was still black with the blood of the Eye. I remembered that I was in the superior tactical position above my challenger, but I did not attack. The wind shoved me up and sideways. I turned and recovered. Beneath the rushing sound of the wind I heard the rhythmic, rattling sound of Eia's breath. Specks of light lay along the edge of ids blade: reflected stars. My wings tucked in; I dropped below ids powerful stroke. I dug into the wind and climbed upward again, turning. I could almost hear Feili's voice shouting, "Turn, again, faster; you'll have to do better than that Del, or you're for the scavenging."

I had made my turn faster than Eia. I dove in on ids left, away from the blade hand, attacking the storm darkness of ids black wing. Id jerked the membrane out of my reach, spoiling ids unfinished turn but avoiding my weapon. I dropped, but not swiftly enough, and felt a foot slam into my back. The wind jerked me earthward. Gasping for breath, I fought the wind, stroke after stroke, locating by s'olel the firm rush of an updraft. My back felt as if a falling boulder had hit it.

It seemed a long time before I was stable again. The earth was a shadowed mystery below me. At one hand glass glittered faintly where a deadly mountain rose skyward. Wind currents tossed me softly. Eia? I looked up, almost too late, and dropped and turned as id dove past me, knife hissing through a freakishly still moment of air. I slashed out, and felt the terrible giving resistance of contact as I wrenched my blade across ids backstroking hand. Glittering and turning, something fell earthward: ids untethered black blade. I took a breath of relief. And maybe I had not hurt idre too badly. . . .

Eia tumbled after the falling blade.

"Eia!" I cried hoarsely. Ids wings struggled to spread and break the dive. But they could not; id was exhausted and ill, id was falling too fast . . . "Eia!" Like a dropped stone, id fell into the black night, toward the deadly embrace of the mountain. The wind howled in my ears and I did not hear the impact. But Eia was gone.

Something was wrong with my wings. I turned my head, and saw a long gash through which stars shone. I had not even felt it when Eia's black blade cut me open. I did as I knew Feili would instruct me: I glided, losing altitude slowly, flying conservatively and keeping in control. Somewhere below and behind me, Eia lay. I would not be able to find my way back to idre in this darkness. And if id were not already dead, the elements would finish my killer's work for me. Tears froze on my face, burning cold.

*   *   *

After I had landed, I huddled on my belly with my arms and legs under me and my wings spread to cut the vicious wind. I lay there a long time, stupid with the fierce shock of grief. "Delan," someone said. I was hearing voices, I thought. I was delirious.

"Delan." Something small tugged on my fur. I turned my head. An onfrit had huddled against my shoulder.

"Ch'ta? I left you at the Triad. I told you to stay there."

"Bad onfrit," Ch'ta said severely.

I laughed hysterically, hugging Ch'ta in my elbow. He was hot as a coal in the fire. I lay down with the roll of tape in my hand, to hand him little pieces of it to hold the edges of my gashed wing together. It had to be done before the blood was dry, or I might never fly again. Ch'ta's tiny clawed hands were gentle and careful. I did not feel the pain very much, perhaps because I did not care. I felt not at all myself: cold and still inside, light-headed and empty.

When he was done, I gave him a piece of flight bar. He ate hungrily, looking around himself with an anxious, alert gaze. I ate, too, unaware either of the taste or of the satisfaction. Ch'ta lifted his head sharply and began to chirrup, a shrill, clear sound. A reply rumbled on the wind. I turned my head as the long, tall bulk of Brother Och treaded softly out of the darkness.

"Brother," he said in satisfaction. "Och find you."

"Great winds!"

He patted me with callused hands. "Brother call me, I find."

I hugged him. He steamed and panted in the cold. He smelled musty and sweet, like moldering leaves. He nuzzled me, like a draf hoping for a treat.

"How did you find me?"

"Follow smell. Find little flying brother. Little brother

know where to go. Run, run, long way, many nights. I am Och, good nose, find anything anywhere."

My astonishment abruptly turned cold inside of me. I said, "There is a Walker near here, a bad Walker. Can you smell out his trail and then come back to get me?"

"Yes," said Och hesitantly. "Why find bad Walker?"

"He killed my friend."

Och hissed fiercely. "Och will find," he said, and was gone, soft-walking, setting feet down securely, seeing clearly in the darkness that blinded me.

"Delan," I said to myself. "What are you doing?" But I knew. Pehtal was nowhere nearby. It was up to me to do something to prevent Teksan from escaping. Given a chance to pause and concentrate, he would open a Door and be gone completely out of reach. He could hide at the far ends of the earth. Perhaps he could even go to another planet. And someday an Ula would take in a weary, wounded stranger and the whole cycle of hatred would begin again. Or, even worse, the Ula would fail to take the stranger in, out of fear. Then Teksan would have truly won, won in a way he had probably never even imagined.

I stroked Ch'ta's soft head. "Little brother, if you go away can you come back to this place again?"

"Yes," Ch'ta said with his mouth full.

"Then go to the Ula. Find Eia's friends and bring them here. Tell them Eia fell out of the sky here. Tell them to look over by the mountain. Will you do that, Ch'ta?"

"My Eia?" the onfrit said. "Yes!"

Unhesitating, he braved the gale, fluttering on the wind like a bit of paper tossed from hand to hand. I watched after him until my eyes ached with peering into the starry sky. A pale sliver of moon hovered on the horizon. The barren glass felt like ice under my knees.

I huddled on the ground again and waited for Och to return.

He came in a cloud of steam, patting me with his tough hands. "Found smell."

"Show me the way. Go slow, brother. I cannot see in the dark." I got to my feet and followed him.

Sometimes the wind brought me a faint sound: voices on the wind, Aeyries in flight. The wailing darkness pushed and shoved me as I walked. My wing began to throb with dull and distant pain. I walked carefully on sharp pebbles until the way became smooth under foot. Teksan was following a narrow, twisting path. With his night vision, he would be able to move quickly. How could I hope to catch up with him? Perhaps he had already paused to work his magic. Would I be able to follow him into the Void? But I sensed no tremor in the fabric of the Universe. I walked on, unsuccessfully trying to force myself to stop contemplating what it would be like to be lost in the Void, suspended indefinitely in that timeless cold.

I walked into Och. He had paused on the pathway, the front third of his body raised as he peered ahead, arm-legs crossed over his chest as a Walker would do. I patted him on his flank, feeling the fur standing out in tension. He turned to me. "Bad Walker, not far. Smell danger, brother. Bad danger."

"You stay here. He is my enemy, not yours."

"Bad Walker hurt you. Smell hate."

"He cannot hurt me," I lied. "I am stronger than he is."

Och stepped aside to make room for me to pass him. We were in a narrowing ravine, and my wings brushed one steep wall as I edged past my guide. On the other side I thought there might be a water channel, but the water could not be heard over the shrill wind. Och caught me by my clothing and snuffled against me, then let go, saying, as if my smell had told him something important, "Yes."

I walked on, alone. My sensitive feet found the smooth way, recognizing at once whenever I strayed because of the subtle roughening left by the sucker plants on the glass. Ahead of me I saw a glimmering, water in starlight. The walls of the ravine brooded over a pooling spring. Something rustled in the darkness. I held my breath, listening. There was nothing, neither sound nor motion, only the impenetrable dark and the howling wind.

I shut my eyes and spread my wings. And turned, and twisted aside, and felt the sharp edge slip past me. My knife came into my hand. I struck at the turbulence which was Teksan, and missed, but not by much, I judged. I heard his breath hiss out between his teeth. I backed away hovering out my wings again, reminding myself to breathe, keeping my eyes closed.

A slight extra pressure against my wings told me he was coming at me again. Aiming for the torso, a slashing motion, I thought. My wings pushed me forward. His right arm crashed against my left as I blocked his blow. Forward again, point first, softly, softly, push with the wings—

"Aaah," he said, jerking away. Cloth tore, and my blade skittered across bone. He pulled out of my range, but I could hear him breathing hoarsely. I am stronger than he is, I am stronger. . . .

"Delan," he said.

"No. No bargains."

"But I can give you—"

"No." I curled my wings around the wind. "You will come back to the Ula with me. Or I will kill you."

He gave a snort of laughter. I struck. Pain shocked through my wing; the tape had given way. My attack went awry and I missed. A redness washed across my closed eyelids. For a time, a long time, I was utterly disoriented and could not even locate the ground. *Breathe.* I instructed myself. *Breathe deeply.*

I felt the blow. I felt the blade go in, a cold shock and then the fire. Rage and pain shook me through like a hellwind. I slashed down viciously, and felt horrible things happening under my blade. Teksan fell away, crying out. I heard his weapon ring on glass. I leapt forward, and paused.

I could not kill him. The man had tortured and raped me, but I could not kill him.

My feet slipped. The glass surface was spattered with blood. I sought more solid footing. Teksan groaned and muttered in the darkness. I felt something happening, something terrible and twisted being created out of the hatred that empowered my enemy. "No," I protested wearily. "I can't—"

Out of nothing it materialized, a huge, eldritch, mewling thing, pale as carrion and dripping green shrouds of mucus.

Only the memory of the innocent Och awaiting me on the path kept me from running. I would not bring this Thing upon him. Screaming with panic, I ran and slammed my blade into the awful stink of it. My weapon passed through without impact, as if through a shred of mist. The Horror's laughter rattled inside my head. One of the green strands brushed my arm, and I smelled my fur burning. And then, in an awful shudder of pain, my flesh.

"Breathe," the voice said calmly in me. "Stand back and breathe. You are stronger, stronger, stronger." Shaking violently, I backed up against the wall of glass, and took in a deep breath, and let it out, and took in another deep breath, and let it out. The Thing came at me.

A thing of thought could only be defeated by a thing of thought. Aeyrie magic begins where Walker magic ends.

It came, spreading burning tentacles to engulf me. I raised my blade, my red glass shard that I had stumbled across one lucky winter day, long ago now, when I was only a child. It had come clean of blood as, unaware of what I was doing, I rubbed it on my clothes. Now starlight glittered on its surface. Light, sunlight, sunrise in the mountain peaks, blazing across the surface of the glass! Many times had I seen it, delighted in it, and stored it away in my memory to make myself rich, that glorious flash of brilliance, the light tumbling down the mountainside. Sunrise! The ravine flared with remembered daybreak, and my knife was the sun.

Then it was dark, even darker than before, but the Horror was gone. My knees gave way under me. The mountains clasped me close. I stared at the stars. Blood trickled down my side. Pain blossomed out from my charred arm.

Someone whimpered and stumbled across the ground. Crawling, feeling with his hands. A knife in one hand. His hands touched me. I cringed within, but I had nothing, no strength with which to move away. He was sobbing. For a moment I saw his face: staring, blank, burned eyes. His knife found my throat by feel. He rested the point on that soft place where during lovemaking the heart thunders. Then he leaned his weight forward.

Chapter 17

A monster leapt out of the shadows. The metal knife flew out of Teksan's hand to chime and rattle on the bare glass. Teksan tumbled away after it, tossed lightly aside before the Orchth's massive strength. The monster leapt after him into the gloom. Teksan cried out once.

I stared into the murky darkness, stunned. The scream of the wind and the chaos of my fear abruptly gave way to silence. I lifted my shaking hand to touch myself. My fingers on my throat brushed the crusted wound and matted fur where Eia's blade had gashed me. But in that secret, soft place my heartbeat still vibrated wildly to the uneven rhythm of stark terror. I did not understand how I could still be alive.

"Brother," rumbled Och.

"Brother." My voice came out hoarse and strange. "You are a better monster than the one Teksan dreamed up." I giggled hysterically.

The Orchth drew close to me. His rough voice said unsteadily, "Heard shout, heard—afraid. Bad Walker dead."

"Thank you," I whispered. "I'm sorry"

The great bulk of him blanked out the stars. His hands patted my legs. He snuffled at my fur, voice rumbling in his throat. He found the deep wound in my side, over which I was clutching one hand convulsively.

My voice said calmly, "Don't worry—Aeyries heal fast. Get the tape out of the leg pouch, though. I want to fly again someday."

For the second time that night, I trusted the delicate task of wing taping to a sentient beast. Despite being distressed and upset, Och nonetheless was able to understand what I needed him to do. I clenched my teeth and would not cry out, but I could not keep from shuddering when he hurt me. Afterward he carried me in his arms to the spring, so I could wash my burned arm in it. The frigid water left me shivering violently. Teksan's body lay beyond my sight, but blood stank in my nostrils. Abruptly, I was crying in Och's arms, my voice raw and childish in my ears. But I remembered to eat.

I opened swollen, aching eyes to frosty daybreak. I ached and throbbed and burned and hurt in such pain that I could feel nothing else. My hand on my face came away wet with sweat and tears. I turned my eyes into the fur of my companion. He lay half on top of me to keep me warm. He held me, close and careful, concern rumbling in his throat. Certainly, he had not slept.

I thought indifferently: I am going to die. I wish it would happen faster.

Och's tongue licking the raw burn on my arm awoke me again. I clamped my jaw shut on a shout of pain, but my muscles quivered wildly until he stopped. "Brother?" he said helplessly. His eyes were squinted to narrow slits against the sunlight, despite the shadowing of the overhang under which we had sheltered. I blinked at his blurry image, but my vision would not clear. I was desperately thirsty.

Get up, Del, it's not going to get any better.

I dug my hands into his fur. "Stand up, Och. Help me."

His incredible strength pulled me halfway to my feet. I struggled the rest of the way myself before I blacked out. When the darkness cleared, Och was clutching me firmly to his chest. I pulled my feet under myself, my knees trembling.

A frightening amount of blood had dried in my ragged clothing and clotted in my fur. But the dully throbbing cut in my side appeared to be closed, and what I could see of my wing showed no gaps where the membrane edges had parted under the tape. There the pain sang intermittently, sharp and sudden. Where the Horror had touched me, the burn had become an ugly, weeping wound, with the singed fur curled at its edges and the flesh swollen. It was that pain which bent my mind to longing for death so that I might escape it.

But I was no longer Teksan's victim, to die from his hatred. I could endure the pain. Lian would heal me and make it stop hurting, if I could only get to her.

Och shaded his eyes with one hand, blinking and squinting. He could not travel under the sun, but I could not afford to wait until nightfall. With my knife I cut a strip of astil from the leg of my garment and used it to blindfold Och. He did not like it much, but submitted. We took one step in tangent with each other, and then another. The pool near which Teksan's corpse lay was already behind us. I did not look back.

We both drank from the little spring that ran beside the path in its carved channel. I passed out with my face in the water, but the cold brought me back. Choking, I got my feet using Och's strength, and he held me against his side again. We began to walk haltingly, one step at a time. Eventually, he grew accustomed to trusting me and our pace picked up to a crawl. When tears drew cold lines down my face, Och began singing to me.

He sang, "Orchth arenuchmm oorghtchgrdmmm."

I am the shadow-walker, the night is sweet and silent.

We walked that way all afternoon, me guiding him, him holding me on my feet: with strength, with music, with gentle verbal prods. Soon the way was slick with ice, and later I walked in snow. I fainted with monotonous regularity. Even when I was conscious, I was aware of little more than the massive effort it took for me to put one foot in front of the other. Sometimes I heard Och's simple poetry, though whether or how I understood it I did not know. How I kept us on our pathway I also did not know. The fire of pain burned me to ashes, and blew the ashes away.

Och stopped. "Delan?"

"What?"

"Dark now?"

The sun had set, but I had gotten so stupid I didn't notice. Through the blur of my vision and the mist of twilight, I saw the mountain where Eia had fallen. I fumbled at the knot of Och's blindfold with numbed and strengthless fingers until it came off and Och blinked at me in the fading light. He touched his padded fingers to my damp fur. I was so miserable that I had scarcely noticed I was crying again. "Ride me home," Och said.

My mouth formed the words with effort. "Can you find where to go?"

"Yes. Och take care of brother." He lay down on his belly so I could crawl onto his back. He burned hot under my chill. His muscles rippled, and he was up, moving stiffly at first, able to go on all six limbs now that he did not need to hold me up. Soon we glided like liquid between the darkening mountains. With my hands dug into his thick fur, I shut my eyes.

Slivered moons moved with weird speed up the side of the sky as I slipped in and out of the feverish sleep.

Och's distressed hissing woke me once. Except for the moon and the stars I could see only darkness. "What is it?" My voice whispered hoarsely. My hands ached with holding onto his fur.

"Blood." The glimmering snow was churned and stained. He sprang forward, eager to be away.

I shut my eyes, and tried to sleep again. But Teksan's Horror haunted me, and the memory of the feel under my blade as his flesh parted. I jerked awake, sobbing. It was a frigid night, but I burned hot with fever. I wondered in a panic what had happened to the stars.

Somehow I knew that this journey would never be over. Och and I would travel in unbroken darkness, and the sun would never rise. We would travel until there was nothing left of me but bones, still riding through the black night.

And then, suddenly, there was light and startled voices crying out in H'ldat. Och reared up, covering his eyes with his hands, nearly dislodging me. "Don't hurt him!" I screamed hoarsely at the winged people as their shining knives came into their hands. "Don't hurt him, he is my friend, don't hurt him!"

"Orchth," a soft, wondering voice said. A'bel.

"Brother?"

"It is I. Stand still, we are your friends. Let us help Delan. Somebody get a blindfold, mute the light!"

A hand softly touched my shuddering back. "Del?"

I looked into a blaze of gold, a drawn, weary face. red-lined amber eyes. "You're safe," Feili said. "How are you hurt?"

"Wings," I whispered. "Deep cut in side. Arm burned. Cut in neck."

"All right, I have you. We'll take care of you. Let go, Del. Let go."

My hands were reluctant to loosen their cramped deathhold in Och's fur. I slid sideways until the waiting arms caught me. Yet it seemed I kept falling, deeper and deeper into a softness that welcomed me, that called my name and took me in like the beloved who has come home at last.

Lian, looking very old. "It is a bitter burn. It must have been the l'shil and the Orchth who fought the sorcerer."

"In all our seeking, how could we have missed them?" Feili, wind tangled and sweat stained, sitting on a stool, weary head resting on an open hand.

"The Orchth told A'bel that they sheltered most of the morning, some way from the pool. Del was asleep or unconscious. You would not have seen them from the air."

Something touched the burn on my arm. I shuddered and moaned weakly. Lian's familiar, comforting voice said, "I'm sorry, wingling. I have to hurt you a little. But then the pain will be gone."

Cold, cold, extinguishing the fire burning in my arm. Soft bed, soft blankets, soft light.

I whispered, "Lian, Pehtal—"

"Id took a bad fall, but will be all right. Id is sleeping now."

"Did Ch'ta show you . . ."

"Yes. We found Eia."

I knew, I heard it in her voice. Eia was dead.

Darkness embraced me again.

Someone was weeping. The sound was choked and muffled, as if the one who cried did not want to, and yet could not help it. My eyes felt glued shut. What was wrong with me? Fragments of memory flittered nonsensically in my brain.

The person sobbed again. I wrestled my eyes open. A pair of air lamp flames flickering faintly in the corner. A glimmering bottle half full of clear liquid hung suspended over me, attached to my arm by a slender tube. I stared at it in bewilderment.

I turned my head. At the sound of the bedsheet rustling, the weeping person stiffened, and dropped ids hands hastily from ids mouth. Black, black, stormcloud black, exhaustion-ravaged and bent under the weight of ids wings, Tefan Malal Hana raised ids face. "Delan?" Ids voice cracked.

I could not summon up more than a whisper. "Hana."

"They told me to leave you alone. They told me you are in danger yourself, you are so worn out. They said you couldn't do anything, but I had to come here. I'm sorry."

"What?" I said.

Hana hesitated. "Id is dying."

"Who?"

"My l'frer. Eia."

My heart turned over within me. "But—I thought id was already—I saw id fall onto the mountain!"

"Feili and I brought idre in at daybreak, alive. They connected our veins together, but my blood was not enough. I would give my l'frer more—" Hana stopped, breathing unevenly. "But Lian says it would be no use. That Eia would live if only id could desire to live. Pehtal insisted before that battle that only you could help idre. Delan, is there anything you can do?"

I sat up, stiff with bandages. My head seemed to float above my shoulders. "Wait," Hana said, and gently peeled the tape from my arm, and slid the needle out of my vein.

"Help me."

Hana lifted me to my feet, careful of my bandaged wounds, and then supported most of my weight as we walked. One step at a time, we crossed the room. I seemed insubstantial to myself, worn thin as last year's dishrag. Hana felt rock hard against me, but id swayed under my weight, and ids mouth was narrow with effort. I did not feel any pain. Lian had probably dosed me thoroughly out of her drug box. Where my thoughts should have been was nothing but mist. Even my passion had lost its intensity. The only thing which remained intact was my obstinacy. I would finish this thing.

"It is not far," Hana said as we stepped into the hallway.

I sighed. "Good."

The skylights let in gray dawn. Weariness and grief haunted the hallway like ghosts. An Aeyrie sprawled on a bench, wings hanging to the floor, with a blanket tossed over idre. Farther on, a pair of Triad Walkers sitting on the floor against the wall had fallen asleep on each other's shoulders. Blood spattered their clothes, and healing supplies stuck out of their pockets. Hana and I stumbled past them, and they slept on.

Hana laid a hand on a doorknob and whispered to me, "I think Gein is with idre now. You might have to walk a little on your own."

Id opened the door. Gein perched on a stool, wings drooping like Hana's in utter exhaustion. Id turned ids head slowly as we entered, but did not speak or look surprised.

Hana's free hand rested on the hilt of ids blade. "Get out." Hana suggested.

"Hana—" Gein sighed. "I'll stay."

"You won't interfere."

"Probably I won't. We'll see."

"Get out then."

"No. I am a healer, and Eia is my charge."

The tension between them was bowstring tight, but I was not much interested in it. On the bed, a body lay very still, with a tube running to idre from a bottle, and a neat tray of supplies nearby. I took a step forward, unbalancing Hana, who had to walk with me to keep from falling over. I wondered vaguely what made Hana think idreself capable of violence when id was little stronger than I.

Eia lay curled on ids side. On the pillow, nestled in ids tangled mane, Ch'ta also slept, too deeply. Eia's fur was dull. Ids dusky skin had a waxy look to it, as if no blood flowed there. A stove warmed the room, and blankets covered Eia well, but under my touch ids face was cold. My heart became very still in my chest. And then I saw the faint motion of a shallow, struggling breath.

I brushed with my fingers the fine bones that stood out in the inanimate face. "Eia? It's Del."

Eia took another breath, and lay still again. Id was so cold; id needed to be warm. Gein hissed anxiously behind me as I crawled onto the bed, under the blankets, curling my wing around Eia's bony shoulders, careful of bulky bandages. "Eia," I said. I longed for id to move, to open ids eyes and look at me, to smile. "Eia," I said more loudly, but id was too far away to hear me.

I lifted my head.

Hana said, "I am here."

"I want your knife."

"My knife?"

"Quickly, Hana, I am so tired!"

Id gave it into my hand. It shone in the lamplight. I looked into the deadly sharp sliver, but there was nothing to see. I stared until my eyes hurt; wishing, longing, for what I was not certain. I became vaguely aware of something happening in the room, of the door opening, of voices raised in surprise and shock. Hana argued in a fierce, hushed voice, protectively screening the bed with ids spread wings. But I stared into the glass, until my eyes went out of focus, and abrupt despair extinguished my urgency. Was it even possible to scry a mere shard? Of course it wasn't.

Someone touched my shoulder. A darkness suddenly swirled in the blade.

I dove into it as unthinkingly as I had dived from the window two nights ago. The Void spun me like a whirlwind. I fought my spirit's wings open, and rode the wind in, in to the lightless center. Cold it was, cold beyond imagining, death cold. But the darkness cracked open and a rift of blinding light sucked me through.

I entered Eia's cave in the maze. It was a sunrise. An exuberance of light poured across glass through the doorway. I thought: *it is so cold here, too long since the hearthfire burned*. I laid tinder in the little stove, and took the tinderstick on its chain. The sparks would not catch, so cold it was. I breathed on them: burn, burn. Finally I took a glowing coal out of my own breast and tucked it under the tinder.

A little flame flickered and flared. I tended it, adding fuled piece by piece, careful not to smother the little fire. The stovepipe warmed under my hand. Flame crackled. I sat on the stool nearby with the firebox open, watching the blaze closely so it should not burn down.

Heat flowed out of the little stove to meet the brilliant sunlight. The cave warmed around me. I set a pot of water to boil. I found a tin of spicy tea, and set the pot to steep.

The sunlight flowing like bright water through the cave opening was blotted out. Eia folded ids wide wings, and sunlight poured in again, flowing around ids darkness. Ice glittered in ids fur, edging the black with silver.

I said: *Sit down and rest. I have a hot fire burning.*

I am awfully cold, id said.

Eia took my place on the stool, and hovered out ids wings to the heat of the stove. Firelight flickered in glossy fur. I poured the tea, and gave idre a cup. I stood close to idre, sipping the hot drink. It was like no tea I had ever tasted, hot and soft as sunshine pooling on a parlor floor.

Eia said, *This is good. Del, where have I been so long?*

I don't know. Lost. But you are home now.

I put my hand on Eia's shoulder. The ice was melting and ids fur was beginning to steam. Ids face turned to me, deep-eyed, smiling, utterly unmasked. I saw respect, regret, and weariness. I saw pain, and love.

After a long time I said, *I have something for you. You have? A present?*

I put my hand into the firebox. The burning coals caressed my hand with their fierce flame. I took one of the coals into my hand. It glowed like a little sun, transparent as red glass, flames floating and trembling around it.

Eia said, *Oh Del.*

I put id's heart into ids chest. Smoky eyed, Eia stood up, pulling me wildly close to Ids hot fur: *Del. Oh. Del.*

A soft voice asked, "Are you still with us?"

I looked up at Pehtal. One bandaged arm was strapped to ids chest. The other hand lay warm on my shoulder.

"Sh'man." My voice came out thin and ragged.

"Sh'man," Pehtal greeted me, softly.

In the edge of my vision, Hana turned swiftly, wings tucking and folding. I held up the knife, my hand shaking. Hana took the weapon from my hand. There were tears on ids face again. Id did not understand. I tried to speak, but how could I begin?

Under my wing a voice whispered. I drew my wing aside. Eia looked into my eyes. "Del," id said.

Hana's hand came out to touch Eia's shoulder cautiously, as if id were some breakable, precious thing.

Eia said, faint and weary, "L'frer? Why are you crying?"

I said, "Hana, you had better tell Lian."

Hana looked confused. "Id—she—is . . ."

"Tell Lian what?" Lian came forward, grim and exasperated and pale, with black smudges under her sea-green eyes. Eia turned ids face and looked at her, blankly, and then with a sudden, deep gladness.

She dropped to her knees. "Eia?"

Under the blankets Eia's good hand moved to touch mine, to stroke my fingers briefly and leave behind a startling, intense burning: Don't you worry, Del. "Lian. I don't want to remember. How badly did I hurt Delan?"

Lian blinked. Her exhaustion was such that her smile came slow and did not linger, but her eyes stayed bright. "Not anything like as badly as you could have."

"Id will fly again?"

"Oh, yes."

Eia sighed. Then, "And I?"

"You, too, will fly again, thanks to many healers, your l'frer not the least among them."

Eia's head turned again. "Hana, why aren't you in bed?"

Hana made an outraged choking sound, which would have been laughter on some other day.

"There was a battle. Walker and Aeyrie. Did I dream it?"

Lian looked down at her fingers twisting in the blanket. "No. Only a few dead, though. All the surviving Teksan-dre are—guests of the Ula. Eia, you were right about a lot of things."

I realized belatedly that the room was very full of people, for they came crowding up around the bed. The taiseoch t'Han was there, and the taiseoch t'Fon as well, standing back a little as if not certain what to do now that id was in the same room with ids estranged offspring, who seemed likely to live after all.

Gein hesitantly put a supporting arm around Hana, who swayed on ids feet. And yet another stood beyond the others, a beautiful stranger, quiet in body but with dark, restless eyes that sought mine out and then looked away as if it were an accident, only to determinedly turn back again.

I might have been looking at myself through a mirror which scried the future. No wonder everyone was certain of my parentage. The taiseoch t'Cwa stepped forward, with my own shyness, my own hesitation which comes from seeing and knowing too much, my own bravado.

Pehtal turned as the Silver came up to ids side. "Taiseoch," Pehtal greeted idre. "Delan, I present the taiseoch t'Cwa, Gina Theli Ishta. Ishta, this is Delan."

"Ishta Meili Delan," id said.

I whispered, "Yes."

My parent smiled painfully. Ids hand came out to touch my fur, dark and light as ids own. Softly, id spoke in H'ldat the traditional words for greeting an infant newly hatched: "Welcome. Don't be afraid. The world is a good place."

Epilogue

I am thirty years old now, by Aeyrie standards still in my youth, with my life not even a quarter over. Yet I awoke one morning a few months ago to the feeling that I had lived too long.

I had been preoccupied with an art exhibition in the Walker capital city of Nemdor-By-The-Bay (where A'bel and I put Och onto a ship one joyous, unhappy day), and had been deceiving myself into believing that I was only tired. But when I took up my paintbrush again that cold spring morning, I realized that I had ceased to be able to paint. That was the day I began to write this chronicle.

Since then, I have become able to paint again.

I have already painted sunrise on the mountains, many times in many forms. That we have hope in our barren, all too violent land is a truth that needs to be repeated. But this time I painted the sunrise within: looking from inside the cave at the stormcloud Black landing on the edge, wing membranes smoky with the light burning on the glass behind and before. It has been a difficult painting: to capture the translucence of the glass and of the Aeyrie's wings is not simply a matter of putting paint on canvas, but of understanding light.

I know, and yet I do not know, what the painting

means. Though I am famous as a painter, I am also a seer. I scry my canvas like Glass, and sometimes I learn a secret about myself, and sometimes I learn the future. Other times it takes someone else to tell me what I have painted.

So my magic and my art cannot be disentangled from each other, and each time I let go of one of my paintings I question myself. Why are Walkers buying my paintings? What is the message I am sending out, and what will happen to those who study my work? Is it a ridiculous egotism to imagine that my paintings are forces of change? But I have not forgotten that awful night I challenged the Horror with the brightness of the sun. And I know that in every painting I issue that challenge anew.

Here it is again, the brightness illuminating the dark cave, the dark wings. In all the years of painting, this is the first time I have painted Eia.

I had been painting all day when Eia came to me to tell me id was leaving. Id came into the art room where I was finally getting around to cleaning my brushes, since the light was gone. Even Stotla had not outlasted me.

I could always tell when Eia had come from the Quai-du floor, for id rippled with power much as Och did. Three months we had been together, healing, loving as soon as it was possible, but sharing far more than just our room and bed. Winter had given way to spring. The taiseochs had met, and met again, Pehtal included among them. Now the Walkers of the land were out of hibernation. The eggs had been laid shortly after the battle of t'Han, and had incubated on their parents' hearths since then, surrounded by stones that controlled the heat. At last they had put out the chemical message that brings the parents into milk, and been slitted open to release their wiggling prisoners.

Most of the Triad-re were gone, Gein, Lian, and Feili among them. At least Hana and Gein had parted friends, their wounds closed, their scars remaining.

Love is not a prisonkeeper. I swore I would remember that lesson.

Three months Eia had been unfolding before me, bright and shadowed, angry and gentle, restless and driven. Therefore I knew that id would leave Ula t'Han, just as id knew that I would not. My first painting ached with too many good-byes, those that were said, and those that would soon be said.

"Can I see it?" Eia asked. Id stood a long time before the painting. I finished cleaning my brushes, and put my arm around idre.

"You're going to leave when Pehtal does," I said.

Id nodded, and would not look at me.

"It is true what you said. We each need to fly our own winds."

"I wish I could stay with you."

"I would rather you didn't stay in the wrong place just to be with me."

Eia turned to me, smiling slightly. "Sh'man l'shil," id mocked me gently. "You are supposed to beg me to change my mind."

"Someday I might beg you to come back," I said.

But I never did.

I immersed myself in art, and magic, and the Aeyrie culture. Almost a year later, the manuscript that I had saved, valuing mindlessly without even knowing its contents, had its first printing on the Triad Press. Eia sent me a copy. The next printing was made on another press; the one at the Triad just wasn't big and fast enough to keep up with the demand for copies. *L'shile Caih: The Novices of Peace,* Eia called the book, which, like its title, was written in both languages. But Pehtal calls it *H'loa Prlea,* after the first warm wind of spring, on whose back the wintering spores of the sucker plants ride in to their planting. Out of the mating of that book with the Community of the Triad and the memory of Teksan's War hatched the Alliance Movement.

When Eia's second book, *Shadrale Caih: The Partners of Peace,* was printed, the Aeyrie separatists and the Walker supremists both attempted to assassinate idre. But Quai-du masters do not kill easily. The Aeyries created a new title for Eia, which the Walkers translate as "Stormtamer." But it means much more than that, having to do with flight dancing and riding close on the edge of the wind so its force gives dangerous beauty to the dance. The Walkers, not so accurately, address Eia as Ambassador.

I realized finally that my obstinate pursuit of Eia's life and sanity was not merely the madness of a l'shil in love. It had been the act of a wingling mage, one who knew without knowing that Malal Tefan Eia was the hinge on which the future turned.

I thought I had finished this chronicle, for it had served its purpose in giving me a painting. But last night something important happened, which uncovered that painting's meaning.

I came down late from my work, to try to make a meal out of the leftovers in the kitchen. The dark common room was empty except for one person, huddled over a book with a lamp drawn close for light. I went quietly, respecting ids concentration, wondering briefly why id was not using the library.

"Del?"

I stopped, and turned. The solitary Aeyrie had lifted ids face out of the shadows. "The Ula-dre told me you are painting again," Eia said. "That's good; your letter worried me."

"Eia," I said stupidly. But even as I stared in wonder I was thinking about how ids face had changed from how I remembered it. There were lines in it, and shadows, pain and weariness, too much work, too little rest. I could put these things in my painting. I could put in the things that suggested the worn out traveler was coming home for a night's rest: a comfortable stool, a hearthfire burning.

"You have to stay until the painting is finished," I said firmly as Eia came up to me. But it was meant as a joke; Eia went ids own ways, always.

Eia paused, looked at the hand id had extended in dignified greeting, put out ids other hand as well, and embraced me. "Why?" Id asked against my neck.

"Because it's a portrait of you."

"Will you give it to me?"

It was no small request. To my embarrassment my paintings generate enough Walker money to support a small Ula, as Eia knew well. "Yes," I said.

"I'll stay, then."

"You will?"

Eia pressed ids face to my shoulder, laughing at my astonishment. "This is much easier than the usual methods I have to use to see one of your paintings."

Laughter died, and I felt a slight quiver in ids flight muscles as I stroked my hand down them. "My parent Tefan is dead," Eia said.

"I know."

"You did not come to the Burning."

"It was a bad time to leave my work. But I would have, had I known you wanted me there."

"The people of t'Fon, my l'frer among them, begged me to stay. Hana never wanted to be taiseoch, and thinks id is not suited for it."

"What did you say?"

"I said no. I told Hana to make the best of it.

"Since the beginning it has been Tefan preventing the Aeyries from all flying the same wind. But Hana fought in the war, and called a Walker 'sh'man' in the end. I flew to t'Cwa then, to talk to Ishta. And your taiseoch t'Fon also seems to be in agreement at last. It might be years yet before the Walkers and the Aeyries have a treaty, Del, but at last I believe it can happen."

Id paused, and said in the amazed voice that people always used when discussing this subject, "I met your child."

"Ishta's child," I corrected. The year *L'shile Caih* was printed, I had begotten Laril on a Silver cousin, who dutifully laid the egg on the taiseoch's hearth. It was the only thing Ishta ever asked me for, that I, the child id never had, give idre an heir. By Aeyrie logic it is the obvious solution, but, being a Walker by culture, I suppose I will never stop feeling a little strange about it.

"Great winds, what a little hellion. Are all your offspring going to be like that?"

I said, "I certainly hope not. How could I paint?"

Eia made supper for me. Perhaps it is part of Teksan's legacy that I hate cooking so much that I simply will not do it, even if that means I do not eat properly. We sat together among Eia's books and papers, and Eia told me the news as I ate.

"Gein and Feili hatched their second. Lian is well, glad to be able to concentrate on the sick and the children, and leave the administration of the hospital to Gein. Pehtal and A'bel are well also—the three of them are writing a history of Triad. Pilgrim seems to have some kind of treaty with a Mer Gestalt, and as a result is giving birth to her own herd. There are four Triad Mers now. One of them apparently is bonded already with Gein-Feili's eldest. Who knows what will come of it?"

I saw my next painting. "A new race."

"What?"

I suddenly found speech impossible. My heart pounded within me: terror, joy. When had I stopped growing? When had my beloved Ula become too small for me? When did my continuing need to study and claim my heritage become mere lack of courage?

Eia looked at me, shielded and controlled, keeping some powerful thing carefully in check.

"I think it is time for me to go back to Triad," I said. "Past time, even."

"Del, I have been so afraid—" Eia's wild hands displaced the papers, shoving the book dangerously near the table edge. "Great Winds, I was ready to plead with you, to beg you, to sit with you day and night until you agreed to come with me!"

"Why?" But I looked into Eia's face and knew.

The rising sun just spilled its rich light across this paper. Eia is asleep in my bed, tangled and ruffled and smiling in ids dreams. I have yet to sleep, but it was not pain that kept me awake. I have seen, this night, to the other side of loneliness.

On one level, each of my paintings is a self portrait. I, too, am finally coming home.

Glossary

Aeyrie — a sentient species of winged hermaphrodites who live in remote communities in the mountains. Although they are a creative and ingenious people, their inability to grow their own food makes autonomy impossible.

Ahbi — the lucky moon.

Abki — the dark moon.

ast — a blooming sucker plant native to the Glass Mountains, the stems of which are processed to make astil, a tough, silky fiber.

caricha — an edible sea coral.

c'duni — a sweet bar of food eaten in flight for quick energy.

ch'ta — charismatic, having a strong and energetic personality.

cleata — Giant sea lizards, whose shed skin is a tough, water-resistant material often used to make shoes.

c'lol-fe — "The wildness which comes after the confinement of winter."

crich — a powdered, dried fungus, the smoke of which is a mild hallucinogen.

Derksai — one of three lowland areas inhabited by Walkers, where the land is arable.

Digan-lai — a primitive, cave-dwelling Walker people, who make their living primarily by gathering and processing astil.

draf — a six-legged, shaggy beast of burden.

-du — a suffix meaning "having to do with flight."

em'an — an empath, one who has the gift of knowing another's feelings.

Fon — The Sun.

forty-day — The Walkers divide the year into ten periods of forty days each. (The Aeyries think in terms of four seasons, each lasting one hundred days, and the Mers think in terms of winter and summer migrations.)

glass — a hard, durable crystal of which most of the world is composed, which occurs in a wide range of colors.

H'ldat — the native language of the Aeyries.

H'loa Prlea — the first warm wind of spring, the bearer of plant spores.

H'shal — any common room of an Aeyrie community.

hunter worm — a web-spinning worm which captures and devours flying insects.

h'ta — art.

id, idre, ids — the H'ldat pronouns.

kip — a herd animal raised for wool and milk products.

l' — a prefix indicating that what follows describes a person.

l'din — a gardner, a botanist. Also the name of the community where Teksan lives.

l'frer — a sibling, a nestfellow.

l'per — a parent.

l'shil — a newly adult Aeyrie, a wingling.

lightwands — a reedlike plant, the stalks of which are dried and burned from the end for light.

Lla — the tiny moon.

Magic — Unusual talents are considered normal among the Aeyrie population. Those with sufficient intelligence, creativity, and courage may find themselves "growing into" magic (as opposed to learning it). The talents of a particular mage develop as part of the maturation process, and will be unique to them. (However, a few abilities, such as scrying glass, are relatively common.) See "Sorcery."

medog — a large, stupid, grazing animal, with prehensile toes, native to the Glass Mountains.

Mer — a sentient, air-breathing species which inhabits the ocean. Mers live in Gestalts, or herds, in which their telepathic links with each other result in a highly intelligent group consciousness. However, they normally have little concept of their existence as individuals.

onfrit — sentient, sociable, winged animals, with a facility for languages, the traditional companions of the Aeyries.

panja — a sucker plant with sweet-smelling blossoms.

Quai-du — the traditional Aeyrie martial art.

-re — a suffix indicating association (i.e. a Triad-re is a member of the Triad community.)

se'an — a person with the gift for knowing another's thoughts, a telepath.

shadral — a partner in activity.

Sh'man — a title indicating great respect.

S'olel — "The knowing which is feeling," kinesthetic knowledge.

Sorcery — the Walker art of spells and potions, of which acts of sadism are an integral part, which is viewed by most Walkers with superstition and awe. The Aeyries believe that the rituals of sorcery access the sorcerer's inborn talent, but in such a way that the magic and the person are perverted by the process. See "Magic."

t- — "Of" (prefix)

taiseoch — the hereditary chieftain of an Aeyrie community.

Ula — a traditional Aeyrie community, built atop a hollow glass mountain.

waterwyth — an eel-like freshwater creature.

DAW

Savor the magic, the special wonder of the worlds of
Jennifer Roberson

THE NOVELS OF TIGER AND DEL

☐ SWORD-DANCER   (UE2152—$3.50)
Tiger and Del, he a Sword-Dancer of the South, she of the
North, each a master of secret sword-magic. Together, they
would challenge wizards' spells and other deadly perils on a
desert quest to rescue Del's kidnapped brother.

☐ SWORD-SINGER   (UE2295—$3.95)
Outlawed for slaying her own sword master, Del must return to
the Place of Swords to stand in sword-dancer combat and
either clear her name or meet her doom. But behind Tiger and
Del stalks an unseen enemy, intent on stealing the very heart
and soul of their sword-magic!

CHRONICLES OF THE CHEYSULI

This superb fantasy series about a race of warriors gifted with
the ability to assume animal shapes at will presents the Cheysuli,
fated to answer the call of magic in their blood, fulfilling an
ancient prophecy which could spell salvation or ruin.

☐ SHAPECHANGERS: BOOK 1   (UE2140—$2.95)
☐ THE SONG OF HOMANA: BOOK 2   (UE2317—$3.95)
☐ LEGACY OF THE SWORD: BOOK 3   (UE2316—$3.95)
☐ TRACK OF THE WHITE WOLF: BOOK 4 (UE2193—$3.50)
☐ A PRIDE OF PRINCES: BOOK 5   (UE2261—$3.95)
☐ DAUGHTER OF THE LION: BOOK 6   (UE2324—$3.95)

DAW
New Worlds of Fantasy

STEPHANIE A. SMITH

☐ SNOW EYES   (UE2286—$3.50)
When the mysterious mother who abandoned her returns to claim Snow-Eyes for the goddess known as Lake-Mother, Snow-Eyes is compelled to go with her to the goddess' citadel—there to face betrayal and a confrontation with her own true nature.

☐ THE BOY WHO WAS THROWN AWAY (UE2320—$3.50)
The spell-binding sequel to SNOW-EYES! Gifted with a musical magic and a shape-changing talent he can scarcely control, Amant struggles to rescue his cousin caught in a terrifying spell halfway between life and the realm of Lord Death.

MELANIE RAWN

☐ DRAGON PRINCE   (UE2312—$4.50)
In a land on the verge of war, Rohan and his Sunrunner bride would face the challenge of the desert, the dragons—and the High Prince's treachery! *"Marvelous . . . impressive . . . fascinating . . . I completely and thoroughly enjoyed DRAGON PRINCE."* —Ann McCaffrey

TANYA HUFF

☐ CHILD OF THE GROVE   (UE2272—$3.50)
☐ THE LAST WIZARD   (UE2331—$3.95)
Magic's spell was fading, but one wizard had survived to wreak madness and destruction. And though the Elder Races had long withdrawn from mortals, they now bequeathed them one last gift—Crystal, the Child of the Grove!

DAW

DAW Presents
Epic Adventures in Magical Realms

MERCEDES LACKEY
THE VALDEMAR TRILOGY

Chosen by one of the mysterious Companions, Talia is awakened to her own unique mental powers and abilities, and becomes one of the Queen's Heralds. But in this realm, beset by dangerous unrest and treachery in high places, it will take all of her special powers, courage and skill to fight enemy armies and the sorcerous doom that is now reaching out to engulf the land.

☐ ARROWS OF THE QUEEN: Book 1   (UE2189—$2.95)
☐ ARROW'S FLIGHT: Book 2   (UE2222—$3.50)
☐ ARROW'S FALL: Book 3   (UE2255—$3.50)

VOWS AND HONOR

☐ THE OATHBOUND: Book 1   (UE2285—$3.50)
☐ OATHBREAKERS: Book 2   (UE2319—$3.50)

PETER MORWOOD
THE BOOK OF YEARS

An ambitious lord has meddled with dark forces, and an ancient evil stirs again in the land of Alba. Rescued by an aging wizard Aldric seeks revenge on the sorcerous foe who has slain his clan and stolen his birthright. Betrayed by a treacherous king, can even his powerful friends save him as he faces demons, dragons, and wrathful fiends?

☐ THE HORSE LORD: Book 1   (UE2178—$3.50)
☐ THE DEMON LORD: Book 2   (UE2204—$3.50)
☐ THE DRAGON LORD: Book 3   (UE2252—$3.50)
